Claimed by the Enemy

Shauna Roberts BHS Class of 1974

Shauna Roberts

http://www.ShaunaRoberts.com

Nicobar Press

—

Riverside, California

http://www.NicobarPress.com

Nicobar Press
http://www.NicobarPress.com

First printing, July 2014

ISBN 978-1-938125-13-3

Map of ancient Mesopotamia prepared by Shauna Roberts
based on a map by John D. Croft,
http://commons.wikimedia.org/wiki/File:Sumer1.jpg.
Modified with permission under Creative Commons Attribution-ShareAlike
3.0 Unported license.

Map of modern Iraq prepared by Shauna Roberts
based on a map by Karl Musser,
http://commons.wikimedia.org/wiki/File:Tigr-euph.png.
Modified with permission under Creative Commons Attribution-ShareAlike
2.5 Generic license.

For my own hero, David A. Malueg

— Table of Contents —

— Ancient Sumer, Akkad, and Elam —

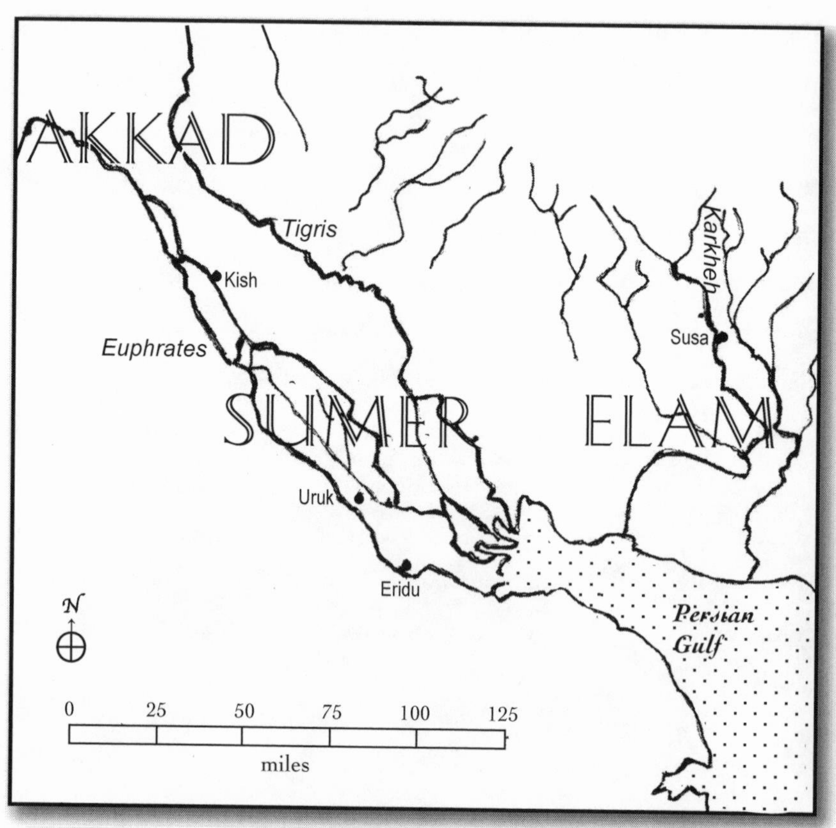

LEGEND

CAPS .... region
San Serif italic .... rivers
Bold italics .... bodies of water
• .... ancient city mentioned in novel

Note: The Persian Gulf extended much farther inland in 2350 BCE, and the courses of the Euphrates and Tigris Rivers were different. Cities that sat by a river then are usually far from a river today.

– Modern Iraq and Iran –

LEGEND

BOLD CAPS .... modern country
Bold italics .... bodies of water
▫ .... ancient city
• .... modern city
? .... location is uncertain
⌜ ⌝ .... area in map on page vi

— Characters —

Duplicate sets of the tables to clip out are provided starting on page xv to help you keep the foreign names straight.

Abba	the Sumerian word for Father
Abi	(Elamite) Nindalla's older daughter from Prince Humba
Ama	the Sumerian word for Mother
Bar	(Elamite) Nindalla's younger daughter from Prince Humba
Bau-iggal	(Sumerian) Ur-sag-enki's younger sister
Daanan	(Elamite) wet nurse for Enki-kiag
Dagu	(Elamite) chamberlain of Susa
Earabi	(Sumerian) an old man from Eridu who lives in Anshan
Ebarti	(Elamite) king of Susa, father of Humba, Ka'a, Kumdupum, and other children
E-kug	(Sumerian) one of Nindalla's older sisters
Enki-kiag	(Elamite) Nindalla's son
Enkidu	(Sumerian) in legends, the friend of King Gilgamesh of Uruk
Gan-utu	(Sumerian) an old woman from Eridu who lives in Anshan
Gilgamesh	(Sumerian) an ancient king of Uruk whose legends tell of his adventures with his friend Enkidu and his attempts to find eternal life

Gunidu (Sumerian) master of a tablet house in Susa

Habarane (Elamite) an orphaned royal princess adopted by Nindalla

Humba (Elamite) Nindalla's husband, crown prince of Susa

Idi-Ishtar (Akkadian) Ur-sag-enki's lieutenant

Il-alsu (Elamite) one of Ur-sag-enki's scouts

Intarza (Elamite) Dagu's daughter

Ka'a (Elamite) Humba's sister, Nindalla's sister-in-law

Kuk-kalla (Elamite) one of Ur-sag-enki's scouts

Kumdupum (Elamite) one of Humba's younger brothers

Midu (Elamite) Humba's concubine

Namazu (Sumerian) a Sumerian exile living in Anshan

Nindalla (Sumerian) a princess of Eridu; now princess of Susa

Nu-nu (Sumerian) Nindalla's youngest sister, who has been missing since the Akkadian conquest of Eridu

Qisim (Akkadian) general under Sargon of Akkad, now governor of Anshan

Pinririna (Elamite) counselor of King Ebarti

Ri-ti (Sumerian) queen of Susa; Humba's mother and Nindalla's mother-in-law

Sagburru (Sumerian) E-kug's midwife, sent to Nindalla

Sargon (Akkadian) king of Akkad and conqueror of Sumer, the rest of Mesopotamia, and parts of Elam

Shatirra (Sumerian) Ur-sag-enki's older sister

Sisi (Sumerian) Nindalla's children's former nursemaid

Sukura (Elamite) Daanan's sister, hired as a nursemaid for Abi, Bar, and Habarane

Tirushaki (Elamite) a priest of Inshushinak, liaison with high priestess

Ur-sag-enki (Sumerian) a captain in the army of Sargon of Akkad, now governor of Susa

Zag-sudta (Sumerian) one of King Ebarti's counselors

Zana (Elamite) high priestess of the temple of Inshushinak in Susa

– Deities –

Damgalnunna (Sumerian) wife of the god Enki

Dimme (Sumerian) a demon or evil goddess whose deeds included killing newborns and harming mothers

Enki (Sumerian) patron god of Eridu; god of the *abzu*, the ocean under the earth. He is associated with masculinity, fertility, fresh water, wisdom, magic, and the achievements of civilization. His symbols include flowing water, fish, turtles, and the goatfish.

Enlil (Sumerian) god who decrees the fates

Ereshkigal (Sumerian) queen of the Underworld and goddess of death and birth

Inanna (Sumerian) goddess of love, sex, and war. She is associated with the power of female sexuality, military might, royal power, prosperity of the land, and the planet Venus. Her symbols include weapons, the lion, an eight-pointed star, red and blue, and the gems carnelian and lapis lazuli.

Inshushinak (Elamite god with a Sumerian name) patron god of Susa; god of oaths and a judge in the Underworld

Ishkur (Sumerian) god of storms

Ningirin (Sumerian) goddess of incantations

Nintu (Sumerian) "lady of the birth hut," an ancient mother goddess known by many names. She is associated with pregnancy and birth. Her symbols are a capital Greek omega and a knife.

Pinikir (Elamite) mother goddess, goddess of love and sex, and the highest-ranking deity in Elamite religion

— Place Names —

Akkad	the region of Mesopotamia including and north of where the Euphrates and Tigris Rivers come closest together; the region immediately north of Sumer in what today is Iraq
Anshan	Elamite city located south of Susa in what today is Iran
Elam	a kingdom in western Iran that included Susa and Anshan
Eridu	port city in southern Sumer in what today is Iraq; founded in 5500 B.C., making it one of the oldest cities in the world
Kish	the northernmost city of Sumer; Sargon was the king's cupbearer there before staging a coup and becoming king of Kish
Meluhha	the Indus Valley region in what today is India
Sumer	the southernmost region of Mesopotamia in what today is Iraq
Susa	ancient Elamite city, founded by 4200 B.C. in what today is Iran
Mesopotamia	"the land between the rivers," the region between the Euphrates and Tigris Rivers in what is today Iraq, Syria, and Turkey
Uruk	a major city in Sumer on the Euphrates River

— Characters —

The following duplicate sets of the tables of characters, gods, and places are provided to help you keep foreign names straight. You can cut these out on the dotted line and keep them hand as you read.

Abba the Sumerian word for Father

Abi (Elamite) Nindalla's older daughter from Prince Humba

Ama the Sumerian word for Mother

Bar (Elamite) Nindalla's younger daughter from Prince Humba

Bau-iggal (Sumerian) Ur-sag-enki's younger sister

Daanan (Elamite) wet nurse for Enki-kiag

Dagu (Elamite) chamberlain of Susa

Earabi (Sumerian) an old man from Eridu who lives in Anshan

Ebarti (Elamite) king of Susa, father of Humba, Ka'a, Kumdupum, and other children

E-kug (Sumerian) one of Nindalla's older sisters

Enki-kiag (Elamite) Nindalla's son

Enkidu (Sumerian) in legends, the friend of King Gilgamesh of Uruk

Gan-utu (Sumerian) an old woman from Eridu who lives in Anshan

Gilgamesh (Sumerian) an ancient king of Uruk whose legends tell of his adventures with his friend Enkidu and his attempts to find eternal life

— Characters, page 2 —

Gunidu	(Sumerian) master of a tablet house in Susa
Habarane	(Elamite) an orphaned royal princess adopted by Nindalla
Humba	(Elamite) Nindalla's husband, crown prince of Susa
Idi-Ishtar	(Akkadian) Ur-sag-enki's lieutenant
Il-alsu	(Elamite) one of Ur-sag-enki's scouts
Intarza	(Elamite) Dagu's daughter
Ka'a	(Elamite) Humba's sister, Nindalla's sister-in-law
Kuk-kalla	(Elamite) one of Ur-sag-enki's scouts
Kumdupum	(Elamite) one of Humba's younger brothers
Midu	(Elamite) Humba's concubine
Namazu	(Sumerian) a Sumerian exile living in Anshan
Nindalla	(Sumerian) a princess of Eridu; now princess of Susa
Nu-nu	(Sumerian) Nindalla's youngest sister, who has been missing since the Akkadian conquest of Eridu
Qisim	(Akkadian) general under Sargon of Akkad, now governor of Anshan
Pinririna	(Elamite) counselor of King Ebarti
Ri-ti	(Sumerian) queen of Susa; Humba's mother and Nindalla's mother-in-law
Sagburru	(Sumerian) E-kug's midwife, sent to Nindalla

— Characters, page 3 —

Sargon	(Akkadian) king of Akkad and conqueror of Sumer, the rest of Mesopotamia, and parts of Elam
Shatirra	(Sumerian) Ur-sag-enki's older sister
Sisi	(Sumerian) Nindalla's children's former nursemaid
Sukura	(Elamite) Daanan's sister, hired as a nursemaid for Abi, Bar, and Habarane
Tirushaki	(Elamite) a priest of Inshushinak, liaison with high priestess
Ur-sag-enki	(Sumerian) a captain in the army of Sargon of Akkad, now governor of Susa
Zag-sudta	(Sumerian) one of King Ebarti's counselors
Zana	(Elamite) high priestess of the temple of Inshushinak in Susa

— Deities —

Damgalnunna (Sumerian) wife of the god Enki

Dimme (Sumerian) a demon or evil goddess whose deeds included killing newborns and harming mothers

Enki (Sumerian) patron god of Eridu; god of the *abzu,* the ocean under the earth. He is associated with masculinity, fertility, fresh water, wisdom, magic, and the achievements of civilization. His symbols include flowing water, fish, turtles, and the goatfish.

Enlil (Sumerian) god who decrees the fates

Ereshkigal (Sumerian) queen of the Underworld and goddess of death and birth

Inanna (Sumerian) goddess of love, sex, and war. She is associated with the power of female sexuality, military might, royal power, prosperity of the land, and the planet Venus. Her symbols include weapons, the lion, an eight-pointed star, red and blue, and the gems carnelian and lapis lazuli.

Inshushinak (Elamite god with a Sumerian name) patron god of Susa; god of oaths and a judge in the Underworld

Ishkur (Sumerian) god of storms

Ningirin (Sumerian) goddess of incantations

Nintu (Sumerian) "lady of the birth hut," an ancient mother goddess known by many names. She is associated with pregnancy and birth. Her symbols are a capital Greek omega and a knife.

Pinikir (Elamite) mother goddess, goddess of love and sex, and the highest-ranking deity in Elamite religion

— Place Names —

Akkad — the region of Mesopotamia including and north of where the Euphrates and Tigris Rivers come closest together; the region immediately north of Sumer in what today is Iraq

Anshan — Elamite city located south of Susa in what today is Iran

Elam — a kingdom in western Iran that included Susa and Anshan

Eridu — port city in southern Sumer in what today is Iraq; founded in 5500 B.C., making it one of the oldest cities in the world

Kish — the northernmost city of Sumer; Sargon was the king's cupbearer before staging a coup and becoming king of Kish

Meluhha — the Indus Valley region in what today is India

Sumer — the southernmost region of Mesopotamia in what today is Iraq

Susa — ancient Elamite city, founded by 4200 B.C. in what today is Iran

Mesopotamia — "the land between the rivers," the region between the Euphrates and Tigris Rivers in what is today Iraq, Syria, and Turkey

Uruk — a major city in Sumer on the Euphrates River

— Chapter 1 —

Eridu, Sumer, 2300 BCE

Eridu, the Mighty Place, the Noble Place, most ancient of towns, home of the great god Enki, the Lord of Fresh Waters, sprawled on a high hill atop three thousand years' accumulation of homes, businesses, and temples. To the south, verdant marshes thrived and the peacock-blue sea churned. To the west, the sluggish, muddy Euphrates River meandered toward the sea, splitting and reuniting, branches running through the city. Irrigation canals diverted the Euphrates' nutrient-rich water into desert fields, where it nourished figs, flax, plums, mint, apples, barley, date palms, chickpeas, emmer wheat, onions, sesame, cucumbers, rosemary, and many other crops.

Although it was spring now, the salty and sweet waters moderated the heat in this favored city. Still, it was too hot on this New Year's Festival day for any water to linger in the shallow moat around Enki's towering temple.

The people streaming to the temple for the festivities—city residents, marsh dwellers, herdsmen, farmers, villagers—didn't care. They would work in heat much worse during the coming summer. Today was for spectacle and, for some, a once-in-a-lifetime marvel.

At the back of the crowd, just arrived with his family from their farm a two-hour walk away, stood a tall twelve-year-old boy, one of the black-headed people, whose name was Ur-sag-enki.

The boom of the kettledrums resonated inside Ur-sag-enki's chest, and tambourines tinkled his name. He stood high on the balls of his bare feet. Tall as he was, he could not see over the thick crowd of grownups, some made even taller by their hats of felt.

Bouncing with excitement and frustration, he looked to either side for a way around. But enthusiastic people crowded against the mud-brick houses on either side of the wide dirt street. Some children had climbed onto the flat roofs of the few one-story homes for a better view. No one but him paid any attention to the huge houses, as if two-story houses with white plastered walls were as common as reeds.

An animal-horn trumpet brayed. Ur-sag-enki could resist the call of the instruments no longer. Pulling his two giggling sisters behind him, he squirmed his way through the smoke of burning cypress and a mass of people of every station and occupation. He played a game of guessing who each was as he passed by. The smiling woman who smelled of beer: a tavernkeeper. The man with flour smeared on his face and caught in the matted black hair of his chest: a baker. The man wearing only a loincloth who smelled of fish and salt: a marsh dweller.

"Don't push!" Abba shouted from the back of the crowd, his deep voice carrying over the chatter. "Or you'll be cleaning the chicken run until the rainy season!"

Ur-sag-enki ignored his father. He and his sisters squeezed through the crowd, stirring up dust with their feet; a woman in a bright-yellow tunic tutted her disapproval. She smelled strongly of sesame oil, and he slowed to look at her shiny skin. A woodseller bowed over by the weight of the wood on his back clouted him. Even a beggar frowned at him and wrinkled his nose at his manners.

He ignored those grownups too. He was in Eridu for the New Year festival, his first time ever. Maybe his only time ever. He was going to see the parade around the temple, no matter what Father threatened.

As several trumpets blasted, he and his sisters reached the broad avenue that circled the high wall around the House of the Aquifer, the temple where the great god Enki lived.

Shading his eyes against the harsh desert sun, Ur-sag-enki's mouth dropped open in wonder. The temple loomed high above the tall wall as if stretching toward the heavens, its baked bricks golden in the sun. Curved walls tilted inward so that the temple narrowed as it got higher. He tipped his head back and back and back to see the small sanctuary at the very top.

"Look at this," Shatirra said. His older sister pointed to the broad, straight avenue that crossed in front of their bare feet, so unlike the narrow, meandering dirt paths they had trudged to get to the city. "Bricks! The street is made of baked bricks."

He whistled. "The king of Eridu must be rich."

"The gods have smiled on our city and our king." Shatirra's eyes widened under their straight, dark brows. "Eridu is a city of wonders."

Trumpets sounded again. Ur-sag-enki put his hands over his ringing ears. Around him, people quieted and turned to face forward.

As dust shimmered in the air above the street, slaves drove bleating, wild-eyed white goats toward the temple. His small sister, Bau-iggal, sucked her thumb, her gaze darting everywhere.

Ur-sag-enki boosted her onto his shoulders. "Now you'll be able to see everything."

Shatirra tried to put her arm around his shoulders but settled for his waist. "You're getting too tall, little brother. If you keep growing so fast, soon I'll have to reach up just to embrace your knees."

"Don't complain." Ur-sag-enki puffed out his chest. "When I'm grown, I'll protect you and Bau-iggal. Your husbands won't dare beat you. I'll frown if they speak even a harsh word."

The sacrificial goats ran past, followed by sweating slaves tugging a wheeled cage that stank badly enough to wake the gods. Inside paced a cat nearly the size of a cow, with teeth like sickle-swords. It shook its thick golden neck ruff and growled.

Bau-iggal whimpered and grabbed Ur-sag-enki's hair.

"Hush, hush, little one," Ur-sag-enki said, jiggling her on his shoulders. "I'll keep you safe from the beast."

After the huge cat passed, the musicians marched by, banging drums, blowing reed pipes, and plucking lyres. Dancers whirled and spun, their clothes a cloud around them. They accented their moves with sistrums and clappers. Both musicians and dancers, the women in their white shifts that glowed in the sunlight and the men in their white kilts tied with sashes, seemed like gods.

Behind them strode the high priestess of Enki. She held her head high as if the parade watchers were beneath her notice.

Ur-sag-enki gaped at her splendor: Her shift sparkled with gold embroidery, and a gleaming ornament of gold beads and orange and blue stones covered most of her forehead.

The priests of Enki marched behind her, row after row, naked as plucked ducks from their shaved heads and chins to their bare feet. Ur-sag-enki's head spun, yet the procession continued, marvel after marvel: jugglers, men who ate fire, a woman with green-painted eyelids who carried a snake that twined around her arms.

At last the parade seemed to end. Yet most of the crowd stayed, watchful and eager.

Shatirra turned. "Wait," Ur-sag-enki said, taking her arm. "What if there's more to see?"

She laughed. "I've seen so much my head hurts. But I'll stay if you can bear to see more."

Trumpets blasted, and cheers erupted. Ur-sag-enki rose to his tiptoes and strained his neck. "Soldiers!" he said to his sisters.

As the people around him cheered, the fierce-eyed soldiers marched proudly, hefting a bed on their shoulders. Not a bed to sleep in: It had no legs. Instead, a long pole ran along each side and rested on the shoulders of the soldiers.

The men were magnificent. Their oiled, bulging muscles gleamed, and they wore new leather kilts whose bronze-studded flaps swayed with each strong step.

Ur-sag-enki's chest clutched, and his head dropped. When he was grown up and a farmer, his muscles would be dust-covered, not oiled. His back would be bent from hoeing and shoveling, not straight with pride. His wool kilt would be stained with dirt, crushed plants, and splashes of muddy water from the irrigation ditches. Farmers were important, but they weren't magnificent.

Shatirra bumped him with her elbow. "Look up, silly boy! You're about to miss the king!"

He looked up and then looked higher. Above his head, the king stood wide-legged on the bed carried by the soldiers as proudly as if he owned the whole world. He towered over his people, thrusting his brawny arms out high, a mace in one hand and a sword in the other. Wide bands of gold covered his arms from wrist to elbow.

A wave of cold ran up Ur-sag-enki's back, and he shuddered. *All our enemies surely surrender when they see our fierce and powerful king.*

He was not the only person affected by the glory of the king. The cheering petered out. Some women gasped or covered their faces. Other people fell to their knees. Babies howled.

"It's like looking at a god," Shatirra choked out, tears streaming from her eyes.

He reached for her hand, and she clutched his tightly as the king on his bed slowly passed by.

At last the king was beyond them. Ur-sag-enki let out a breath he hadn't realized he'd been holding and dropped Shatirra's hand. Many more beds followed, smaller ones carried by slaves. The first held a dignified woman in a lot of jewelry. Her face looked kind. He felt his mouth pull into a smile. *She must be the king's wife.* Cheers rang out again and echoed.

The next several beds held the king's sons and daughters. They moved by slowly. First the oldest son went past and then the other children. All had pleasing, clean faces, and all dressed in white and wore gold jewelry. All sat on their beds with as much dignity as their mother.

Ur-sag-enki yawned and shuffled his feet. His stomach grumbled, and he remembered longingly all the food vendors they had passed when they entered the city. He hoped something good would follow the royal family. Maybe another caged cat! Or a bellowing aurochs with huge curved horns!

Then his gaze locked on a girl in the second-to-last bed. Thick blue-black hair flowed down her long neck to her waist. Her face and chest shone like the moon. Her kohl-encircled eyes were modestly cast down. She was maybe two years younger than his own twelve years.

His breath stopped, and goosebumps pebbled his skin. He forgot all the wonders that had come before. He forgot that he was in a crowd. He forgot he was a simple boy from a farm. He stepped toward her, reaching out his hand.

"Boy!" growled the nearest soldier. "Get back!" He shoved Ur-sag-enki into the crowd.

Ur-sag-enki stumbled. As Bau-iggal screeched, he stepped on the sandaled foot of a man smelling of spices and incense.

"Watch it, peasant!" The merchant elbowed him aside.

Ur-sag-enki grabbed Bau-iggal and steadied her on his shoulders.

The man's daughters tittered.

Ur-sag-enki was too entranced by the girl carried on a bed to be embarrassed. His gaze had never left her: not when the soldier shoved him, not when he stumbled, not when the merchant pushed him, not even when the girls laughed at him. Nothing mattered but the girl in the parade.

"Who is she?" he whispered, his hand shaking as he pointed.

"A princess, silly," Shatirra answered.

"She makes the goddess Inanna jealous," he said.

A hand rested lightly on his shoulder. He glanced behind and then down. Their mother had found them. He brushed his cheek against Ama's hand.

She smiled, her eyes disappearing among her wrinkles. "That's the Princess Nindalla. They call her the Jewel of Eridu."

"Nindalla, the Jewel of Eridu." Ur-sag-enki breathed the words reverently, tasting them on his tongue. His knees wobbled. "When I grow up, I will make her my bride."

The people on either side laughed.

Ama shook him gently. "Hush! Don't make a fool of yourself. The daughters of kings don't marry the sons of farmers."

Nindalla lifted her face. Her gaze caught Ur-sag-enki's—and held. His eyes opened so wide they hurt, and the princess's mouth twitched in amusement. He could not look away, even when his eyes grew gritty in the dry desert air.

She smiled, her eyes crinkling.

He smiled so hard that his teeth bit into his lips and his jaw hurt.

The princess outright grinned. Her sister rapped her arm.

Nindalla jerked into a stiff posture. Her eyes lost their merriment, turning hard as pebbles. Blushing, she dropped her gaze.

His vision blurred. Bau-iggal's weight on his shoulders seemed to double, and he tottered. "Please, Lord Enki, let her look at me again," he prayed aloud.

"Nindalla is promised to a prince," said an eavesdropping woman in a dirty shift.

Ur-sag-enki's stomach dropped. "A prince? Where?" he had to ask, blinking moisture back into his dry eyes.

Ama hissed and pulled his earlobe.

"Far, far away," the woman replied. "So far away they don't speak Sumerian."

Shatirra, leaning against him, shuddered. "She'll marry a man her abba has never met, never judged suitable. She'll never see her brothers again. I'm glad I'm not a princess."

Behind the king's family marched more soldiers, armed with spears they beat against the road. Then the procession ended. People drifted away in clusters, chattering about the parade and the offerings they had brought for Enki and whether there would be any food left.

Ur-sag-enki was stuck as solidly in place as the temple. He stared after Nindalla, memorizing her every curve and angle as her bed was carried farther and farther away. "Nindalla, the Jewel of Eridu," he whispered, wanting to hear the words once more.

When at last the beautiful princess was out of sight, Ama sighed. "Come. We must leave the city now. The goats and sheep need milking." She bustled away.

Ur-sag-enki lagged behind, kicking up dust with his toes. He had to meet the princess. He had to rescue her from the prince of Susa, a barbarian who must baa like a sheep or screech like a monkey because he could not speak Sumerian. But how could he do it?

Shatirra put her arm around him again. "Forget the princess. When it's time, our parents will find you a good bride. A farmer's daughter who knows how to help you on the farm."

He pulled away from her embrace. Shatirra was his best friend. How could she not see what he knew deep in his belly?

"Nindalla is my destiny."

Shatirra rolled her eyes; he glared back.

Bau-iggal laughed and cooed as she bounced on Ur-sag-enki's shoulders. But he and Shatirra did not speak as they snaked through the crowd until they had almost caught up with Ama and Abba.

"I will marry her," he hissed.

Shatirra placed a conciliatory hand on his arm. "Peace, Brother. If the gods decreed it at the cutting of your navel cord, it will come to be."

– Chapter 2 –

Fifteen years later
City of Susa, Elam

Susa dominated the flat, weedy plain surrounding it, rising high on thousands of years of previous settlements. "The mountain that strikes terror," one earlier Sumerian king had called it. Tall brick walls safeguarded the city; another set circled the sacred precinct near the center of the city. A branch of the river to the west ran through Susa. Despite the gates in the city wall, the sons and daughters of Susa considered themselves safe against invaders and besiegers.

Today, the children of Susa were being proved wrong.

On the plain on either side of the river, the immense army of Sargon of Akkad clashed with the desperate men who defended their mother city: King Ebarti, his able-bodied sons, his guards and soldiers, even ordinary sons of Susa. But they could no more prevail than could ants battling a river flood.

Those watching from the ramparts gathered their children and valuables. Some hid. Others fled from the east gate, the soldiers grimly clustered there, too few to stop the determined citizens.

In the sprawling palace in the center of Susa, a birthing hut hunkered in a small, out-of-the-way outside courtyard, purposely cut off from the outside world. The birthing hut was for women only, a structure of reed with no windows. Large enough to hold the laboring woman, her midwife, the incantation priestess, and several attendants who served also as witnesses for royal births, it was also small enough to provide the pregnant woman a comforting, womblike atmosphere with no distractions from her important job of giving birth. The self-contained world contained everything the woman needed: oils, amulets, beer, birthing bricks, and plenty of linens and lengths of fine wool cloth.

Today, though, the outside world intruded all too obviously. Battles are not quiet.

Princess Nindalla waddled in circles inside the birthing hut, passing the time between the contractions that came every fifteen minutes now with the death bite of a leopard. In the heat, the cool dirt felt good under her feet. She was careful not to step her dusty feet onto the woven reed mats scattered about for sitting and sleeping. She also kept her circles far from the chamber pot, which steamed in the warm air with a stench that made her want to vomit.

Once again, she straightened her spine into a posture more appropriate for a princess, knowing that when the next contraction hit, she would hunch again like any woman giving birth.

In the middle of the hut near the birthing bricks, her mother-in-law, Queen Ri-ti; the incantation priestess; Sagburru the midwife; and Nindalla's attendants all argued.

Her incantation priestess was Zana herself, high priestess of the temple of Inshushinak, the city god of Susa. Nindalla would have preferred anyone else. But Queen Ri-ti had insisted on her friend the high priestess, who had disliked Nindalla almost since she had arrived to marry Crown Prince Humba. *I pronounced one word wrong in a ritual as a girl new to Susa, and she holds it against me forever.*

Nindalla kept her face serene even though fear choked her throat and squeezed her chest. Princesses gave birth, as they did everything else, with quiet dignity.

Even when outside the palace walls screams rang, weapons clanged, and soldiers shouted roughly in several foreign tongues.

She stroked one of the amulets tied to her arm, running her fingertips over the soft, warm amber with its carving of a knife. Then she touched the cooler rock-crystal amulet next to it, which was carved with a goatfish.

"Enki, Lord of the Waters, protect my daughters during this time of turmoil," she prayed. "Abi and Bar are brave girls. Too brave and daring sometimes. Please, Lord Enki, keep your gaze on them. Stay their steps and do not let them go to see the uproar outside the walls of the city."

She pressed her lips together. Any good nursemaid would have hidden the children and insisted on palace guards to protect them. But her husband, Crown Prince Humba, had insisted that his old goose of a wet nurse look after all the royal children while his father the king led the sons of Susa to war. Now she had to worry about Abi and Bar as well as the child to come.

Princess Ka'a, Humba's thin, skittish sister, left the arguing women and walked beside her. A loud shout went up outside the city, and Ka'a jumped, grabbing Nindalla's arm.

"I'm so afraid of the Akkadian soldiers. Father says King Sargon is a monster," Ka'a said in her high, whispery voice. "With the baby coming, you must be terrified."

Sagburru the midwife spun toward them, her wrinkled lips pressed together in disapproval. "None of that kind of talk."

Nindalla suppressed a smile. The midwife clearly believed she outranked a royal princess of Susa, at least in the birthing hut.

"Nindalla, why don't you sit and rest?" Despite the midwife's polite phrasing, it was an order.

Nindalla sank gratefully onto a stool. Sagburru anointed Nindalla with sesame oil and said a prayer.

She closed her eyes and let the trickling warmth soothe her dry skin and calm her spirit. She wiped a finger across her chest to pick up some oil and smoothed it across her cracked lips.

"You should have used the midwife I suggested," Queen Ri-ti said, her voice heavy with disapproval. She fussed with her perfectly coiffed hair with a hand heavy with jeweled rings. "The baby would be here by now and we could return to the palace. You are putting us all in danger."

Zana said, "She has always been willful and inconsiderate."

"My apologies, Mother, High Priestess." Nindalla exchanged looks with Sagburru.

The queen's choice of midwife had deserted Nindalla hours ago. Sagburru had trudged into the palace only a week earlier with a letter of recommendation from Nindalla's oldest sister, E-kug, who lived in Uruk. Yet Sagburru remained, her old face determined, her voice comforting her with Sumerian words that brought back memories of her destroyed childhood home.

Home. Beautiful Eridu, with its golden temple, wide harbor, and shimmering marshes. Will I ever feel at home anywhere again?

Nindalla would need to send E-kug a great gift for the loan of her midwife.

"You must drink more," Sagburru said, wiping her own forehead with her arm. "It's almost hot enough in here to bake bread." She filled a fluted silver bowl with red beer and offered it to Nindalla.

She seized the boat-shaped bowl with both hands and sucked the warm, thick, bitter liquid through the long spout as fast as she could. The beer soothed her parched throat.

"Would you like some more, my lady?" Sagburru asked, filling another beer bowl.

"She has had enough. Are you trying to slow this already slow birth?" the queen snapped.

Sagburru offered Nindalla the bowl.

Nindalla cocked her head and listened. Clangs, crashes, and screams penetrated from the world outside the birthing hut. The clamor gave no hints about how the battle was going. Her stomach fluttered even though she was certain that Susa was winning and that the citizens were safe behind Susa's strong walls.

"No more beer for now," she said, although her dry mouth begged for more. She added in a low voice that she hoped the others wouldn't hear, "If we are in danger, I don't want to slow my labor."

Several screams rang out. Ka'a clapped her hands over her ears. "I cannot bear it. Not any longer. I am going to scream myself if the noise continues. I must know what's happening in the city."

"*Outside* the city," Nindalla corrected. She clenched her hands to keep them from shaking. "*Outside* the city. Our husbands are returning to Susa with Akkadian prisoners of war." She would not, could not, let herself believe anything else, not while her daughters were in the palace and she had a son to bear.

"The screams are closer than—"

"Don't. Not in here," Sagburru snapped at Ka'a. She again anointed Nindalla with oil.

Nindalla shivered. The oil felt wonderful as it ran down her heavy, naked body, and it would help the child come faster.

An animal-horn trumpet brayed. Ka'a burst into tears.

Nindalla's calm shattered like a fallen pot. "Go! Check on my daughters and the other royal children. Make sure they are safe and well hidden."

Ka'a did not make even a token protest. She kissed Nindalla's hand and ran out, leaving the reed door open behind her.

Nindalla met Sagburru's eye. "Perhaps the child is so slow to come because the women's words have made it afraid."

The midwife nodded. "I've seen such happen. Many children hold back if there is fear or discord in the birthing hut."

The queen rounded on her. "Your insolence is unbearable. We will leave. Now." She pulled a pin from her hair and jabbed it back in.

Sagburru pursed her lips. "Two women must stay here to bear witness to the birth."

Nindalla placed her hand on Sagburru's arm. She would be glad if the fearful women left. "When the child is ready to arrive, I will send you to fetch someone."

"As you wish, my lady. Will you mount the birthing bricks now? Perhaps they will remind your body how to push out this reluctant child."

In a flurry of colorful linen and flashing jewelry, the women hurried toward the door of the birthing hut, including Zana.

Sagburru spoke sharply. "You can't leave, high priestess. It's time for you to call on the gods."

Zana's face tightened as if she might refuse such a disrespectful request.

It serves her right to be ordered around by a midwife, Nindalla thought. *She has spent her time in the birthing hut gossiping instead of praying for me.*

The priestess glared at Sagburru and then, at last, began the Sumerian incantation that Nindalla had insisted she chant.

"The woman, it is her day, it is her month.

"May Enki, patron of Eridu, protect his daughter.

"May he chase all demons from this place of women."

Nindalla squatted on the birthing bricks, one foot on each. She put her hand on the bulge of her belly and sang along softly to the rest of the familiar words.

"May Damgalnunna, Lady of Eridu, wife of Enki, protect her daughter.

"May she escort Nintu, Lady of the Birthing Hut, to this place of water and blood.

"May the great mountain Enlil protect the woman, protect the child.

"May Ningirin, Lady of Incantations, protect the woman, protect the child.

"The woman, it is her day, it is her month."

The power of the gods' arrival in the hut rocked Nindalla at the same time as a strong contraction. "It is my day. It is my month," she chanted. "It is my day. It is my month."

Nindalla's body remembered. The birthing bricks rough against the soles of her feet. The burnt smell of the ashes below her, waiting to catch fluids. The sweat running down her face, breasts, and back, splattering the ashes to make dark spots. Today she would welcome the new child.

If she did not perish from the bearing as one of her sisters had. *Why does this child not come?*

"It may be my day and my month, but it's certainly not yet my hour," she panted.

The incantation priestess frowned and tossed her head. Her gold earrings and necklaces rustled and tinkled. "What blasphemy! I will join the queen." She stalked out the door.

"The cowards have all found reasons to abandon you." Sagburru turned her head and spat. "Don't you worry about me. I'll leave only to fetch the witnesses."

"Now we can have peace." Nindalla shook her head. "They complain so much, yet their lives are soft and easy."

"When they have known true sorrow, as we have, they will be as dauntless and long-suffering as we are."

"You suggest I be more patient?" Nindalla's back tightened painfully. A second later, her viscera twisted like laundry being wrung out by a washerwoman. Nindalla rode it out, huffing, counting to sixty in her head. The contraction released her, although she ached all over from the experience. She put her hand to her back and rubbed it. "Sagburru, you have been my only friend today, so I will take your advice and be more patient with my husband's family. I will also pray to Inshushinak that he protect them from ever knowing misery."

The hut became blissfully quiet. The golden light filtering in gilded everything in the birthing hut, turning it into a goddess's sanctuary and filling Nindalla with awe that she had been blessed by the gods with the sacred role of birth-giver.

Only her hard breathing disrupted the stillness.

Softly, sweetly, the midwife sang several birthing songs and praise hymns to the god Enki and the mother goddess Nintu. Nindalla's tight body relaxed. She swayed in time. When the midwife ran out of songs, Nindalla sang the birthing incantation several more times.

A scream rang out.

The incantation on Nindalla's lips died. She could not pretend that the scream came from outside the city walls. It came from nearby, within the walls encircling the palace itself, perhaps even within the courtyard in which the birthing hut stood.

The gates of the Underworld opened, or so it seemed. The air thickened with cries and shouts, wails and screams, and the clanking of weapons. She wrapped her arms around her belly.

"You've had three children, eh?" Sagburru asked loudly.

"Yes. Three daughters." *If only I could be with my girls now to protect them!* With pride she added, "Two still live, strong and healthy."

Sagburru stroked her hand. "Their health bodes well for this child. What are their names?"

"Abi is eight years old, and Bar is four."

Sagburru anointed her again with oil. "Your child is most reluctant to enter the world."

Pain ripped through Nindalla's belly and burned down her legs and across her back. She gasped. "He has changed his mind at last! Fetch the witnesses." She and Sagburru grinned at each other. Then Nindalla remembered her dignity, and Sagburru's face crinkled with worry.

Sagburru handed her a stout piece of bark to chew. "I'll hurry, my lady. Try to restrain the child until I return."

"I will. I need those witnesses. My husband must have no possible reason to deny my son and set me aside for . . . for the children's former nursemaid. Midu."

Sagburru raised her eyebrows. "For a nursemaid?"

Nindalla clarified, bitterness seeping into her words. "She is also his concubine."

— Chapter 3 —

Many breaths went by, and many more breaths. Nindalla counted the time between contractions. They were getting closer together. The world shrank to birthing hut, bricks, and belly. Time lost its meaning, just as it had during her previous births.

Still, it seemed a long time since Sagburru had left her.

She looked up and listened. The light filtering between the reeds of the walls had changed to the soft pinkish-purple of early evening. The sounds of battle had stopped, but the normal sounds of servants and slaves going about their tasks had not resumed. The quiet felt wrong.

She shivered, and her throat and mouth burned with a sour taste. Why was she still alone? "Sagburru! It is my time!" she shouted in Sumerian. "Come quickly!"

Neither the midwife nor anyone else answered her call. Her hand clutched her belly. The baby wanted out. Pain overcame all her training in self-discipline. She screamed like a calf being castrated. When the contraction released its grip, she shouted for help again, this time in Elamite.

Still no one came. Her breath sped up. *I'm on my own.*

Birth was risky enough with a midwife and an incantation priestess present. Her thoughts whirled in panic. *Enki has deserted me. Nintu has deserted me. All the gods have left the birthing hut. My child will be born a monstrosity or dead.*

Terror like a heavy cape of wolf fur enveloped her. She clawed her hands through her hair and moaned even as her pain dissipated under her worry for her child. She had never experienced such fear, not on her wedding night, not during her previous births, not ever.

She eyed the door. *Could I crawl that far? Could I crawl farther yet, across the courtyard and into the palace itself?* She couldn't move even a toe. Fear glued her to the birthing bricks as the new prince struggled to free himself.

The sun was descending for his nightly journey through the Underworld. It would be her time very soon now, midwife or not, witnesses or not. "It is my day. It is my month," she chanted. She forced her arm to move. Balancing on her other three limbs, she stroked an amulet on which was scribed an incantation against demons. "It is my day. It is my month. It is my day. It is my month."

"My lady, do you need help?"

She flinched at the deep voice and looked toward it. It belonged to a bulky man who, even though he stooped, filled the doorway, a dark silhouette against the dying pink light.

She wrapped her free arm protectively around her belly and squinted. The man wore the snug leather helmet of a soldier, but she had never seen the dust-smeared, sweat-streaked, blood-splattered face before. He carried a sickle-sword and a mace with a head of black stone.

She stared at the darkened mace head. How many skulls had it broken? Was hers next? She licked her lips, and her hands balled into fists. She had left her dagger in her quarters.

Her only weapon was her status. "How dare you enter the birthing hut? Leave at once."

The man ignored her order. He stepped inside and let his weapons drop like a man weary of fighting. He tugged his helmet from his head, dropped it without looking where it fell, and raised his palms. "Peace, my lady."

Only now did she notice his language. "You speak Sumerian!" Even his accent was familiar; he spoke the patois of the lower class of her home city. Her chest loosened, and she drew a deep breath despite the muscles squeezing her torso. "You're from Eridu-that-was."

"Yes, my lady. From the home of Enki, praise be to him."

His black hair confirmed he was a Sumerian, one of the black-headed people. He was an ally, not one of Sargon of Akkad's men. A tall and handsome ally, the breadth and brawniness of his shoulders obvious despite the short tunic he wore above his skirt. His dark eyes radiated compassion.

A sigh escaped her. "Your voice is honey to my ear. It has been years since I heard the speech of a loyal child of Eridu."

The soldier winced and looked around the hut. "Where's your midwife?"

"She left and never returned. But you must leave. No men—" She gasped and waited out the contraction, fighting her body's almost overwhelming urge to push. "Men are forbidden in the birthing hut. Go, find the midwife. Or any woman. My child is ready."

The man again disobeyed. He rinsed his hands in a bowl of cedar-scented water and hunkered down in front of her nakedness.

– Chapter 4 –

Ur-sag-enki had been in more dangerous situations, but never one as strange. He squared his shoulders. *I can do this.* He'd helped Ama birth lambs and kids. Once he'd helped the miller with a cow whose calf came out feet first. How different could a human baby be?

A lot different, he learned, as the woman's face twisted into a hideous expression completely unlike the intent, worried look of a laboring sheep. The woman panted as hard as if she had just fought, and defeated, a full company of soldiers. "It's time to lie down," he rasped.

Her head jerked up. Damp black hair swung in front of her face. "Are you a simpleton?"

He frowned. Did she really want to give birth crouching on bricks? Her position looked awkward and hard to stay in. Worse yet, if he could not see her *murub,* how would he know whether the baby was coming out headfirst, tail first, or feet first?

He had seen a human birth once, when his ama birthed his sister Bau-iggal. He shouldn't have been in the house, but a thick sandstorm roared outside. The midwife banished him to a corner to grind seeds.

But he peeked.

Now he remembered: His mother had crouched, and the midwife had caught the babe from underneath.

Underneath! The skin of his arms prickled. This was no lamb that would gently pulse out sideways from its heaving ama into his waiting arms. This baby would plummet from her unseen *murub*. It would hit the ground if he didn't catch it. Sweat dripped over his brow and stung his eyes.

"The child. Is coming," the woman puffed.

"Lord Enki! Lady Nintu! Help me!" He thrust his hands under her. Glistening sweat ran off her body and dripped onto his arms.

Supplies. He would need supplies. "Linens. Water. Oil. Salt. A sharp reed. Binding strips," he demanded, pretending he was speaking to his quartermaster, trying to hide his panic under clipped words. "Where?"

Moaning, she gestured vaguely toward a corner. Her eyes closed halfway, and she bucked like a goat. She strained so hard that her skin turned a mottled red.

Something slimy and pointed bumped Ur-sag-enki's hands. He frowned. The baby was too light. He leaned low to check the woman's *murub*, then nearly jumped away in shock. "My lady! What do I do now? Only the head came out."

She growled a chuckle. "The rest of the babe will soon follow."

Chastened, he clenched his jaw and put his hands beneath her again, supporting the head as he waited. The woman moaned. Other sounds that he hoped never to hear again ripped from her throat.

His vigor drained away as if he had run for miles, and his liver, the seat of emotions, quivered at her distress. It told him to help her. It demanded that he stroke her back, tell her a story, give her some beer. That he do something, anything, to ease her suffering.

I can't comfort her. The child is coming. "Great Lord Enki, you are not a god of the birthing hut, but you are my patron. I need your help now. Guard us from demons, and help the child enter the world. I will sacrifice a sheep to you if you do these things."

The woman grunted like a satisfied pig and sighed, and the infant plopped into his hands.

I caught it! He stared at it, stunned, and hefted it. A solid child. He gently brushed slime from its face and then its body. A boy. He was well-formed, and his hair was black and straight, like his Sumerian mother's.

"Lay it on its belly," the woman said.

Ur-sag-enki did as ordered and stroked the baby's soft back. The tiny form coughed. "Praise Enki!" he exclaimed. Belatedly he remembered the afterbirth was yet to come. He set the baby aside and reached out. The woman pushed again and again. The placenta dropped into his hands as if he had been a midwife for years.

The woman panted. "A prince?"

He jerked; the woman was royal. *Had been royal.* He told her a half-truth. "It's a boy."

"You have the friendship of the royal house of Susa forever. Know that you may call upon me as your sister. Anytime. You will be heard."

When her panting slowed, she threw her head back and tried to brush her heavy hair off her face. Strands stuck to her eyes and her damp cheeks and forehead. She pulled each strand free and pushed it behind her ear. Her left cheek emerged. Her nose and left eye. Her lips. Finally the right side of her face.

"Brother, I will ask my husband, Prince Humba, to reward you handsomely."

His response caught in his throat. He knew those kohl-rimmed eyes, that goddess-like face, glowing despite the blotches from her exertions. Nindalla, the Jewel of Eridu. *My destiny.*

His hands shook. He had dreamed of her for years. Now he knelt by her side as her friend and brother . . . a tongue-tied friend and brother. *How can I possibly tell her that I killed the king of Susa and her husband, the crown prince, in battle? And that I am the new lord of Susa? That her son is prince of nothing? That she and her son live—or die—at my whim?*

— Chapter 5 —

Ur-sag-enki's patron god, Enki, liked to play tricks. The god had finally reunited him with the woman of his destiny—but only after making him her enemy.

Sourness erupted in the back of Ur-sag-enki's mouth. The princess was looking at him, waiting for a reply to her generosity. He had to say something. He swallowed three times before he could force out a polite acknowledgment. "You honor me more than I deserve," he croaked.

"That is my privilege." Nindalla gestured at the infant. "Find the midwife, quickly. She needs to finish the child's entrance into the world before a demon snatches it."

The victorious Akkadian soldiers were sacking the palace. He couldn't leave her alone here. If he had stumbled upon the princess, despite the isolation of the birthing hut, a drunken soldier with bad intentions might as well.

He shook his head. "Too dangerous."

Her eyes hardened and her lips pressed together. Apparently, she was not used to being contradicted. But he was not in the habit of putting women in harm's way. He crossed his arms and answered her glare with a smile that contained no yielding or compromise.

She crossed her arms too and drew herself upright. "If you will not fetch the midwife, then you must do her duties. First, wipe my son clean with linen," she ordered. She watched as he cleaned the baby, which took surprisingly long: The child had nooks and crevices and folds everywhere, from his ears to his toes. At last the baby's skin was clean.

Ur-sag-enki admired his work. The child's black hair shone. In his wide Sumerian face, solemn black eyes looked into Ur-sag-enki's, and a tiny fist grabbed his finger.

Warmth exploded in his belly and spread throughout his body. Fierce joy intoxicated him like good beer. He held the child closer, knowing that he would kill to keep the boy safe, awed by the power of a baby.

Nindalla's tense words interrupted his ecstasy. "Now you must sever the navel cord."

His hands trembled as he set the cleaning cloths aside. Cutting the navel cord was the most dangerous and vulnerable time for the spirit of a newborn. He could make no mistake.

Ur-sag-enki tied the navel cord with green thread in two places a finger's width apart and picked up the sharpened reed. Nindalla crouched like a lion ready to spring, but she said nothing. He knew enough to keep silent too. Noise during the cutting of the navel cord attracted ill luck and demons.

The princess rubbed an amulet tied to her leg as he took a deep breath and sliced between the threads. Keeping the baby on his lap with one hand, he picked up the placenta with the other and slipped it into the waiting jar.

They both held still, waiting. The baby cooed. A cool night breeze fluttered through the birthing hut. No demons appeared.

The princess let out her breath with a sigh. "Now rub him with salt and oil."

He followed her instructions. Then he picked up the binding strips and wrapped them around the child until his arms and legs were as tightly bound as if he were still in the womb. Contented, the baby yawned, his eyes drooping.

"All the boy lacks is a name!" Ur-sag-enki broke into a grin and looked at Nindalla. Their gazes locked as they had once before, fifteen years earlier. She smiled back and held out her arms for the child. Their smiles stretched seconds into years.

They were alone in the world, he and Nindalla. Nothing existed but the birthing hut, the cool dirt of its floor, and the child whose birth bound them.

The room had darkened. Nindalla changed before his eyes. She was no longer a frightened woman who needed his help. Now her oiled, naked body captivated him.

Before he could stop himself, his gaze caressed her milk-swollen breasts, the roundness of her belly, and the sturdiness of her legs. Her neck was still long; her gaze was again lowered in modesty. She eased her knees off the birthing bricks onto the floor and grabbed as many wool cloths as fit in her grasp. "Turn around."

Heat crawled up his neck and spread over his face. It was little comfort that the dark night and his tan would hide his blush. "I'll return soon," he said. He laid the child on a cushion, grabbed the jar with the placenta, and hurried outside.

The stink of corpses greeted him, wafting over the walls from places of carnage. The metallic tang of blood filled his nose, and insects buzzed as they conducted a reconnaissance of the bodies. Grimacing, he surveyed the scene.

Across the dirt courtyard, past some outbuildings and outside a door in the man-height-thick palace wall, lay the bodies of two women. Was one the missing midwife? His imagination filled in what he could not see in the shadows of the moonlit night.

He swayed, remembering other conquered cities, other bodies. His own father cut in half, his parts lying in a puddle of his own blood.

He would have to tell Princess Nindalla what had happened today. That Susa had fallen to the Akkadians. That her husband was dead. That he himself had killed the prince.

The end of the battle filled his mind again. A group of terrified women fleeing the city and dragging children behind them ran right toward him. General Qisig had shouted an order at him: "Kill them!"

"No, sir," he had shouted back. "I don't kill women and children." The women darted past him and lost themselves among the camp followers.

The general's face turned purple. Ur-sag-enki was sure that the general would have him executed. Perhaps the general would kill him himself.

Instead, the general had gestured him over to a line of richly dressed prisoners against the city wall. All had been stripped of their armor, and a gray-haired man already lay dead. Three younger men stood between several Akkadian guards.

The general reached out with his sickle sword and pricked the chest of the man who looked oldest. "If you disobey my next order, I will strike your head from your body."

"Yes, sir," he said in a firm voice even though his knees wobbled.

"Kill Crown Prince Humba."

Praise Enki! The general wanted him to kill an enemy soldier, not innocents. The chosen prisoner held his head high and looked past Ur-sag-enki as if he were beneath notice.

Ur-sag-enki walked up to the man and stuck his dagger into the heart. The prince died instantly.

As Ur-sag-enki had cleaned his dagger, the general said, "You are now the governor of Susa. If Prince Humba's wife lives, I give her to you as a wife."

He shook his head. The general had always been volatile, but receiving such honors after refusing a direct order baffled him. He should have been dead. Instead he ruled a great city and soon would have a beautiful wife.

He must tell Nindalla that Susa had fallen and her husband was dead before she left the birthing hut and saw two bodies, an unpropitious sight. In normal times, a woman rested in the birthing hut for eight days until she was no longer ritually impure. Nindalla could not stay here; he would not let her. It was too dangerous.

But he would not tell her that he had been the one to execute Prince Humba, not yet. It would be a big enough burden for her for now to know she was a widow.

He pulled his gaze from the dead women and circled the birthing hut looking for something to dig with. The midwife would have been prepared to bury the placenta; he just needed to find where she left her digging tool.

Inside the birthing hut, Nindalla sang softly. Not an incantation to protect her baby but a lullaby from his childhood. The song clutched at his chest, warming him with memories of his family. His mother had sung the lullaby to Bau-iggal after she was born. He had sung it to Bau-iggal often himself. He closed his eyes and let the song enfold him, pretending he was again a boy, carefree and beloved.

When the song ended, he sighed. He was a man now, a man with responsibilities, such as the placenta he carried. He continued around the birthing hut. Against the rear leaned a baked-clay trowel. He set the jar down and dug a deep hole near the tall wall behind the hut. Nindalla would want time to clean and dress herself, so he took his time burying the jar. When he finished, he stomped the clay hard so that no animals would dig up the spot. He brushed dust off his knees with much noise and grunting.

He went back into the birthing hut. The woman's hair was neatly combed. She wore a clean shift held together at her left shoulder with a gold pin, and around her neck a necklace of clear beads dangled a carved cylinder between her breasts.

The baby on her lap absorbed her full attention. She explored his face and hair with gentle fingers. She had already outlined his beautiful eyes with kohl.

A fierce protectiveness engulfed him, stronger than any bloodlust he had felt in battle. He had tried to protect Ama and his sisters, but he had been an ignorant boy. He *would* protect Nindalla and her baby. He clenched his fists. This time he would not fail.

Ur-sag-enki cleared his throat. "Such an ugly child! It has the face of a lizard. You have my pity."

"It is malformed as well." She sighed long and loudly. "Get the hideous creature out of my sight. Put it out for the dogs."

If any demons were listening, they would lose interest in the boy, believing him not worth stealing.

Still, it didn't hurt to take every precaution. He looked for a lamp and found several under a bench. He pulled one out, checked the wick and the level of oil in the brownish-yellow clay dish, and struck a spark with his flint. Then he lit a second one. Light gave safety from creatures of the dark.

There was one more thing he could do now. He reached for the amulet that hung from a cord around his throat.

He stopped with his hand halfway to his neck: He was acting as if the child were his.

He was a soldier hardened in battle, yet his belly felt warm when he looked at the mother with her child. He felt soft, content, fulfilled. He longed to touch them, to gather them in his arms, to protect them. His liver so overflowed with love that he would face a lion for either one. It was a good feeling.

But not an appropriate one for a soldier newly promoted to city governor.

He forced his thoughts to cold, heartless strategy. General Qisim had sent him to find the crown princess for a reason. To hold the city, he would need this child alive and healthy and in his possession: The boy was the last of the royal line of Susa. Marrying Nindalla would legitimize Ur-sag-enki's governorship.

His liver twinged, rebelling at the governor's orders. Demons could take the man and his cold plotting! Ur-sag-enki would marry Nindalla because she was his destiny. The gods had decreed it at his birth. The shiny black hair he yearned to touch, the beautiful eyes he longed to look into, the rare smile he wanted to coax out—he had known they would be his since the day of the New Year's Festival. He had never loved another woman, never expected to.

He had been waiting for her.

His skin tingled from his feet to his scalp. He had looked for her in every conquered city, his heart pounding each time he caught a glimpse of long, heavy hair or a certain arrogant tilt of the head. He had been disappointed too many times to count.

Now his restless body longed to jump around or dance. He grinned widely. *I must look like a fool!* But he didn't care. At last the gods had brought him to her! *I will protect her and keep her safe always. I will let no one, not General Qisim, not even King Sargon himself, harm her or her baby.*

He untied the amulet from his neck. It was a baked-clay figurine of a goat, an animal sacred to the god Enki. He wound the leather thong around it and tucked it inside the baby's bindings.

Nindalla looked up and smiled. "You have done well, soldier. Find Prince Humba. Learn what name I should give his son and successor. Then bring my daughters here."

He squeezed his eyelids shut as his body suffered the pain hers did not know to feel. The woman had daughters in the palace, a palace overrun by soldiers drunk on blood and beer and victory. "My lady— " He stopped. He couldn't tell her, not yet. She deserved a time of happiness with her baby first.

He started again. "Too dangerous."

Her smile disappeared. "He has been swaddled. It is time for him to receive his name. If there is danger, my daughters should be with me. Bring them here. Find my husband."

A warm bead of sweat ran down his forehead. He needed some excuse to stay here and protect her, but his thoughts jostled like racing chariots.

"Why are you still here?" she demanded.

Clever Enki sent him an idea. "Earlier you named me 'Brother.' A brother should never put his sister or her child in danger. My lady, I suggest you give the boy a temporary name."

She straightened up and frowned.

Ur-sag-enki kept improvising. "I mean, a nickname. A Sumerian name that I could call him. I speak little of your husband's language."

Her face softened. "A Sumerian name. I could call him by it too." She held the baby up and studied his face. "He shall be Enki-kiag, 'beloved of Enki,' because the god of Eridu-that-was sent you to birth and protect him."

Ur-sag-enki touched the child's head. "Enki-kiag. May Enki watch over you always."

"My daughters—"

"When it is safe, I will fetch them. I promise."

Light flickered through the spaces between the reeds. Torchlight. The heavy steps of several men approached. Ur-sag-enki and Nindalla both turned toward the door.

"Quick! Your helmet. A weapon," she ordered. "You're my guard, understand?"

The men had to be fellow Akkadian soldiers. They were no danger to him. The crown princess was his, given to him by General Qisim with the city of Susa. But if the soldiers were drunk or didn't recognize him, he might have to protect his right to her. He tugged his helmet on and picked up his mace.

He hefted the mace high with both hands and took a practice swing.

His senses became like those of an animal.

The nearest footsteps were familiar.

His stomach sank. He had to block the door, keep everyone out. He took a long step toward it.

Too slow. General Qisim—once his owner, now his commander and a favorite of King Sargon's—stomped in and shoved him inside. The general stood, hands on his hips and feet wide apart, and surveyed the dim hut. "I need a torch!"

At the sound of the general's Akkadian speech, Nindalla gasped, grabbed Ur-sag-enki's sword, and stood.

Ur-sag-enki's stomach clenched and threatened to spew its contents. Dread enveloping him, he touched his thumb to his nose in greeting, then sank to his knees before the general and touched his forehead to the ground in obeisance.

– Chapter 6 –

Light flared, blinding and brilliant.

A cold chill rolling up her back, Nindalla squinted against the glare of the torch just thrust into the birthing hut. The floor seemed as unstable and squishy as the mud along a riverbank. With one hand she clutched Enki-kiag close, and with the other she tightened her grip on Ur-sag-enki's sword.

The soldier with the air of command to whom Ur-sag-enki bowed had cruel lips, a narrow nose, and curly brown hair held in place by a gold ribbon. He was no Sumerian, and he looked like no man of Susa she had ever seen.

He had to be Akkadian.

Her head spun, and the heavy sword pulled her off balance. She struggled not to fall. The world had twisted into something unrecognizable. Her husband should be here. He needed to name the baby. Akkadian soldiers should not roam loose on the palace grounds, giving orders to a Sumerian.

She scowled at Ur-sag-enki. "Why do you grovel? Get up! Kill the accursed Akkadian!" She spat in the dirt in disdain of those who had devastated beautiful Eridu.

The Akkadian studied her. His gaze flicked around the room, alighting on the birthing bricks and the bloody linen. Quickly he backed into the doorway.

Nindalla smirked. She had one advantage: The Akkadian did not want to be tainted by her spiritual impurity.

He signaled Ur-sag-enki to rise and asked him a question. They spoke quickly; Ur-sag-enki's Akkadian flowed as fluently as his Sumerian.

Nindalla knew almost no Akkadian; she caught only her name, her husband's name, and her son's Sumerian name in Ur-sag-enki's answer.

There had to be an explanation. She was no stranger to palace intrigues; still, she could not believe Ur-sag-enki had betrayed her. Not after he aided her. Not after she declared herself his sister. Not after the smiles of shared joy and accomplishment they had exchanged.

Her skin tingled with unease. Nothing made sense. One-handed, she slid the swaddled baby inside her one-shouldered shift, where he balanced unsteadily on her swollen belly. Now she could grip the sword with two hands.

The Akkadian gave Ur-sag-enki an order, and both turned toward her. The Akkadian looked at the sword she held and snorted.

"General Qisim wants me to translate," Ur-sag-enki said in Sumerian, looking everywhere but at her.

"Then translate," she snapped, not lowering the sword even the width of a finger.

Ur-sag-enki flushed. "General Qisim says this: He has conquered the city of Susa in the name of Sargon of Akkad, the Great King; King of Kish, Lagash, Umma, and Uruk; Overlord of Sumer, Mari, and Yarmuti; and now Overlord of Susa."

No no no no no no. It cannot be.

Her chest tightened; she had to force her breath in and out with almost the effort it took to push Enki-kiag from her body.

"Go on," she said between gritted teeth.

"The general has appointed me governor of Susa." At last he looked at her, his eyes full of pain and apology. "The fighting is over. Now is time for peace. You are safe with me."

Nindalla knew better than to believe him. Her father had tutored her in politics before her marriage. He had told her the best way to cement control of a captured city was to eliminate its ruler . . . and all of his heirs.

When the Akkadians captured Eridu, they had done exactly that. They had slaughtered her father and three brothers in battle. They had executed her mother and one of her two unmarried sisters in front of Enki's temple. Her other unmarried sister, Nu-nu, had been missing since.

If Susa had fallen, and the new governor of Susa was here in the birthing hut, it could mean only one thing: King Ebarti was dead, all the princes were dead, and now they intended to kill her baby.

She squeezed her eyes together. Prince Humba, dead, despite his youth and strength and his skill with lance and battle axe. Her limbs felt heavy as bricks. Humba had not loved her, but he had not beaten her either. He had given her three fine children. He had been a strong arm between danger and his family. Now he was gone.

She gripped the sword tighter. She had only one possible course of action: Escape the birthing hut, find her daughters, and hide in one of the secret passages in the palace.

But the soldiers were hardened men filled with the joy of killing, whereas she was wracked with pain and weary to the bone from her long labor. She shook her head. *I must not think about how difficult escape will be. I have a duty to protect Enki-kiag, Abi, and Bar, and I always do my duty.*

She loosened her tight hold on her royal dignity to let the men think her weak and distraught. "What are you saying? Where is my husband? My daughters?" She let the sword wobble in her hands and shrieked her next words as if she had lost control. "Where are my daughters?"

"Calm down." Ur-sag-enki took a step forward, holding his palms face up. "I won't hurt you. In fact—"

Nindalla charged toward the door, swinging the sword wide to clear her path.

— Chapter 7 —

Ur-sag-enki had killed many men with his sword. Now its blade sliced at him.

A younger, less-experienced soldier might have been taken by surprise. But ten years ago, Ur-sag-enki had vowed never to let his guard down again. He jumped aside to stay clear of the swinging sword.

As Nindalla ran past him, he pivoted and lunged. He wrapped his arm around her hip, below the baby, and pulled her against his body, pinning her arms. He kept her tight against his body as General Qisim grasped the hilt of the sword and twisted it from her grasp.

Ur-sag-enki expected her to struggle; in fact, he would have enjoyed feeling her rounded body and beautiful hair rub against him. But she stood tall and raised her head proudly.

"I will not let you kill my son," she said in Sumerian. "I will gouge your eyes out and tear off your balls before I let you touch *Susa's true ruler.*"

The general laughed and spoke to Ur-sag-enki in Akkadian. "Subduing a conquered city is not always easy. Looks as if you'll have your hands full with this one."

The princess's damp hair smelled of perfumed oil, and her skin was soft. The hair on his arms stood up.

"You gave her to me, my lord, and I will keep her *and* my balls," Ur-sag-enki told the man who had once stolen everything from him. "She'll marry me willingly."

"She doesn't look very willing right now, and you did stick a knife between her husband's ribs." The general toyed with his large gold ring, which he had taken off the hand of the dead king of Susa. "The son is more important than the mother in keeping the city calm and amenable to your rule." He looked at Nindalla and narrowed his eyes. "Beware if you don't convince her to marry you. A woman of her spirit and upbringing can be dangerous."

"I'll convince her."

"If you don't, send her to me. I'll give her to my wife. She would love to have a princess as a slave."

Ur-sag-enki swallowed a lump in his throat. "I will convince her." He had to. She was his destiny. He would not let her be a slave.

Nindalla twisted in his arms. "What are you two saying? Speak in a civilized tongue!"

The general frowned at her tone. "You're a commoner and the man who made her a widow. She may not want you. Women are funny that way. I order you: Send her to me in Anshan if she's a problem. We can't lose Susa because of one uncooperative woman."

"We won't," Ur-sag-enki said.

"Good." The general glanced again at Nindalla and smirked. "I'll leave you to get acquainted with the princess and start your . . . persuasion. I'll meet you in the king's audience hall—*your* audience hall—at sunrise."

Treacherous. Her father had taught her to read men, and when Nindalla read the general's face, she saw a master of duplicity.

The torchbearer and the general strode out, and a sigh escaped her. Her knees knocked together. If Ur-sag-enki had not been holding her, she would have collapsed.

Nindalla pressed her palm to her chest, surprised she still lived after raising a sword to the general. Her heart thudded beneath her hand like drums for a dance. The long conversation between the two men, Ur-sag-enki's tight hold on her, the general's smirk: They added up to one conclusion. Ur-sag-enki was a loyal Akkadian soldier, and the general had given her to him.

She was bleeding from the birth, and the aching muscles in her belly still convulsed off and on. She would be spiritually impure for eight days. But despite everything, the new governor would rape her and then kill Enki-kiag. Or he would kill Enki-kiag first for the pleasure of hurting her, then rape her.

Such were the ways of war.

A princess should be dignified, calm, elegant, and an example to others. But she would do anything, risk anything, for her children.

She would even beg.

She made her voice soft and pleasant in the dark hut; she had much experience doing so in Humba's bedchamber at night. "Please, my lord—" she almost stumbled over the title but forced her way through "—do not kill my son. Please, let him go to the countryside and be given away as an orphan."

She gasped when the tight pressure of Ur-sag-enki's arms around her slackened. He took her elbow and made her turn around to face him. She stiffened. They had enjoyed a most intimate event together. Now he was a stranger and an enemy.

"My lady, you don't understand."

Her sister E-kug had written to her about what had happened at Eridu. E-kug had married an official in the royal court of Kish. Sargon had later installed her husband as governor of Uruk, so E-kug was a good source of information.

Ur-sag-enki was wrong. Nindalla understood everything.

How could she not, when she thought about it every day and sometimes dreamed about it at night?

She pulled out of his grasp and knelt awkwardly at his feet, her arms crossed over the baby inside her shift. "Please, please, don't kill Enki-kiag. Let him be raised a farmer's son with no knowledge of his birth. Please."

"Peace, my lady." He knelt beside her. "Enki-kiag is safe as long as I'm governor. I promise."

He looked so earnest that her temper flared. "Do not think me ignorant. I know what the Akkadians did in Eridu."

He shuddered. Vulnerability flashed across his face. Then it hardened. "I know what happened there too. Things will be different here." He bowed his head and was silent.

Her stomach twisted as she waited for him to speak further. She squeezed her fists and her eyes tightly to keep from retching or crying out. *I must be brave. I must be a credit to my lineage.*

"Peace, my lady," he said again. "If I wanted to kill you or your baby, I could have done it when I first found you."

"That was before the general came. He gave you new orders. I could tell from the tone of his voice."

"He told me again how to hold Susa. He still thinks of me as a thick-witted, know-nothing farm boy. He said nothing about killing."

"You betrayed Sumer and our people. You have no honor."

He flinched, and he drew back as if she had struck him. Then his face smoothed into masklike calmness. "I helped you when you were helpless." He reached out to stroke her arm.

Nindalla's jaws ground together so hard her face ached. She fought the urge to pull her arm away from his touch.

"Sister, I want to protect you."

"You deceived me earlier." She lifted her chin and glared. "Why should I believe anything you say now?"

He reached his hands out to her like a beggar asking for alms. "If you don't believe my words, believe my situation. I need you and your son."

"How can that be? My son is a threat to you and Sargon."

He shook his head, his calloused palms still beseeching her. "Not for many years. Meanwhile, if you and the baby are under my protection, I get legitimacy and your knowledge of ruling and of the children of Susa. General Qisim was right in one thing: I *did* grow up on a farm. I need your help."

She spat on the floor. "You're wasting your time if you want to be accepted as governor. The people of Susa will never accept Sargon as overlord or you as his appointee."

"In time they will. Just as people in other conquered cities have."

He sounded sincere. But statecraft required people who were convincing liars. Perhaps his ability to deceive was why the general had appointed him governor of Susa.

She had been trained in deception since birth. She would play his game . . . and win. She gave her voice a little tremble. "We'll be under your protection?"

His body loosened abruptly, and he smiled.

She leaned toward him, drawn by the gentle, wistful smile. Then she cringed. He used charm and kindness as a weapon. Despite a lifetime at court, she kept falling for it.

"Yes, you'll be under my protection," he said in a soothing voice. "So you have no reason to be scared."

He was going to great lengths to convince her that she and the baby were safe. Yet he had not mentioned her daughters.

She pressed her lips together. That did not mean they had returned to their clay. A liar would guarantee their safety, even if they were dead. He might have no idea whether they still breathed or not.

Her head ached. She rubbed a tight spot with a knuckle. "Explain again why you think being our protector will benefit you."

"As stepfather of the late King Ebarti's grandson and heir, I will be accepted as a legitimate governor."

Her thoughts circled, trying to make sense of his statement. "But you are not Enki-kiag's stepfather."

"Sister," he said and paused.

Fear tickled her skin, and her insides went cold.

"Sister, I will be his stepfather once we are married."

She gasped and rose off of her knees without meaning to. The soldier played no game. "Sister" was not only a term of friendship. It was also an endearment a husband called his wife. Abba had often called Ama so.

Ur-sag-enki truly did mean to marry her.

Father had impressed on her that she must make careful choices if she were ever a king's mother and a widow. She would have much influence, but she would also be the target of power-hungry men.

She had always assumed she would be old if she were widowed. Only now did she recall the rest of his warning. As a widow, she would be courted by every man who wanted to be regent.

At least Ur-sag-enki did not hide his motives behind poetry or false words of love. He needed her and would have to protect her. However, she would be valuable only until they united in their marriage bed. Once Ur-sag-enki was legitimately her husband and

Enki-kiag's new father, he would not need her anymore to ensure his acceptance.

Unless he really was as innocent of how to run a city as he claimed. In that case, he had little chance of keeping his seat as governor and she should not marry him if she valued her life or her son's.

Think! I must have other options.

The law here was the same as in Sumer: A widow could not be forced to marry. Ur-sag-enki needed her consent before he could make her his wife.

She relaxed onto her heels again. She would play for time and seek other options.

Ur-sag-enki's emotions whirled and churned like the muddy waters of the Euphrates in flood season.

Nindalla's face, behind the blank air of the aristocrat, hinted that like him, she was deluged with too many thoughts and too many feelings. She closed her eyes, and her shoulders sagged.

Giving birth drained a woman. He could not imagine how she could bear everything else that had happened today. He gave her time and waited for her to respond to his proposal.

"My lord, Enki-kiag needs a wet nurse. I need to see my daughters, hold them in my arms, and hear from their own lips that they are unharmed."

"So you'll marry me. Right?"

"I need an attendant. I need a messenger who speaks Elamite to carry my orders to the cooks and other servants."

"But you'll marry me?"

"I need—" Her hands rose and clutched hair on either side of her head. "I need time."

He moved a little away from her and drummed his fingers on his knee. She must realize she had few options or allies. "I don't have time. Neither do you."

"But my daughters. I have to know they are safe. I can think of nothing else."

"I told you. I'll protect you and your children."

"You do not even know whether my daughters are alive."

His fists clenched and he stood. "Fine!" He rubbed the tightness in the back of his neck. "I'll go get them so we can settle things. What are their names? What do they look like?"

"Thank you, my lord! Their names are Abi and Bar. Everyone in the palace knows them."

"Not anymore," he mumbled.

"Pardon?"

"Not anymore," he said louder, cursing himself for speaking his thought out loud.

Her hand flew to her throat, and her eyes widened. She stared at him, waiting, but he could not bear to tell her.

At last she spoke in slow, deliberate words. "Why is that?"

Why did she have to be so difficult? He answered in tones as controlled as her own. "Because many fled or are in hiding. Because many of those who didn't flee or hide are dead."

She didn't scream. She didn't cry. Ur-sag-enki wished she would. Instead, she gasped like a fish newly taken from the river, her mouth opening and closing, opening and closing. Then with trembling hands she pulled the baby out of her shift and rocked him faster and faster and faster.

"After Eridu, how could you? How could you kill so many? You are not a man. You are a demon."

Ur-sag-enki would have preferred that she stab him through the heart.

– Chapter 8 –

Rocking, rocking, rocking. Nindalla could not stop. She must have committed many sins she did not know of. Why else would the gods punish her by destroying not just one home, but two? She was doubly cursed.

Rocking, rocking, rocking. Gradually the motion calmed her. She breathed deeply of the familiar, homey scent of sesame oil burning in the lamp and of the new smell of Enki-kiag. She yawned. She had been awake for two days and two nights. Outside, an owl hooted. Inside the hut, Ur-sag-enki snored loudly like an ancient dog. He lay curled in front of the door, where anyone who tried to enter the birthing hut would stumble over him. He cuddled his mace and sickle-sword.

Oh, if only she could curse him as he slept unaware! He had deceived her again and again. He deserved for his skin to erupt in boils and for his "cedar tree" never to rise again; he deserved to mistake his sheep and cattle for his enemies and slaughter them.

But she had named herself his sister, and he had come to her aid in her time of need, as would a true brother. She also needed him to protect her from the Akkadians and to help her find Abi and Bar, whether alive or dead. She had to know their fates.

She yawned again and prodded Ur-sag-enki's foot with her own. He bolted upright with a weapon in each hand, roaring an Akkadian battle cry.

Her breath stopped, and she twisted away, shielding Enki-kiag's body with her own.

"What? What?" he shouted, leaping up and looking around.

"My lord, you fell asleep." She took a deep breath. "My daughters. Please, my lord, find them and bring them to me. And find a wet nurse for Enki-kiag. The baby will soon be hungry And bring a servant for me."

He set his weapons on the ground. "I can't leave you here alone with so many drunk soldiers around." He rubbed his eyes with his fists. "You must come with me."

Her stomach heaved. "I am impure for eight days." *And I am bleeding from the birth.* "I cannot leave the birthing hut."

"Who will know? The city is in chaos and full of strangers."

"The gods know if I sin. I will draw their wrath on the city."

Ur-sag-enki spat into the corner. "It's a luxury of the rich to believe so. They have servants and slaves who can take over their duties for a week."

"Hush! Do not speak against the gods' laws while my child remains so vulnerable."

Bitter words rushed from his mouth. "Let me tell you about the birth of my younger sister. My abba had no sisters, and his ama had already gone to her clay, so my ama had no woman with her but the midwife. She could not use the birthing hut because a sandstorm ripped it apart. She had to give birth in the house. Then the midwife left to attend another farmer's wife."

Nindalla's hand flew to her throat. "The poor woman!"

"Ama couldn't lie around for eight days. She went back to her duties. She fed us, tended Bau-iggal, milked the goats, weeded the barley, and helped Abba repair the sandstorm damage to the house and irrigation ditches. Nothing happened because of her sin. We didn't sicken. The animals didn't sicken. The crops didn't wither."

"I do not understand. Where were your servants and slaves?"

"We had none. Poor farmers are one step from being servants themselves."

Nindalla had never considered how hard the purity rules could be for the poor to follow. "Perhaps the gods forgave your mother because of her circumstances."

"Maybe they'll forgive you for the same reason."

Her sick feeling returned. It felt as if a demon had hold of her stomach, twisting and poking sharp fingernails into it. To knowingly commit a sin went against all her training. "As a princess, I have a greater duty to the gods than do other women."

"You're no longer a princess."

It was if he slapped her across the face. She was stunned into silence.

"Look," he said. "It's your choice. If your duty to the gods is your highest duty, I'm happy to go back to sleep. I need rest, and I've got a city to pacify tomorrow. But if your duty to your daughters is higher, then let's go find them."

A choice. Between two duties. Given her by a man who thought so little of his duty as a son of Eridu that he served its destroyer. Who thought so little of his duties as a farmer that he dared presume to rule a city and marry a princess. She despised his morals and his opportunism.

"It's your choice," he said again, yawning. "Just decide before I fall asleep again."

Her parents had never given her a choice. The priests and priestesses never gave her a choice. Her husband never gave her a choice. They told her what her duty was, and she did it. She had not been trained to choose.

Ur-sag-enki's eyelids slid down, and he slumped. He snored several times and then jerked upright. He looked at her as sternly as her father sometimes had. "I need your answer. Now."

"My daughters," she said then jumped in surprise. She had not made a choice yet; the words had just popped out of her mouth. Her head and shoulders loosened. "I choose to learn my daughters' fates."

Like a servant, he brought her a bowl of water for her to rinse her face. He took clean linen and fashioned a sling for Enki-kiag so that the baby would be less of a burden to carry.

Nindalla blew out a lamp. She picked up wool cloths from the pile and went into the darkest corner. Awkwardly, she reached up under her shift and wrapped more fabric about her waist and between her legs.

Ur-sag-enki picked up the one lit lamp and motioned her to the door ahead of him.

She bit her lip. The councilors and noblemen would laugh behind his back at his manners. "My lord, you must go first. You are the governor. I am . . . merely Nindalla."

His eyes flashed surprise. Then he smiled. "You see how much I need you as my wife. I've been trailing behind people my whole life. It never occurred to me that I would now walk ahead." He strode to the door, a swagger in his step.

He still carried the lamp, like a servant.

As he stooped to pass under the reed lintel, she adjusted the baby in her arms and followed him.

Five steps until she sinned. Four steps. Three steps. Two steps. One step.

She was outside. She hunched over the baby, putting an obstacle between his head and Heaven. She stopped, waiting, and licked sweat off her upper lip.

"Are you coming?" Ur-sag-enki asked.

"Yes." She scurried after him, a little unsteady.

She had broken the law of the gods, and not one had struck her down.

— Chapter 9 —

Every dead body was a lance in Ur-sag-enki's side, a reminder of the terrible day ten years earlier when the Akkadians overwhelmed Eridu and murdered Abba before his eyes.

The memories began their siege before he and Nindalla even entered the palace. The date palms cast the courtyard in shadow. As they walked side by side through the dark, Nindalla tripped over a body.

Ur-sag-enki caught her before she fell. She trembled, and for a moment he was back in Eridu on a stormy day, holding his mother up as she wailed over Abba's body.

Ur-sag-enki shook his head. *I'm in Susa with Nindalla.* The courtyard and the palace returned.

It was no surprise she had stumbled. Enki-kiag and her belly blocked her view of the ground. Ur-sag-enki kept his arm around her waist and tried to guide her inside, but she resisted.

"Is it—" She stopped to swallow. "Did I stumble over someone?"

He looked down for the shortest moment possible. "She's not one of your daughters." His voice struggled to leave his tight throat. "She's a grown woman, an older woman."

"I have to see who she is," Nindalla said. "I must name her aloud for the gods to hear and hold the Akkadians to account."

His fists balled, and his arm tightened about her waist. He thrust her away before he could hurt her and punched the wall. "May the gods curse them with pain and sickness!"

Nindalla squeaked. Mud crumbled off the wall. She looked at him with a wary gaze.

"I hate this!" He smashed his fist against his palm. "Why kill women? I've never gotten it. Women don't take part in wars. They're not soldiers. So why kill them?"

Nindalla turned away, her arm tightening protectively around Enki-kiag. She stared at him over her shoulder, her eyes wide.

He forced his rage back into hiding. "You're right. The Akkadians have much to account for." He couldn't stop the bitterness seeping into his voice. "The gods should know about this woman."

Let's get this over with. Stomach roiling, he stooped and rolled the body over. The flickering light of his lamp revealed footprints on the clothes and skin . . . and another woman's body, also dirtied by soldiers' feet. He clenched his fists again.

Nindalla gagged.

I should protect her from these sights. "Sister, let's go inside the palace."

"I have to see their faces," she insisted.

He held the lamp near the second woman's face.

The princess let out a whoosh of breath. "I do not know her."

He held the lamp near the face of the older woman. It disappeared, replaced by the face of a neighbor woman from long ago. He blinked the illusion away.

Nindalla whimpered, and her body swayed, bumping into him. "Sagburru. She is Sagburru, my midwife," she whispered. "She was returning to me with a woman to witness the birth." She shook her head. "They died for nothing. I was no longer a princess who needed witnesses."

He ground his teeth. Sagburru was a Sumerian name. He was responsible for another Sumerian death. He couldn't bear to know any more about her. "Guard!" he called in Akkadian.

A soldier stepped out of the shadows of the long passage into the palace. Even here, the palace walls were as thick as a man was tall. The soldier saluted and asked, "Yes, sir?"

"Move these poor women away from the door."

The man scratched his cheek. "Uh, I'm not supposed to leave my post."

Ur-sag-enki held the flickering lamp close to his own face and tapped his wide Sumerian nose. He said what he imagined General

Qisim might say in similar circumstances. "Look at this Sumerian face and remember it. I'm Captain Ur-sag-enki, now governor of Susa. If you disobey one of my orders again, you'll be scrubbing floors and digging graves."

"Yes, captain. I mean, governor." The soldier rushed past him, grabbed one body by a wrist, and yanked.

"They're not bags of barley," Ur-sag-enki snapped. "She could have been your mother. Have some respect." As so often happened, he felt sick at the orders he had to give.

He reminded himself that he would soon leave war behind and have a family again. After they found Nindalla's daughters, she would marry him. Enki-kiag would know no other man as father. He would get the boy a puppy. Nindalla would bear him many beautiful, laughing sons and daughters.

Spirit fortified, he strode through the door and into a short hall. Nindalla's bare feet padded behind him. At the end of the hall, they turned onto another, longer hall with doors on each side. He opened each one to find an empty, looted room. They passed several bodies, and he turned each over for her to name to the gods.

He felt sicker with each body Nindalla gave a name to. So many women! The men, of course, lay outside, on the battlefield, and just within the city gates. At least none of the bodies belonged to her daughters.

Yawning, he halted in front of the door at the end. *By the gods' navels, I am so exhausted.* "Prepare yourself. I was in here earlier. Many people are dead."

"These are Humba's quarters," she replied, her voice flat. "I have lived here for eleven years."

"They're my quarters now," he said without thinking, then chastised himself as an idiot. *She probably knew everyone lying inside.*

"Is anything of mine left?" she asked bitterly.

"Others have lost more to the Akkadians than you," he snapped. "Be grateful you have a protector and a place to live."

"I grieve for everyone's losses." She stroked her arm and the baby as if comforting herself. Then she blurted out, "You talk about the Akkadians as if they were your enemy. But you belong to their army. You are governor because they consider you one of them. You may not have killed the people we've found, but you are partly responsible for their deaths."

He could no longer control his stomach. He turned away and vomited at the base of a wall.

"You are a complex man, Governor," she said softly. "One day perhaps you will tell me your story."

When he finally stopped retching, she stepped forward tentatively, paused, and then pushed open the door.

He followed her from the gloomy hall into the courtyard, harshly bright with moonlight and torchlight. The reek of blood and shit and piss struck him like a blow, and the room spun. Nindalla made choking noises and then covered her mouth with her hand.

Huge marble vases lay toppled and broken. Palm trees sprawled across the floor, naked roots snaking toward the sky as if to petition the gods for help. Brown streaks across the stone floor showed where bodies had been dragged away from a pile of jumbled arms, legs, and heads.

His new quarters. The place where he would raise his new family, gods willing. In this courtyard, his children would laugh sweetly and play, servants would chatter as they worked, and he and Nindalla would sit by the fountain in the evening to listen to the water ripple and splash.

But not tonight. Cold quiet blanketed the courtyard. The large green bird that had screeched so loudly this afternoon sat silently now, its head tucked under its wing as it slept. The fountain no longer flowed. The only sounds were Nindalla's ragged breathing and the whoosh, whoosh, whoosh of a servant woman scrubbing the floor to remove the blood.

With a bleak face, Nindalla handed Enki-kiag to him. "I will look at the faces of the dead."

He nodded and sat on the stone edge of the fountain. "One day, little man, you will play here." Moonlight bounced off the water in a way that constantly changed yet stayed calm, peaceful, soothing. He bounced the baby on his knee and made circles with his hand in the fountain's coolness. The memories that had threatened to overwhelm him paled and lost their grip on his soul. He imagined shoving them into a sturdy chest and tying it shut with rope.

Nindalla walked to him. "Praise Enki, praise Inanna, my daughters are not in the courtyard."

"Where is their bedchamber?" Ur-sag-enki asked, his voice tight.

"Over there." Nindalla led him across the courtyard. He grimaced. The bottom of her white shift, wet and sticky with mud and blood, clung to her legs.

She led him to a doorway, but a soldier stepped out.

"No one's allowed in here."

"This is my daughters' room," Nindalla said. "I am trying to find them."

The soldier shrugged. "Everything now belongs to Sargon of Akkad and is under the authority of the new governor. If you apply tomorrow, you may be able to schedule an audience within a few months." He looked Nindalla up and down with a contemptuous smile. "I could get you in sooner. For a favor."

The affront and Nindalla's shocked inhalation inflamed Ur-sag-enki's blood like a battle cry. Didn't any of these men recognize their new governor? He shoved the baby into Nindalla's arms, balled his fist, and slammed it into the sentry's face.

The man reeled and fell to the floor, his hand cradling his jaw.

"I am the new governor of Susa, and the woman you insulted is my betrothed." He clenched and unclenched his fists. He imagined tearing the Akkadian apart, first ripping out his entrails and then twisting off his limbs and head. He hadn't been able to do it ten years ago when the Akkadians killed and raped and destroyed in Eridu. But now he had the strength and the authority.

But also the wisdom not to.

"Why is your heart so arrogant when you yourself are so lowly?" he asked the soldier. "You're nothing but a skulking jackal. Get out of my apartments."

The man scuttled along the floor, then got up and ran. Ur-sag-enki took a few steps forward, but Nindalla was not beside him. He turned. Her eyes were wide, and the skin under her left eye twitched. She exuded the metallic, salty scent of terror.

"That braying ass is gone. I told you I'd protect you."

She remained where she stood, shrinking into herself.

"What's wrong?" he asked.

"You sounded just like Prince Humba did when he was in a rage."

Something in his chest pulled tight. It wasn't the surly soldier who had put such terror in her eyes and scent.

It was he, Ur-sag-enki.

– Chapter 10 –

Nindalla's heart beat like a captured bird, so hard and fast that she was afraid it would fly out of her chest and escape through the open roof of the courtyard into the heavens. Ur-sag-enki had seemed an easy-going, simple man. She had assumed that when she eventually outwitted him, he would take it in stride.

Had she misread him? He had displayed a hot temper to the two guards. If his temper always burned so, it would be a danger to her and her children if she succeeded in avoiding marriage. His temper would be a worse danger if she did not succeed.

She took a deep breath and hung the baby's sling again around her neck and shoulder. She slithered between Ur-sag-enki and the wall into her daughters' room. No torch or lamp burned inside. She took a few steps into the blackness then stopped to wait for her eyes to adjust.

Firelight from the courtyard barely entered the room. She saw only grays and blacks until Ur-sag-enki entered with a torch.

Nindalla moaned. Dark edged her vision, and it took all her strength not to collapse. She would see this scene in nightmares for years. How could she not? She already dreamed too often of the sack of Eridu. But this horror was worse than anything she had imagined for Eridu.

Sisi, the girls' nursemaid, lay on the floor, crumpled like discarded linen. A jump rope circled her neck and was twisted cruelly behind it. Saliva dribbled from her mouth. Even in death, she kept her hold on a kitchen cleaver, its edge reddish brown and thick with blood.

The monster who strangled her, an Akkadian soldier, sprawled across Abi's bed, his face frozen in agony and his hands rigid above his sliced-open abdomen.

Her fists clenched, and she longed to pound on his face until no one could recognize him. "Inanna, queen of Heaven, hear me!" she prayed, looking up. "May his father say, 'I had no son.' May his wife and sisters go in pain and fear to the Underworld as Sisi did."

She swallowed and looked around for the girls. They were nowhere in sight. Their jewelry boxes lay overturned and empty. Their clothes and linens had been pulled from chests. The girls' little reed table and stools had been slashed apart with a sword. Tops, balls, and dolls lay strewn on the floor.

Nindalla put a hand to the painted wall to support herself. *I am a princess. I do not cry. I do not cry.*

"Abi! Bar! Are you here?" Her throat was so tight her intended shout came out a whisper.

"Your servant guarded your daughters well." Ur-sag-enki rolled the dead soldier off of the bed and then lifted the nursemaid onto it. He composed her limbs so that she looked as if she were sleeping, but he left in her grasp the cleaver.

"My girls were not here." Nindalla picked up a necklace of three strands of rock crystal beads and closed her hand around it. "At least, they should not have been. Humba's elderly wet nurse was to guard all the royal children." She called out their names again. Still no answer.

"Then what did this servant protect with her life?"

Nindalla shook her head. So many emotions had coursed through her in the past few hours—terror, exultation, confusion, anger, relief, disgust—that she felt drained inside and out. Gingerly, she sank onto a servant's bed, first wadding the sheets under her tender *murub*. The wool cloth she had wrapped around her waist and between her legs pressed wet and cold against her. She grimaced.

"Search under the beds and behind the cushions and chests," she ordered. "Pick up the linens to see whether they are underneath."

He frowned. His eyes looked as tired as she felt. "No more orders. You owe me respect."

Yawning, she leaned back against the smooth plaster wall and closed her scratchy eyes. Yet another reminder of her changed status and of how she depended on this traitor for everything. She forced out the words. "My lord Ur-sag-enki, would you be so kind as to search the bedchamber for my daughters?"

"Of course, Sister."

She immediately fell into a dream of watching Abi jump rope in the courtyard. But Ur-sag-enki made such a racket that staying asleep was impossible.

With a sigh, she opened her eyes again and studied Ur-sag-enki's face. What a contradiction the man was! His countenance was kind, if sad, and he clearly had a soft spot for children. His dark eyes were the highlight of a handsome face. Kindness, love of children, handsome—all traits she wanted in a husband. Yet he had joined the Akkadians and fought against his own people. She did not want to ask what terrible thing he had done to win the governorship of Susa.

"Women give life. Men take it away," she murmured, half asleep.

"Hmmm?" Ur-sag-enki hoisted a pile of sheepskins as tall as Nindalla, and probably as heavy, and looked behind it.

"A saying of my mother's."

He knelt in front of a reed chest, lifted the lid, and began removing the clothes inside. "No more taking lives for me, gods willing."

Nindalla sat up. Rulers could not rule without being willing to kill. "Are you saying you will not protect Susa if necessary? That you will desert your new home and family as you did your old one if enemies attack?"

"That's not what happened. You have the wrong idea about me." He finished emptying the chest and scanned all the walls and the ceiling. "Your daughters aren't in here, not unless they're the size of fleas."

"I know all I need to know about you." She forced her body to stand, and she kneaded her tender lower back. "Let's try my husband's quarters—your quarters—next. They love to play there."

He yawned, took the torch from its holder on the wall, and led her across the courtyard. "Here's what I know about *you*," Ur-sag-enki said, sounding exhausted. "You're the coldest and most selfish woman I have ever met. You've not asked one question about how Susa or its children fare. You stepped around the dead nursemaid as if she were a goat carcass. You haven't even cried for your dead husband. Even a bad husband deserves a few tears if he gave you children."

"Who are you to judge me?" Nindalla asked through clenched teeth. Splashing reminded her that the servant woman was still scrubbing the floor. She waited until they were in Humba's quarters before continuing. "Death and death and death!" She slammed the door. "There is no end to death. I have not cried since the sack of Eridu. An event that appears to have had little effect on you. Again I ask, who are you to judge me?"

"Who am I? I am the governor of Susa!" he shouted.

Enki-kiag woke and cried out.

Ur-sag-enki's fists clenched. The torch wobbled, and Nindalla lunged forward to steady it. In Susa, as in a Sumerian city, the worst disaster that could befall was fire.

Nindalla knew she must apologize, quickly. But she was too tired to find the right words, and the wrong words that sprang to her tongue would only increase his anger if voiced. She struggled to compose her face, too exhausted to let go of the torch or to move away from him.

The tense moment of angry intimacy stretched out. His gaze locked with hers. Nindalla refused to look away. Until they married, she was not required to defer to him. As a royal widow, she was a prize to be won, and so far he was not winning.

Enki-kiag whimpered, and Ur-sag-enki's gaze dropped to the baby. His eyes softened, and his gaze caressed the child's face.

Warmth burgeoned in Nindalla's belly, and she sucked in her breath. Her anger flew from her. *Humba never looked at our children with such affection.* She blinked. Already she had discovered more good traits in this lying stranger than she had ever noticed in her husband.

Ur-sag-enki raised his face to gaze at her with the same tenderness with which he had looked at the baby.

Nindalla's face heated: They stood only two foot-lengths apart in Ur-sag-enki's new private chambers, close enough to feel the warmth of each other's bodies—and she had shut the door.

"Welcome, Governor," a high, childlike voice said.

They jumped apart, Ur-sag-enki managing to keep hold of the torch.

A woman who was anything but childlike slunk from the bedchamber, her overabundant jewelry sparkling in the torchlight. Nindalla balled her fists and narrowed her eyes: The earrings and necklaces were her own.

No dirt or blood stained the woman's shift, which was pinned so low that her right breast showed, and her hair and cosmetics looked freshly done. The heavy, earthy scent of myrrh wafted ahead of her.

Ur-sag-enki's gaze followed her. Wordless, he gaped.

Nindalla made no effort to soften her words. "You disgusting pig!" she said to Ur-sag-enki. "You are not content with coveting Prince Humba's wife. You have already moved his concubine into your chambers!"

— Chapter 11 —

Ur-sag-enki looked from one woman to the other and decided his wisest position was anywhere but his current one: standing between them.

He strode to the rack of swords leaning against the wall before challenging the alluring intruder. "Who are you? What are you doing in my bedchamber?"

"And why are you wearing my jewelry, *Courtesan*?" Nindalla asked. "Take it off. Take it off now and give it back."

The woman half-closed her green-painted and heavily kohled eyes and leaned against the wall in a snakelike curve. Her narrow shift strained against her body. Dark-brown curls broke free of her put-up hair. "I'm Lady Midu. I thought I could be useful. I know the palace—and these chambers—quite well."

"It's the middle of the night."

She smiled more seductively than before—which he would not have guessed was possible.

Ur-sag-enki had little patience left to deal with a scheming opportunist. He himself had done the unthinkable in Eridu to keep himself, his mother, and his sisters alive and fed after the Akkadian conquest. It was hard to find sympathy for Lady Midu, who apparently thought she could buy her safety easily and enjoyably, in his bed.

The torch flared and crackled, and both women jumped. The seconds of extra light revealed a different Midu. Her lip quivered, and crescents of purple shadowed under her too-bright, bloodshot eyes. He winced. Like all the sons and daughters of Susa, she hoped to find a way to stay alive under Akkadian rule. Lady Midu was probably only the first of many desperate citizens who would visit him in the days to come.

He sighed. "You're here and you want to be useful. Fine. Is that the princess's jewelry?"

Lady Midu pouted her henna-stained lips. "Prince Humba asked me to protect some of the royal treasure because Lady Nindalla was indisposed."

He scowled and crossed his arms. "Give it back."

Her hand flew to her face, and she flushed. Looking down, she pulled off and handed the earrings to the princess and then lifted the necklaces over her head.

As she reached out her arm toward the princess, he said, "Now you can help us find Princess Nindalla's daughters."

Both women exclaimed, "No!"

The necklaces slipped from Midu's grasp. "Find? The girls are missing? What happened?" She turned to Nindalla. "What kind of mother loses two children?"

Nindalla's gaze looked over her shoulder. "My children are no concern of yours."

Midu straightened and frowned. "You may have forced my removal as nursemaid. But you cannot force me to stop loving the children."

Nindalla snorted.

"The more searchers we have, the sooner we'll find the children," Ur-sag-enki said. He turned to Nindalla and reached out his hand. "Sister, shall I conduct the search in these rooms as before?"

"Yes!" She lowered herself slowly onto an inlaid wood bench, winced, and squirmed as if to find a comfortable position. "Yes, thank you, Governor. Brother. You have been so kind to me." Her head lifted arrogantly, she glared at Lady Midu.

Midu patted her hair as she turned back to him. "What can I do?"

Praise Enki for her help! He might get a little sleep before his meetings. "We'll start in this room. Search along the wall starting in that corner."

They searched the entry room, the bedroom, the storerooms, and a small chapel with a painted, jeweled statue of a goddess.

No children.

He helped Nindalla up and told her to call the children's names in every room—it was a rare palace, he had heard, that had no secret rooms or passages—but no muffled voices answered from behind furniture or within the walls.

They searched the remaining rooms off of the courtyard: Nindalla's suite next, then Enki-kiag's future room, then well-stocked storage rooms and small sleeping quarters for servants, and finally, well away from the others, a large room whose floor sloped toward a hole in the middle. Nindalla said the room was for washing and for pissing.

No children.

Luxury beyond his wildest dreams in his new quarters, but no children.

They returned to the courtyard. Yawning, he gazed toward his personal suite. His dark, quiet bedchamber, with its real bed with a wool-stuffed mattress and linen sheets, awaited him. He turned with reluctance to Nindalla. "Where should we search next?"

"Perhaps the king's chambers?"

He had been in them briefly, immediately after the battle, but no longer remembered the way. He took a torch from its bracket on the wall. "Lead the way, Sister."

"Bring the lamp," she told Midu, who picked it up without protest.

They left his quarters. He shortened his stride so that Nindalla could stay slightly ahead of him.

They encountered no one as they walked. Most of the torches had burnt out, leaving corners and doorways dark enough to hide a man or a wild dog. He pulled his sword. Such large spaces should bustle with people and ring with talk. It was eerie to find them empty but for an occasional prowling cat; eerier yet to hear the susurrations of the mice, snakes, scorpions, and other vermin that fled from the torch and their footsteps.

"Why did you not take the king's chambers for your own?" Nindalla asked. "They are bigger and next to your audience chamber."

Because General Qisim had promised me the crown prince's widow if she would have me. I want her—you—to feel safe and comfortable. Out loud he said, "We need the king's quarters for important guests. General Qisim may visit. Maybe even King Sargon."

She gasped and clutched Enki-kiag tighter. "Before that Akkadian murderer comes, please send me far away on a diplomatic mission."

"I can't send you away. I'll need you here to brief me on protocol and manners. Also to remind me to smile and bow at the tyrant who sent his army against our beloved Eridu."

"Yet you joined that army."

Heat flooded his ears, and he dropped his gaze. He couldn't explain. The story hurt too much to ever tell anyone. "I recognize these statues. We're near the king's rooms now, right?"

She adjusted Enki-kiag's sling. "Around that corner with the woven hanging. The rooms will take time to search. There are a half-sixty or so."

"Half-sixty and seven," Lady Midu corrected.

Ur-sag-enki groaned inside. The way things were going, he wouldn't get any sleep tonight.

He immediately felt ashamed. He didn't know where the children were hiding, but he was sure they were more scared than they had ever been in their lives. If they still lived. General Qisim had ordered no looting or pillaging for the first time in Ur-sag-enki's memory. But clearly many soldiers had disobeyed.

"What about—" Nindalla hesitated then loosed a flood of words. "What about Queen Ri-ti? My sisters-in-law? Others of the royal family?"

"The general was harsh."

Midu sucked in her breath.

Nindalla didn't speak for long seconds. "How harsh?"

He tightened his grip on the torch. "He ordered all adults in the royal family, except you, executed."

Both women gasped. Midu exclaimed, "May the gods smite the locusts who name themselves Akkadians!"

"May the gods hear your words and have mercy on those who toil for them," Nindalla said. "Governor, why was I spared?"

"The general says you have 'tactical importance.' You were to be under my protection."

"Protection." She sniffed. "So I am a prisoner. Or at least a hostage."

"Neither," he snapped. "As I told you, you're free."

"An easy thing to say to a woman who has just given birth and cannot test where the bars of her cage are."

"Be glad you live! Be glad I was the one to find you and the general gave you to me. You are the luckiest woman in Susa. You should be grateful, not complaining."

"You belittle my losses. You may rule now in Susa, but you do not get to dictate whether I mourn."

Lady Midu cleared her throat as delicately as a cat. "I will go ahead to the king's chambers," she said. She scurried toward the weaving and turned the corner.

"I don't blame her," Ur-sag-enki said. "I wouldn't want to listen to us squabble either."

He expected a sharp retort. Instead, Nindalla touched his arm and then hurried her steps. "I apologize," she said. "I am exhausted and consumed with worry for—"

Lady Midu screamed, a loud scream that didn't match her tiny voice. It was as if a newborn lamb roared like a lion. The cry went on and on, echoing in the broad passageway, finally ending in a gurgled whimper.

Ur-sag-enki raced toward the sound, raising his sword as he rounded the corner.

Behind her face paints, Lady Midu looked as pale as milk. Her right hand clasped her left wrist as if she was praying, but her hands shook so badly that he could hear them thudding against her breastbone loud enough to set a rhythm for dancers. She stood over a pile of bodies carelessly thrown in a pile like discarded toys. All but one were children.

Great Enki, let none of these children be Nindalla's. He took Lady Midu's elbow and turned her away. "Don't look," he ordered. "Go to the door of the king's chambers. Wait there."

No longer the seductress, she nodded, tightlipped, and stumbled down the hall, clutching her arms to herself.

Nindalla caught up with him. Her eyes widened, and drew her breath in sharply. Her knees crumpled. He caught her. She buried her face in his short tunic for several long breaths.

She swayed, whispering, "I wonder whether the Akkadians piled up the bodies of my family like this."

He dared to stroke her back.

She didn't protest. At last she drew her head away and looked again at the bodies. She stiffened, but she maintained her gaze.

"The elderly woman was my husband's wet nurse. When last I saw my daughters, they were under her care." She tried to lower herself down. The effort tore a groan from her. She cradled her swollen belly with one hand and balanced the baby with the other.

He cupped his hand under her elbow. "No, Sister. Stand where you are. I'll show you their faces."

Nindalla nodded, her face the color of undyed linen. Her lips pressed together tightly.

The children all wore short skirts of finely woven wool, but five had darkly tanned skin. Ur-sag-enki guessed they were boys. One still held a small bow in his hand. He picked each boy up and showed his face to Nindalla.

She named three as her nephews.

He laid the boys face up in a row along the wall. He smoothed their hair back and wiped their faces clean with his hand so their parents, if they had survived, could easily find them.

Sweat trickled down his back. Now he had to turn over the faces of the girls. Any one might be Nindalla's daughter. Their stiff little bodies made a compact pile. Their arms and legs were wrapped around each other as if each girl had tried to protect the others.

He disentangled the top body and brushed the hair from the face. He showed Nindalla.

She glanced at the face, shook her head, and said a name.

He put the child's body next to the boys' and lifted another corpse from the pile. Again, he showed Nindalla. Again, she shook her head and muttered a name.

Three bodies left. And a doll. He placed the doll in the line of children. As he picked up the third girl, his hands shook. He had to take a deep breath before he could turn her over.

Nindalla shook her head and whispered a name.

Sweat poured freely from him now. His liver ached for the children and their parents. Only two girls remained. Would they be the ones?

He stood over the bodies protectively. As long as he didn't turn them over, Nindalla could hope her daughters lived.

"Please show me their faces. I must know. I must know now."

He wanted to flee the corridor and hide. Showing her these children horrified him more than any battle ever had. Slowly, with unsteady hands, he propped up the fourth girl.

Nindalla stared. Her eyes flared wide. "Praise the gods! She is not my daughter." She covered her mouth with her hand and shook her head. A tear rolled down her cheek. "How terrible the times are when one rejoices that one's niece is dead."

They both looked at the last child, the smallest yet, who had been beneath the four older girls.

Nindalla's shoulders drew together. "This one looks too small, and the stitching on her skirt is crude. But let me see her."

Ur-sag-enki picked the toddler up. Her body was soft and floppy and warm. Holding his breath, he tickled the girl under her chin.

Her eyes popped opened, wide, curious, and free of pain.

He laughed. "Praise Enki! Praise Enki! This child lives! Is she your daughter?"

Nindalla shook her head. "She's another niece." Tears sprang to her eyes and ran freely down her face. She clutched Enki-kiag so tightly that he fussed and squawked. "Ka'a's daughter, Habarane."

"Praise Enki and whatever god rules in Susa!" he said. "I will sacrifice a fine bull to them for safeguarding this innocent."

Nindalla knelt by the girl. She wiped dust and blood from the toddler's face with her hand and wiped it off on her costly tunic. Then she stroked the child's head.

"Habarane," she cooed. "This is your new cousin, Enki-kiag."

The little girl's eyebrows furrowed while she studied the baby. Then a slow smile grew on her face. She reached tentative fingers out to stroke his face. Enki-kiag turned toward her fingers, his lips pursed and smacking. Habarane laughed.

The tired lines around Nindalla's eyes and mouth softened. "I will keep my niece with me," she said, embracing the child along with the baby and rocking back and forth. "If she is an orphan, I will raise her."

Ur-sag-enki felt as if he had been struck by a thunderbolt thrown by Ishkur the storm god. He'd accused Nindalla of heartlessness. He'd been wrong. She had the cool-headed, weary bravery of a warrior who, like the Gilgamesh of legends, had seen much and endured much.

"I will carry her for now," he said, picking the child up. *Why did I think Nindalla would not have been affected by the destruction of Eridu?* He himself had changed much since then. He had become slow to anger and quick to return to calm. The things other soldiers complained about—rough ground, scorpions, biting flies, boring rations—he shrugged off. Losing everything had made him brave. He was a fool not to have recognized the same bravery, born of the same cause, in Nindalla.

"What sons you and I will have!" he exclaimed. "They'll have the courage of lions!"

– Chapter 12 –

The man was possessed by a demon! Nindalla could think of no other cause for Ur-sag-enki's odd, ecstatic outburst or for why he looked at her as if he had stumbled onto a prize bull at an auction. Her face flared with heat and she looked down as a modest woman should. She was not used to the attention of men. She had no idea what to say or do in response.

She changed the subject. "Please, let us keep searching."

"Of course." They headed toward the heavy door where Midu waited, hugging her arms to herself.

Nindalla had never been beyond the daunting portal of the king's private chambers and treasure house. The costly cedar door loomed above them, adorned with—and strengthened by—bronze plaques.

"I ordered two of the palace guards stationed here," Ur-sag-enki grumbled. He shoved the door. It swung open.

Nindalla peeked in. The entry had a huge wool carpet on the floor and was filled with prizes of war and gifts from other rulers. Weapons. Chairs of blackwood. Chests of cedar. Statues of men and gods. *Many children could hide here unseen.* She licked her lips and stepped across the threshold, hope outweighing dread.

"I know my way around." Midu smirked. "Prince Humba brought me to drinking parties and strategy meetings. I refilled the beer jugs, replaced clogged straws, and kept the platters full of food."

Nindalla narrowed her eyes at her recital of her usefulness. But she would not disagree; she needed Midu's knowledge of the rooms. She would tolerate the woman if doing so would help her find the children. "Where do you suggest we look first?" she asked in a warmer voice than the concubine deserved.

"The treasure room. What little girl wouldn't enjoy playing with all the jewelry there?"

"Is there a tablet room?" Nindalla asked. "Abi is just learning to read."

Midu wrinkled her nose. "That dusty old place? Besides, Abi is a girl. She needs to know only how to be beautiful."

"In Sumer, wives are expected to be wise counselors to their husbands. I will bring up my girls to be assets to their future families—" She looked pointedly at Midu "—not vain and foolish."

Midu reared like a desert cobra. "Assuming you do not lose them again."

Ur-sag-enki broke in. "We'll start searching here, in the first room, and work our way back as necessary. Princess, call out for your daughters."

"Abi! Bar!" Nindalla called as she had so many times already. Her throat felt rough, and her voice had lost its power. Soon she would have nothing left but a whisper. "Abi! Bar!" she called again without waiting for the answer she had almost given up hope of hearing.

"Hush." Ur-sag-enki laid the drowsy Habarane under a table. "I heard something."

A muffled, high-pitched voice cried out. Abi's voice. Wherever she was, she was alive!

Nindalla could not breathe, could not move, could not talk. Hope raced through her blood and made her dizzy.

"It could be a different girl," Ur-sag-enki warned.

She ignored him. She stumbled to a low tablet table along the wall and laid Enki-kiag there. Then she dug through the nearest pile of pillows and cushions, throwing them every which way, shouting, "Where are you?"

"In a chest," Abi shrieked.

"There must be half-sixty in this room alone," Ur-sag-enki said, laying the toddler he carried down next to Enki-kiag. "And look at all those doorways!"

Abi's muffled voice came from everywhere and nowhere. She needed her to keep talking.

"Abi, sing for us. A long song."

A thin voice started a wobbly version of a praise-hymn to Inanna.

"Good girl," Ur-sag-enki called. "Keep singing so your mother can find you."

The singing grew louder and more confident. Ur-sag-enki went from chest to chest, throwing open the lids.

She held her breath as each lid flew up and then let it out in a whoosh of disappointment when no child's head popped up. Her tired womb ached from her hard breathing.

At last every chest stood open. Abi's voice sounded louder; she must be in the entry with them.

"Take out the contents," Nindalla ordered, then winced. She had again told the new governor what to do.

But he seemed not to notice. He tore through a chest, flinging aside gold goblets and jeweled headdresses and treaty tablets as if they were worthless trinkets. Her girls were not among the other treasures.

Nindalla clicked her tongue in disappointment. "Sing louder, Abi."

"Bang on the chest too," Midu said.

Thud. Thud. "Good girl!" Nindalla called. She turned toward Ur-sag-enki. "No reed chest could make such a deep sound."

He nodded. "Wood."

"But which one?" Nindalla looked from chest to chest, looking for some sign of her daughters. "There!" She pointed to a huge chest of cedar inlaid with ivory and lapis lazuli. She had been in the audience chamber when the ambassador from the king of the Gutians had presented it. Now, it shuddered with each of Abi's thuds.

She rushed past Ur-sag-enki to the chest. She pulled linens out as fast as she could and dropped them on the floor. Ur-sag-enki joined her.

She reached again. The colorful Meluhhan cotton fabric on top quaked. She thrust her hands in the chest and felt for skin and warmth.

A hand thrust up into the air. Then Abi pushed her way free. Her face popped up and then an arm, purple fabric wrapped around it. She looked tired, distressed, but uninjured. "Ama! I thought you had forgotten me."

Nindalla blinked back tears and laughed shakily. Her emotions battered her like waves in the sea by Eridu, rocking her body. "Never! I would never forget you."

"Abi! I am so happy to see you," Midu said.

Ur-sag-enki lifted Abi from the chest and put her in Nindalla's arms.

She embraced Abi so tightly that the girl squealed. She loosened her grip and stroked Abi's hair, her back, her arms, as the child raced through a recital of what had happened. Nindalla followed none of it except that Abi's Uncle Kumdupum, who had not gone to battle because he was crippled, had hidden the sisters.

No other sound, not even the sound of breathing, emerged from the chest.

Nindalla comforted herself with the warm body in her arms. *At least one of my girls lives.*

Ur-sag-enki held up his hand for silence, and Abi's story trailed off. He smiled at her until she smiled back shyly, turning her face into Nindalla's shoulder. "I'm glad you're safe, little one," he said. "Where's your sister?"

Abi pointed to the chest. "I'm sorry, Ama. Please still love me. I tried to take care of Bar."

Nindalla's entrails turned cold, and her eyes squeezed shut. She could barely choke out a reply. "Of course I still love you, my honeycomb. I am proud of you for not crying. You behaved like a true princess."

Nindalla's own eyes filled with tears. A pit seemed to have opened in her chest and threatened to swallow her. Today the gods had given with one hand and taken away with another. *My poor, sweet Bar!* If only she had defied Humba and convention and taken the girls with her to the birthing hut. If only she had insisted that someone besides Humba's ancient nursemaid guard the royal children. If only she had done *something* different so that her child would yet live.

She drew a deep, shuddering breath and swallowed the lump in her throat that threatened to choke her. She was a princess. She must lock away her mourning and maintain her dignity. She must be happy with what the gods left her, a daughter and a healthy new son. Habarane would be like another daughter.

No child could ever replace Bar.

Ur-sag-enki emptied the chest quickly, as if he wanted to find Bar's dead body sooner rather than later. "Here she is!" he shouted, lifting a small body out of the chest and above his head in triumph. "Midu! Fetch beer. Hurry."

"She's beyond beer now," Nindalla said, her voice sounding as dull as a cracked bell. Her head sagged. Hair fell in front of her face, and she let it hang there. Bar was gone. Another sorrow she must bear.

The concubine went to another room and returned with a small beer pot frothing over the top.

Ur-sag-enki dipped his fingers in the beer and dribbled the liquid into Bar's mouth. After several tries, the girl's throat appeared to swallow.

The room seemed suddenly brighter. Nindalla leaned forward, licking her lips, but then berated herself. *I should not be so foolish. I see only the light of the torch flickering on Bar's skin, nothing more.*

Still, she could not budge her gaze from Bar's body. As despair warred with hope, the ache in her chest increased.

Ur-sag-enki dripped more beer into Bar's mouth.

Bar lifted her head and latched on to Ur-sag-enki's wet finger with her mouth.

Nindalla gasped. *Impossible. No one wakes from the dead. I am seeing what I want to see.*

The little girl turned an angry red and howled.

Nindalla forgot where she was, who she was. The world contracted to one hungry, thirsty child who needed her. Trembling, she pulled the heavy beer pot away from Ur-sag-enki and dribbled beer into Bar's mouth herself. Through eyes blurred with tears, she caressed each precious feature on her child's face. *Bar lives! Bar lives! The gods are kind: Bar lives!*

"I'm thirsty too," Abi pouted.

Humming a praise hymn under her breath, Nindalla let Abi suck a few swallows from the straw before pulling the beer pot away.

"I want more, Ama," Abi said.

Nindalla smiled more broadly than appropriate for a princess. "You can have more in a bit. You do not want to be like a silly ass that drinks too much and gets colic, do you?"

"No, Ama."

Nindalla sank to the baked-brick floor. She was so happy she felt no pain as she sat. "Praise the gods you girls are safe!"

"Your face is glowing," Ur-sag-enki said softly.

Bar pulled free of him. Nindalla drew both her daughters close, shut her eyes, and buried her face in each neck in turn, deeply inhaling their scent. They smelled of sesame oil and the bland, stale smell of child sweat, of the herbs of their clothes chest and her own perfume, of their wool clothes and the ashes used to clean them. Beneath, each had her own scent, unique in the world. Like a ewe, she would be able to find her own offspring by scent alone in a field full of children.

Smiling, she hugged the girls more tightly, remembering the first time she had smelled each one. She could sit like this forever, her world encompassed in her arms, pretending nothing had changed.

"I'm glad that's done with! When should we get married? Tomorrow?"

"What?" Her eyes flew open. Her memories disappeared like clouds. She was back in the world of earth and sky, a new widow who had just given birth in a conquered city. Her body seemed to have turned to stone, so heavy it felt.

Ur-sag-enki gave her a crisp nod, his chest puffed out in apparent self-satisfaction.

She sighed. Now she remembered: She had hinted she would give him an answer to his marriage proposal after they had found her missing daughters. *I must put him off.* Her hand found the cylinder seal hanging on her chest and fingered it; her sleepy mind struggled for a good excuse to delay.

Midu saved her. "Governor! She must spend a week in the birthing hut. She should not be here now, contaminating everything and everyone and endangering the little prince."

Nindalla nodded agreement.

Midu continued, batting her malachite- and kohl-enhanced eyes at Ur-sag-enki. "A woman cannot marry for three months after the death of her husband."

Three months! Nindalla needed to ensure her children's safety much sooner than that. She tried to interrupt. "Under the circumstances, many things take precedence over mourning."

Midu talked over her, drowning out her words. "Governor, you could do much better than someone who looks like a bloated cow." She stroked her too-tight shift.

Nindalla winced. Prince Humba was dead, yet she and the concubine were still in competition. As women, they had few choices. Each had to find a new protector or risk destitution. Neither had time to mourn. If she returned to the birthing hut, Midu might succeed in seducing the governor. Nindalla would have one fewer option for protecting her children.

She let go of the children and reached out her hand to Ur-sag-enki. She held it just so, in a graceful gesture her mother had taught her, her wrist turned to reveal the vulnerable spot of pulsing blue veins.

"Brother, could you help me up? I am weary, so weary."

His gaze caught and snagged on her wrist. He grasped her hand with his own, put his other arm around her waist, and helped her to her feet.

"Would you do me another favor?" She smiled, not seductively, but sweetly. "Would you carry Enki-kiag and Habarane to my rooms? I must hold Abi's and Bar's hands."

Her ploy worked. He gave her a smile of such joy that her own smile turned real and grew. He picked up the sleeping little ones so carefully that neither woke, and he glided out the door, Midu forgotten.

What gentleness and grace! Nindalla's fist pressed against the warmness burgeoning in her chest. She stared after the new governor.

"Shame on you, Princess," Midu hissed. "Your husband's body is not yet cold."

"And neither is your lover's," Nindalla replied. "Never scold me again. I am a princess of Sumer!" She glared at the woman until she dropped her gaze.

She could not bear the woman's presence any longer. "You may go ahead of me, Midu. I do not want our slow pace to inconvenience you."

Midu smirked and sauntered out.

Once she was out of sight, Nindalla urged the girls to hurry. They caught up with Ur-sag-enki. She let go of Abi's hand and slipped her arm through Ur-sag-enki's. He looked down on her with tenderness and hugged her arm to his body.

Her legs ached with the urge to run, and her lungs craved outside air. She was like a mouse trapped in a room, exploring every corner looking for a way to escape or a place to hide. She had again escaped marriage, but her reprieve from his proposals would be brief.

She walked a delicate thread. She must keep Ur-sag-enki wanting her enough to tolerate her requests for delay, but he must not desire her so much that he would not take "no" for an answer. Whatever she decided, she would need the governor's good will.

Her stomach lurched. If she accepted the suit of a foreign prince, her situation could be worse.

"Where's Abba?" Abi asked. "Who's this man? Why is he touching you?"

"Where's Abba?" Bar echoed.

Nindalla bit her lip. Beneath her hand, Ur-sag-enki's arm stiffened. *By the gods, what can I say that will make sense to them?*

"Do you remember that your father told you that he was going to fight the Akkadian army?"

Abi nodded "yes." Bar sucked her thumb, her eyes wide.

"Abba fought them to protect Susa. He was a hero. But the Akkadians won."

Abi's eyes widened. "Is Abba a prisoner?"

"No. He, he—" Nindalla's eyes filled with tears. She couldn't finish the sentence. To lose a father, uncles, and a grandfather all at once was horrifying.

"He's dead, is he not?" Abi asked. She dropped her head and choked out, "Must I behave like a princess now?"

Nindalla stroked Abi's black hair. "It is acceptable to cry when one's father dies. There are mourning rituals for us to perform that I will explain later." *When—if—we get his body back.*

Bar asked again, "Where's Abba?"

Nindalla swallowed a lump in her throat. "He is gone, my sweet."

Abi narrowed her eyes and looked sideways at Ur-sag-enki, studying him from head to toe. Then she crossed her arms and frowned.

Before Abi could voice her disapproval, Nindalla said, "May I present Governor Ur-sag-enki? He will rule Susa now instead of your grandfather. You may call him 'Governor.'"

Abi fixed her gaze on the hand Nindalla rested on Ur-sag-enki's arm.

"The governor put aside his duties to help me find you. Was that not courteous of him? We all owe him much thanks. Please say 'thank you' to the governor."

"Thank you." Bar pulled on Habarane's leg and whispered loudly, "Say 'thank you.'"

"Thank you," Habarane said. She looked around in confusion then rested her head again on Ur-sag-enki's broad chest.

The governor's hand cradled her head instinctively.

"You must have little children of your own," Nindalla said.

"No." He bit the word off hard. He appeared on the brink of saying something more.

Nindalla leaned toward him, eager to hear his explanation of his ease with children.

Instead, he said, "Abi, don't you have something to say?"

"Thank you, Governor Ur-sag-enki, for finding me." Abi said. "You must be very nice to my mother. If you're not, I will, I will . . . bite you and kick you in the knees!"

Nindalla winced. "Abi!"

Ur-sag-enki crouched at Abi's level and looked her in the eye. Gravely, he said, "I'll keep your warning in mind. But I assure you, I intend to treat her very well and protect you children."

– Chapter 13 –

Before daybreak, Ur-sag-enki set off for his audience hall. He stood tall and held his shoulders back to look confident in spite of the bees buzzing in his guts. Despite the early hour, servants already bustled through the corridors of the palace, and General Qisim, dressed in full military regalia, waited for him at the dais in his audience hall, tapping his foot, impatient as usual.

This was his own audience hall, where he would rule Susa! He would be a fair and just ruler, unlike the harsh, vindictive King Sargon, who often appointed friends and supporters to leadership posts, regardless of their abilities.

He took a deep breath, smelling incense and the sesame oil in the many lamps, and looked around. He had not seen the audience hall in good light before. The large room had a high ceiling and plastered walls painted with zigzags, dots, and stripes. Stone sculptures stood by the walls, interspersed with figurines on brick pedestals. On the dais stood a large wood chair decorated with silver and inlaid with mother of pearl. All for him, the governor of Susa. He suppressed a grin.

Not even reed stools were provided for his advisors. They would have to stand.

He approached the general slowly, evaluating the two men who stood close to him: a small priest with a huge wart on his nose and a richly dressed civilian with a hard, pinched face.

Priests were often hard to read because of their temple training. This one was not. His hunched shoulders and jerky movements showed he was unsettled, as he should be the day after an invasion.

But his high chin and tightly pressed lips suggested a determination to do what was necessary.

The other man, though, the wealthy civilian—he bore watching. He held himself proudly, and his full linen robe, held together at the right shoulder with a huge jeweled pin, had more linen than necessary. He alternated between leaning toward the general fawningly and hectoring him with a wagging finger.

Ur-sag-enki noted that General Qisim accepted both tolerantly, with an amused smile. *A leader is not intimidated by others. The council chamber is like the army that way.*

Elsewhere in the vast hall, soldiers and servants put things to rights, dragging bodies out, setting furniture and statues upright, and scrubbing the stained marble floors.

He arrived at the dais, climbed up two stairs, and stopped on the third. He still towered over the general but not as much as usual. He saluted his superior with a crisp hand motion to his nose.

The general nodded, first to acknowledge his salute, then to direct Ur-sag-enki's attention to the priest and civilian.

The skin under the civilian's right eye twitched, forcing his eye partly closed. He prostrated himself on the floor in front of Ur-sag-enki. "Lord, I am Dagu, your chamberlain and humble servant," he said in Akkadian. His voice was deep, gravelly, and arrogant. "I am at your service in any and all matters."

His skin tingled. *How did this man survive?* As chamberlain, Dagu should have been at his king's side during the battle. But Ur-sag-enki hadn't seen him there. Now Dagu stood unharmed, speaking passable Akkadian. Even though he had a king to mourn, his hair was combed, and he had not torn his robe. This man merited watching.

"Rise, Chamberlain Dagu." Ur-sag-enki jerked his thumb toward the workers setting the hall in order. "Your doing?"

Dagu bowed over his hands.

"Excellent. When General Qisim and I finish our meeting, you will attend me in a tour of the palace and city."

"As you wish, my lord."

"First, you will make sure the former king's chambers are guarded by two trustworthy men at all times. I ordered so yesterday, but the chambers were looted."

"That will not happen again, my lord." Dagu bowed again and strutted off.

So far, so good. Two hours of sleep, a cold bath, and some cheese, cucmbers, and dates from the kitchen had revitalized him enough to start his new duties.

"You have good men in place here," Qisim said, gesturing toward the priest. "Tirushaki comes on behalf of Susa's patron god, Inshushinak. He offers the full support of the god and the temple. He will be your liaison with High Priestess Zana."

"Thank you for meeting with me," Ur-sag-enki told the priest.

"It is my pleasure." The little man rubbed his palms together and cleared his throat. "I happened to notice in the main square of the city—" he cleared his throat again "—a rather large pile of corpses."

General Qisim yawned. "Yes? What of it?"

Tirushaki coughed. "The soldiers won't let anyone near. There are ceremonies to be performed, you understand. To release the spirit of the breath so that it may travel to the Underworld. We need to have the bodies to bury. And before we can bury them, we need to identify and prepare them."

"No," the general said.

The priest blinked several times. Beads of sweat popped up on his forehead. "But those people . . . the spirit of their breath will be trapped in all of them. Their ghosts will torment their relatives."

The general shrugged. "King Sargon's orders."

Veins bulged on Tirushaki's forehead. "I must protest."

General Qisim could be as rude as he liked without repercussions. Ur-sag-enki would be the one to deal with angry citizens. He spoke before the general could.

"I must talk with the general now, Tirushaki. But allow me to escort you to the door." When they were out of the general's hearing, Ur-sag-enki said, "We all have our duties and responsibilities, right?"

The priest nodded.

He continued. "The king must make his victory clear. You must get the bodies of the dead so that you can perform the necessary rites. I must take control of Susa and restore normal life to its people as soon as possible. Three people, three different duties."

"Yes, my lord. How can you 'restore normal life' when people don't know where their family members are and bodies accumulate in the main square?"

"I'll order the guards to allow families, if accompanied by a priest of Inshushinak, to identify their loved ones now. After General Qisim leaves, families may claim the bodies."

Tirushaki wrinkled his nose. "The bodies will stink by then."

"We can't break the king's orders. We can only find a way around them. Do you have a better idea?"

"No." Tirushaki looked around to make sure no one was listening and spoke in a lowered voice. "You'll allow us to perform all the proper ceremonies? Even for King Ebarti and his sons?"

"Yes. But there's a price. The priests of Inshushinak must find and identify every royal body. High Priestess Zana and the most prominent citizens of Susa must see them as well. I want no pretenders to the throne to challenge me. It's time for peace and for the people of Susa to live without fear."

After a pause, Tirushaki said, "Your terms are wise. I accept on behalf of the temple Inshushinak." He cleared his throat. "You have odd ideas for a soldier."

"I'm done with fighting. I will rebuild Susa, and it will be my home."

"Stability. Good. We were expecting a governor who would use us and take our wealth." The priest continued out the door.

Ur-sag-enki called to a passing servant. "Bring beer for the general and me! The best you have. That *I* have."

He strode back to General Qisim, enjoying the sound of the slap of his feet against the stone. He would never again have to prowl or slide around an enemy encampment. He was a governor now. He could walk and talk as loudly as he wanted.

"My apologies, general. I wanted to pacify the priest. I need the temple on my side." He led the general behind his chair, where the soldiers and servants could not hear their conversation. "I don't trust Chamberlain Dagu."

Qisim laughed and clapped Ur-sag-enki on the back. "Good. You shouldn't trust any of the nobles or civil servants. Such people don't understand loyalty as we soldiers do."

"Even Princess Nindalla? I have to be wary in my own bedchamber?"

"With her beauty and proven fertility, she can marry anyone she wants. If—*if*—she marries you, it will be because she thinks it best for Susa and her son. You'll be able to trust her then."

"Until her son grows up and asserts his claim to the throne."

"You'll have made a loyal Akkadian subject out of him by then. Just as I did with you."

Ur-sag-enki's entrails twisted. He was a son of Eridu first and a Sumerian second. He was no more a loyal Akkadian subject than an army ass was. "My loyalty is to you, General, not to King Sargon or to Akkad."

The general grinned and threw his arm around Ur-sag-enki. "I know. I didn't save you for your size and strength alone. I saved you for your defiance, even after Eridu had been crushed beyond hope, and for the hatred burning in your eyes."

"Why?" Ur-sag-enki looked around the luxurious hall that was now his, courtesy of the general's recommendation. What a strange fate the gods had decreed for him at the cutting of his navel cord.

"I knew if I could win you over, you would be loyal to me for life," the general said. "Your princess will be the same."

"I delivered her baby. I helped her find her daughters. Yet she balks like an ass."

Two servants lugged in a large red ceramic beer jug with two long copper straws sticking out. A raised rope design decorated the jug's neck. They set the beer jug down, jiggling the dark froth on top. The servants scurried away and returned with two well-made reed stools, which they put on either side of the beer jug.

"Please, general. Have a seat." Ur-sag-enki waited to sit until the older man had settled his bulk on his stool with a groan. The stool squeaked under him.

"You need to woo the princess." The general pulled one of the bright copper straws toward him. "Make her believe you want her for more than the legitimacy she brings to your governorship. Women are odd that way."

Ur-sag-enki grimaced. "I know nothing about wooing."

"Then learn quickly." The general took a long draft. "Excellent beer. Have you tried the wine yet? The Elamite royalty are known—that is, were known—for their prodigious consumption."

Ur-sag-enki winced. He had assumed everyone here, commoner to king, drank beer, as was the custom in Sumer and Akkad. He must remember that wine was the high-status drink in Susa.

He sipped beer through his own straw. The general right; it *was* delicious. It was *kash-ge-du-ga*, sweet dark beer, thick and warm and frothy, aromatic with the scent of resin and barley-sweet with no bitterness. He would not be drinking wine if his brewers were this good. But he would use straws of reed like a soldier; the slight metallic taste of the copper straw detracted from the good beer. "How long will you be staying in Susa, Governor?"

"Only until tomorrow. Then back to Anshan. You need to establish firm control of Susa quickly."

"I will," Ur-sag-enki said, hiding his doubts behind a firm tone.

"A word of advice. Dagu's loyalties may shift with the wind, but for now, you're in charge. Use Dagu; learn what he knows. You'll be a better leader," General Qisim said. "Oh, and put a spy on him. And maybe on your princess, too, until you win her."

The burden of governorship weighed heavier on his shoulders than ten capes of the finest fleece.

— Chapter 14 —

Nindalla reached within the sheets for her knife, which she slept with always. She grasped the handle, took a deep breath, and leapt out of bed.

"Who are you?" she demanded, her eyes tearing from the twinge in her belly and back from her sudden movement.

The plump young peasant had laughing eyes and a florid face, and she held Enki-kiag to her breast. Unperturbed by the knife, she answered in Sumerian. "I'm Daanan, my lady, the little prince's wet nurse."

"You are?" She had no memory of hiring this woman. She looked around her bedchamber. While she had slept, someone had straightened the room. One would never guess that soldiers had looted it. In the corner, Abi, Bar, and Habarane played with dolls under Midu's supervision.

She brushed her hair out of her face. She apparently had slept long and hard. "Daanan, how did you become my son's wet nurse?"

Daanan beamed. "The new governor chose me himself! He came to the kitchen this morning for a bite. He asked who spoke Sumerian, and several of us stepped forward. He talked to all of us. When he found out I was weaning my three-year-old, he sent me here." She smiled shyly, revealing two missing teeth. "I'll work very hard. And I'll take care of you as well until you have maidservants of your own again." Her gaze flicked to Midu and back, and she mouthed the words, "Besides Lady Midu."

Nindalla pressed her palm to her heart. She was not dreaming. Ur-sag-enki had done her yet another great kindness. "You are the rain to my desert, Daanan."

Daanan blushed the bright carmine red of pomegranate arils.

Nindalla leaned toward the wet nurse. "Did my girls' nurse or tutor survive? Or any of the royal nurses or tutors?"

"I don't know, my lady. Some of the staff ran away before the soldiers arrived. We in the kitchen hid. We knew we'd be needed soon enough." Daanan leaned in and said in a hushed, fearful voice, "The Akkadians are piling the dead in the city square. No one knows who is dead and who is alive. So many people are chewing fennel seeds to calm their stomachs that the streets smell of it."

Nindalla pulled the sheet higher around her. "That is an outrage! How will I send my husband's spirit of the breath to the Underworld without his body?"

"Everyone is wondering the same thing, my lady. My husband was in the army and hasn't come back. He could be in that pile."

"The Akkadians are demons!"

"As you say, my lady."

"May it be the gods' will that you find your husband alive."

Daanan nodded and bit her fist. Tears ran from her eyes, dripped down her face, and splashed on Enki-kiag.

"What about your child?" Nindalla asked gently.

"The gods were merciful. My son lives."

"You will be safe here. The governor put Enki-kiag under his special protection. Perhaps your son could come to be his playmate?"

"You honor me, my lady." She bit her lip. "But what about the rest of my family? We have no men left."

"Governor Ur-sag-enki will restore order soon," Nindalla surprised herself by saying. She hoped she spoke truth. "We must pray. Later this morning, I will send offerings to the temples of Inshushinak and Inanna for both of us."

"Thank you, my lady."

"As for your family . . ." Nindalla thought about what servants she needed and whether she could presume on Ur-sag-enki to pay for them. ". . . I cannot protect your entire family. But I have an extra daughter now, and the girls' nursemaid has returned to the clay. Do you have a mother or sister who could come care for them until I know which of my servants yet live?"

Daanan snuffled and wiped her nose on her arm. "My sister Sukura! My lady, I will love and serve you forever if she can stay here until the city is safe."

"I will arrange it, Daanan."

Exhausted, Nindalla lay down again and closed her eyes. Her swollen, painful breasts ached to feed her son, and her arms and legs were so heavy she felt she might never rise. Yet she needed to recover quickly, as quickly as animals and slaves did after giving birth. Her children needed her, and so did the palace servants, especially the ones who had not yet been found.

She mentally catalogued the places they had searched the previous night, wondering where her people would have hidden. She remembered the unknown servant cleaning blood from the floor when she and Ur-sag-enki arrived the previous night. Her servants may have been killed and their dead bodies already removed, to lie in a pile in the city square.

Images blurred; she no longer knew what she had seen and what she was imagining. *I'm so exhausted. Enki-kiag's birth already has the feeling of a dream.*

Her thoughts clouded until she struggled to remember the new baby. It was no use. She fell back asleep into a familiar dream. *Flames roared through Eridu, burning every reed structure and setting the precious cedar doors of Enki's temple alight. Pigs and goats raced down the brick streets, shrieking and bleating. Grinning Akkadian soldiers kicked open the doors of houses to slaughter the people inside. The sun burned hot and orange. The sky turned crimson. The streets ran with blood.*

She woke screaming and ran to Enki-kiag's room to hold the innocent in her arms.

— Chapter 15 —

The scent of fire still floated on the cool early-morning air, and a few ashes landed on Ur-sag-enki's skin. But no screams pierced the air, only the harsh calls of the wheatear bird. A few finches bravely chirped. All in all, the city was recovering.

Ur-sag-enki studied the neighborhoods he passed through on his way to the soldiers' camp set outside the city walls. He gave Lieutenant Idi-Ishtar the orders he had promised Tirushaki the priest. Filled with dread about what awaited him in his audience hall, he headed back to the palace, clutching one of his amulets.

He stopped to chat with each huddled cluster of citizens foolish enough to brave the streets and told them when they could claim their dead. Each group had at least one man who spoke Sumerian and could translate.

All were angry, of course. But he could stretch the king's orders only so far. At least he had faced them man to man. It was the first step to earning their respect and obedience.

He doubled back to the city square to see the pile of bodies and to pay his respects to the dead. The pile stood higher than he had guessed possible, and already it reeked. The gods in Heaven must be able to smell it.

He hoped the general would leave soon and he could get all these people buried. Nothing would incur people's wrath more than seeing their loved ones' heads bouncing down the pile and rolling around on the ground.

He prayed out loud to Enki and to Ereshkigal, the dark sister of Inanna and queen of the Underworld. A few citizens arrived with priests, but they kept well away from him. *I'm praying to Sumerian gods in a foreign language. For all they know, I'm cursing them or their dead.*

He ambled over to one group. He gestured to the priest and then to the pile. "Inshushinak," he said, hoping the priest would understand.

The priest nodded and clasped one hand over the other, the same position of prayer used in Sumer. Ur-sag-enki followed his example and stood respectfully as the priest called upon the local god.

He was sad and somber and ready to sleep by the time he reached the palace. Grimly, he climbed the steps and strode to the audience chamber. When he entered, Dagu the chamberlain was frowning and tapping his foot. A basket of clay tablets waited by his side.

"Show me the palace, the temple, the city. Don't spare me the worst," Ur-sag-enki ordered. "I need to see everything the army damaged, and I need your advice on how you and I can start fixing it."

Dagu puffed with pride. "I have taken the liberty of preparing preliminary reports, my lord." He gestured at the basket.

"Good job. We'll talk as we walk."

Dagu grasped the basket's handle and led him past the former king's quarters—two guards now stood there—to a nearby room. Its door was almost as grand as the cedar door to the king's quarters. Dagu rapped.

A clean-shaven priest opened the door. He wore a simple linen kilt, but the embroidery had been worked in gold thread. Behind him, the wood-paneled space glowed with gold-plated statues and lamps. A screen hid the cult statue from profane view, but he noticed it stood on a dais higher than Ur-sag-enki's own. Stone and clay statuettes of worshippers prayed shoulder to shoulder, nearly filling the space between the door and the dais.

"You see, my lord, we have our own temple to Inshushinak here in the palace." Dagu's smile held satisfaction and pride. "It may be much smaller than the main temple, but I made sure it was as richly furnished as the main temple. Our cult statue is dressed in the finest of wool and linen and eats the finest foods."

Dagu turned to the priest and spoke in Elamite, the language of Susa. Ur-sag-enki had picked up bits and pieces of several languages over the years, including Elamite, but as the chamberlain and priest talked, he understood only his name and a few other words.

Akkadian and Sumerian would not be enough here. He would need to learn Elamite properly to speak to the lower classes. More importantly, he needed to understand Dagu when the chamberlain spoke to underlings.

Dagu led him out of the palace and through a maze of roads toward the golden ziggurat, which loomed above the rest of the city like a date palm above a man. The chamberlain talked about the cities from which they imported stone and bronze and other goods.

Ur-sag-enki let him babble. He memorized the layout of the streets, assessed their defensibility, and noted where roads began their climb up the temple mound. They reached the high, well-built wall surrounding the temple grounds and entered through the open gate.

Locked warehouses, kitchens, tablet rooms, and sleeping quarters for the staff and the high priestess lined the walls on either side of the huge courtyard. Directly in front of him stood a two-story temple with niched walls. Most of the buildings lay in the shadow of the tall ziggurat, which rose in stepped layers and had a small, painted shrine at the top.

A horde of priests scurried about the courtyard and in and out of the temple and outbuildings, taking notes on clay tablets, leading sacrificial animals, and giving instructions to slaves. The bent-over slaves staggered under their burdens of large baskets of grain and tall jars of oil.

Several priests came over to greet Dagu, and they spoke in Elamite under a palm tree.

Ur-sag-enki looked about for Tirushaki, but did not see him. Among the deep voices of the priests he caught a new sound, the higher tones of a woman's voice.

"Now you'll meet the high priestess of Inshushinak, Lady Zana." The chamberlain led him toward the voice. "Unlike Sumerians and Akkadians, we worship only a few deities in Susa. Most are minor and going out of style. One might almost say we have a single god. Inshushinak."

"So the high priestess here has as much power as in a Sumerian city."

"Yes. She and we of the palace work together often."

Ur-sag-enki's palms dampened. *I must make a good impression. Her help will be important in rebuilding the city and earning people's loyalty.*

They found the owner of the voice, a short woman with gray-streaked brown hair whose shift was fastened by a jeweled pin of gold. Ur-sag-enki met her withering stare with what he hoped was its equal.

Dagu bowed and said in Sumerian, "Lady Zana, may I present Lord Ur-sag-enki, our new governor."

"Governor for the time being," she said in a voice so beautiful and luxurious that Ur-sag-enki was enthralled despite her insult. She stared at his black hair and wrinkled her nose. "You are a Sumerian, yet you work for the Akkadians." She studied him at insolent length. "You're also wearing a skirt instead of a robe. What were you two days ago? A peasant?"

"A captain under General Qisim in the army of King Sargon of Akkad," he stuttered, overwhelmed by the captivating power of her voice.

She raised her eyebrows, and heat rushed to his face. He bowed belatedly.

"My lady, may I take him to the top of the ziggurat so that he can see the city and outlying villages?" Dagu asked.

"Now? While we are busy disbursing barley and beer to the homeless? While corpses lay in the square? While so many people are missing? While the lucky survivors fix up and straighten their looted homes?" She turned her gaze on Ur-sag-enki. "Before this Akkadian puppet proves he can hold Susa against loyal sons of Susa?"

Tongue-tied, he bowed again. For the first time, he noticed their feet. *I'm barefooted, and they're both wearing sandals of beautiful leather.* His face got even hotter.

Zana looked back at Dagu. "You are rather premature."

Ur-sag-enki found his voice and rushed to speak before the chamberlain said something that would make him look even more foolish and lowly. "My lady, returning life to normal for the people of Susa is my first priority. I asked Chamberlain Dagu to show me the city so that I would know the extent of the damage and where the situation was worst. I hope the temple of Inshushinak will help with putting the city to rights."

Her head tilted as she studied him. "We will continue with our relief efforts, and we will consider any plan you submit."

– Chapter 16 –

The wind blew cold and strong, almost strong enough to blast Ur-sag-enki and Dagu off the steep, narrow steps that climbed the ziggurat. Ur-sag-enki pulled his cape closed over his tunic and hunched forward to fight the gusts better.

When they at last reached the top, the gusts chilled his sweat until he shivered. *We must be 150 arm-lengths high!* Rubbing his arms, Ur-sag-enki circled the painted shrine. His first view of his city took his breath away. It spread below him like a model, well-ordered and neat. Its yellow and whitewashed brick buildings glowed in the sunlight. He could see far beyond the thick city walls across well-watered plains to hazy mountains in the east. A canal zigzagged within the walls through the western edge of the city. Sparkling rivers ran from north to south on both the west and the east sides of the city walls.

The city had been well protected, but somehow General Qisim had known of a ford to the north, and they had crossed the western river there.

About half-sixty villages were scattered around the city, surrounded by greening fields. Neither the villages nor the fields had burned. Some fields on the western side had been trampled by the armies, but Sargon's troops had taken Susa too fast to cause damage elsewhere.

"Praise the gods! Most fields stand unharmed," he exclaimed. It was a pleasant and fertile land, one he was happy to make his home.

A gust of wind threatened to topple him over the edge, so he moved toward the small shrine. He leaned his weight against an outside wall and braced his feet as Dagu did.

"Dizzy, my lord?" Dagu shouted over the whine of the wind. "I would not blame you if you were unsteady, given your humble origins. You've probably never been higher than the roof of your farmhouse."

Ur-sag-enki rubbed his arms. He felt more than unsteady. He felt tiny compared with the vastness of the city and its outlying villages, like a bead dropped into a storage building of grain. So many people, all depending on him, a farmer's boy risen beyond his station. But he could not let Dagu's disrespect stand.

"On the contrary, I have marched through mountains that make this ziggurat look like a pimple. Sometimes at night."

Dagu cleared his throat and pointed toward the west. "My lord, I suggest that the western gate be our first priority. The Akkadians damaged it. That gate is vital to our defenses."

Ur-sag-enki shook his head. "No point in repair. I'm going to knock the city wall down."

"You'd be a fool to do so," Dagu burst out.

Ur-sag-enki looked down his nose at him. "Those are my orders."

"Excuse me, my lord, but if the wild tribes in the mountains learn of weaknesses in our defenses, they'll attack."

"You're under Akkadian protection now."

"But my lord! I must protest!"

"Sargon doesn't allow any captured city to keep its walls. Three companies of seasoned Akkadian soldiers will be stationed here. Six hundred troops. They should be a match for disorganized mountain tribesmen with stone weapons."

The wind calmed, and Ur-sag-enki took advantage of the pause to return to the edge. He spread his feet wide and leaned his weight back for better balance on the treacherous space. He surveyed the city neighborhood by neighborhood, and his stomach knotted. Although soldiers had mostly spared the villages and their fields, the city was a different matter. Two neighborhoods had been reduced to char. Along the canal, people collected mud in baskets to repair their houses, ignoring floating bodies. The market squares appeared empty.

He squinted at one. Only a few vendors had set up booths, and only a few customers wandered among them. The broad streets could handle huge crowds, but few people trod them.

Dagu joined him with his basket, standing close and just behind him. It was not the first time Ur-sag-enki had been used as a wind block. His large size seemed to invite it.

Dagu nattered again about imports and exports and ambassadors that might visit.

Ur-sag-enki ignored him. As a soldier, he had watched General Qisim. He had learned how to assess a situation and to set priorities. His first priority had to be calming the citizens and giving them back the life they were accustomed to.

Dagu's voice became louder and more enthusiastic, and he rested his hand on Ur-sag-enki's back.

What presumption! Ignoring Dagu, Ur-sag-enki continued his survey of the city. In Susa's main square, soldiers were still tossing bodies onto the pile of slaughtered Susians. Even up here, the wind brought occasional whiffs of the smell of rotting flesh. By the time the general left and the citizens began claiming their dead, the stench would be unbearable. The dead would create other problems as well.

The pressure of Dagu's hand on his back increased. *He's not being overfriendly. Is he so uncomfortable with heights that he must brace himself against me?*

"Chamberlain, vermin will soon be swarming everywhere in Susa. Have our storehouses checked and repaired immediately, and warn the high priestess to attend to hers as well."

Dagu pulled a flattened lump of clay from his basket and pricked symbols on it with a reed.

Meanwhile, Ur-sag-enki studied the city further. Not since the sack of Eridu had he seen the full extent of an Akkadian conquest. He had always marched on to the next town. He drew a deep breath; it tasted of the ashes of Eridu.

Dagu's hand returned to Ur-sag-enki's back and pressed hard. *By the gods, is the little man trying to force me over the edge?*

He turned and picked the chamberlain up. Dagu sputtered while Ur-sag-enki carried him to the shrine.

"How dare you?" Dagu said. "I am not a child to be carried about. A civilized man would have asked me to join him at the shrine."

"Next time you try to kill me, I won't be so forgiving." Ur-sag-enki dropped Dagu by the shrine's wall. "Now, how is the food supply? How much grain survived? Are the wheat and barley fields harmed? Did enough farmers survive to care for the crops?"

Dagu looked at him with a mix of innocence and outrage on his face. Anger reddened his cheeks. "I did not try to kill you. I was only—"

Ur-sag-enki crossed his arms and interrupted. "The food supply?"

Dagu pinched his lips together, rummaged through his basket, and pulled out a tablet. "As you noted, the army destroyed few fields. However, after the victory, the Akkadians killed or enslaved many of the farmers."

"That's their habit," Ur-sag-enki said bitterly.

Dagu's gaze flicked up from his tablet, his eyebrows lifting. "An odd criticism, given you are an Akkadian soldier."

Ur-sag-enki said nothing.

Dagu continued. "The palace warehouses are intact. I have already inquired at the temple about their stores and looked around the grounds myself. As you perhaps noticed, the soldiers did not breach the temple wall, and the temple gate held. Even so—"

Ur-sag-enki was tired of being talked down to. He might know little of governing, but he knew soldiering well. "I was in Sargon's army ten years. Of course I noticed."

The chamberlain's face tightened. "As I was saying, even so, we won't have enough food for winter."

Ur-sag-enki took a deep breath. "The dead won't need food."

"I took them into account, my lord." Dagu's voice didn't waver, as if the dead were just numbers.

"How many orphans?"

Dagu shrugged. "Uncountable, my lord."

Ur-sag-enki had hoped against hope there would be few . . . even though he knew better. Susa faded from his sight. Dirty, naked children filled his vision, the ziggurat of Enki soaring high in the background. Two children roasted a rat over a fire. The others saw him. They ran toward him, crying out that they were hungry.

He shook his head until he was on the top of the ziggurat again. In Susa, he had the power to make a few things right. "Is there a shrine to Enki here in Susa?"

"Yes, my lord. Princess Nindalla had it built."

"Gather up the orphans and take them there. Tell the high priestess to care for them in Nindalla's name until they can be adopted."

Dagu made a face as if Ur-sag-enki had ordered him to eat maggot-ridden meat. "Collect the orphans myself, my lord?"

"Yes. Uh, I mean, you'll be in charge. Give the task itself to someone you trust." He shook his head at his stumble. He should have guessed that a chamberlain did not do menial tasks, but delegated, just as an army captain did.

"I will choose some men to round up the urchins, my lord," Dagu said, trying to look down his nose at him despite his short height. "May I inform the high priestess how she is to feed them?"

"From her stores, of course." Among the seemingly tens of dozens of things he had to do, he now would need to visit Enki's high priestess and soothe any anger over this charge. He needed to earn good will everywhere. He continued, "Also, send her good beer and oil from the palace. Tell the high priestess to have the children plant gardens on the temple grounds."

"Herself, my lord?"

"If she wishes. Or she may delegate." Ur-sag-enki added with an edge to his voice, "of course."

"As you wish, my lord."

"I've seen what I need to see. Let's get back to the palace."

"My lord?"

"Yes?"

"You are the governor, of course. I only advise. But I would be remiss if I did not point out that in a disaster one must set priorities. Orphans are not a priority."

Ur-sag-enki stared over the city and plains to the mountains, once again seeing flames and hearing crying children.

"My lord?"

"Did you have too few beggars and thieves in Susa before that you want to add to their number now?"

Dagu's haughty pose drooped a little. "No. That's not what I meant to suggest."

"Good. Let's go now."

"After you, my lord."

Ur-sag-enki threw back his head and laughed. "Chamberlain, if you think I will ever let you walk or stand behind me again, you're a bigger fool than you take me for."

⁂

When they reached the bottom of the many flights of stairs, Chamberlain Dagu hurried through the bottom floor and courtyard and out the gate, leaving Ur-sag-enki behind.

"What is he fleeing?" a man's voice asked.

Ur-sag-enki turned. "Tirushaki! How good to see you again. I'm glad to hear of the relief efforts of the temple. If we all make an effort, the city will be back to normal soon."

"Is the chamberlain ill?"

"No. He's . . . just in a hurry to do his part to rebuild."

Tirushaki gave a bark of laughter before his face sombered. "News came while you were at the top of the ziggurat, and High Priestess Zana sent me to talk to you."

"How can I help the high priestess?"

The priest licked his lips. "In a disaster many rules can be broken. But some cannot."

"Go on."

"The high priestess says Lady Nindalla committed a great sin by leaving the birthing hut early. Her sin will bring Inshushinak's wrath down on Susa."

Ur-sag-enki shrugged. "What's done is done."

"The high priestess says Nindalla must return to the birthing hut for eight days and then be purified."

Ur-sag-enki shook his head. "Too dangerous. The city is still in disorder."

The priest hunched his shoulders, looking miserable. "I think so too. I've been out in the city, and the high priestess has not. I suggested that it was too risky for the princess to be in the birthing hut or for any of the palace women to, uh, go to the, uh, bleeding hut. But the priestess is adamant."

Ur-sag-enki bit back a curse. In his experience, it was King Sargon's wrath that destroyed cities. The gods had nothing to do with their fate. Even wise Enki, one of the greatest of the gods, had not been able to shield Eridu from Sargon. *The priestess wants me to understand her power here, even if it puts the palace women in danger.*

Tirushaki interrupted his thoughts. "Shall I send a servant woman to tell Lady Nindalla that she must return to the birthing hut, my lord?"

He groaned. A week without seeing her would be torture. Risky too: He needed her advice on court matters, and she still hadn't agreed to marry him.

"No. I'll tell her. I need to see her anyway about urgent matters."

— Chapter 17 —

The queen of Eridu hurtles onto the platform in front of the temple, pushed by two laughing Akkadian soldiers shouting unintelligible insults. She keeps her head high and proud. When the young princess is thrown onto the platform too, the queen helps her up. Two crimson suns shine in the sky, too brilliant to look at. The best archers in the army step out of the crowd, aim, and shoot. Aim and shoot. Aim and shoot. By the gods, why don't the women die? They stand in agony as they are pierced again and again. . . .

A soldier yanks the queen and princess onto the temple platform by thick ropes tied around their necks. The queen stumbles and falls. Her scraped knee gushes brilliant crimson blood that covers the platform and runs over every side. The soldier drags her the rest of the way to the sky-tall post. He ties the women to it. He strips their clothing off, even their cylinder seals. They are no one now, and they are naked. Purple and green bruises mottle their bodies like spots on a leopard. The laughing crowd of soldiers throws mud and filth at them. Then someone picks up a sharp-edged rock. . . .

Gasping and choking, Nindalla bolted upright, rocking the bed and nearly dumping herself on the floor. Her sweat-drenched shift clung to her. *Not again. Not now.*

Over the years, she had dreamed less often of the destruction of Eridu. Now, after the Akkadian conquest of Susa, her bad dreams came more frequently, as lurid as ever, fed by first-hand reports, second-hand reports, rumors, and E-kug's account—augmented by her own wild imaginings of all the ways her family could have died.

No one touched by the disaster at Eridu ever broke free of its effects. Most survivors were eager to tell their stories to anyone who would listen, as well as to answer her questions, the ones she asked every diplomat, every messenger, every merchant, every refugee: How did the Akkadians kill my parents? Has anyone seen my youngest sister, Nu-nu? Do you think she could have escaped?

She slumped, resting her arms and head on her knees and listening to the girls and Lady Midu murmur as they played with dolls.

I can't escape the Akkadians, even in my sleep. Praise Enki that the children are safe.

So far.

She was tired, so tired, and she ached from the birth. Lady Midu's voice grated like pottery shards underfoot. She wanted her gone.

I can't think of my own needs. Others depend on me. I must do what is best for them.

Daanan's cheerful humming entered the room. "News, my lady."

Nindalla opened her eyes. The wet nurse had Enki-kiag at the breast, and she stroked his glossy hair as he suckled.

Her own breasts, painfully full of milk, responded to his rooting and grunting. Milk spurted through her shift. She crossed her arms over her chest to hide the wet spots. Still, she could not take her gaze off her son. He was so beautiful. Her body missed him and longed for him.

Daanan had swaddled him tightly in a sheepskin to warm him and squeeze him as if he were still in the womb. Nindalla wished he still were there, safe within her.

"My lady, there's no harm in your feeding him too." Daanan pulled the baby free and held him out. His lips remained pursed and sucking on nothing.

Fingers tingling, she took him. He smelled of milk and sheepskin, sesame oil and baby poop. Ordinary, everyday smells. As she unhooked the pin that fastened her shift at the shoulder, she marveled that anything ordinary could still happen in these odd times.

Enki-kiag took to her breast easily and eagerly. She supported his heavy head, her hand in his hair. It was as fine and soft as thistledown. "Feeding him feels so right. How can it be wrong?" she murmured. "Daanan, do not tell anyone I did this."

"My lady, who could I tell who would care?" Her eyes shone with pity.

Nindalla's head jerked up. As disrespectful as it seemed, she sometimes forgot her sisters-in-law and Queen Ri-ti had returned to the dust. She supposed it was because she had not seen their bodies. And because so many people had disappeared from her life that it was hard to keep track of what had happened to each.

"You said you have news."

"Much news. A messenger came with this for you. I sent him to the kitchen for a good meal and to wait for your response. I hope that was right."

"Yes, thank you." She shifted the baby to support him with her elbows and free her hands, and she took the envelope eagerly. It was inscribed, "Messenger messenger say unto my sister Nindalla a princess of Susa in Elam what E-kug says."

Nindalla slit open the leathery clay envelope with her dagger. Bits of clay crumbled onto her, the bed, and the floor. Inside was a soft clay tablet the size of her thumb and inscribed in her sister's twisted cuneiform.

She put her finger under each character in turn, saying its sounds out loud, piecing together the meaning of the whole. "It is urgent. Say to your lord husband that Sargon takes large army to Elam."

She gasped, and the room spun around her. She steadied her head with her hand. If only E-kug's letter had arrived earlier! Perhaps King Ebarti could have found allies or hired mercenaries.

"Are you ill, my lady?" Daanan asked.

Nindalla shook her head. "Only surprised to hear from my sister so soon after her last letter." She set the tablet down on the bed and edged it under the sheet. She would erase it later when she was alone. E-kug had risked her life to write such news. "Daanan, do you have more news?"

Daanan hesitated for the length of an eyeblink. "Two men came by while you slept to pay their respects and ask whether they might call on you."

Nindalla sighed. "So begins the parade of suitors who wish to be the father of a king."

"Begging your pardon, but you're lucky to have suitors. You won't end up like some women whose husbands died."

"Do not tell me again about my good fortune. My losses may be smaller than some women's, but that does not mean they feel small to me."

Daanan bowed. "I'm sorry, my lady. I won't speak of it again."

Nindalla caressed Enki-kiag's ear. It was as soft as wheat bread dough and as perfect as the rest of him. He was asleep, still connected to her, still sucking every so often as he drowsed. "Who are these suitors?"

"Two of the king's counselors. Lord Pinririna and Lord Zag-Sudta son of Uruk. What should I tell them?"

Counselors. Ur-sag-enki might keep them for their knowledge or replace them with men he trusted. Either would be a risky husband politically, at least for now.

"How did they seem to you?"

"My lady?"

"Did they look at Enki-kiag or ignore him? Did they speak to you politely or brusquely? Were they dressed appropriately to their station?"

She wrinkled her nose. "They were old!"

"Yes. I believe both have grandchildren." Nindalla lifted and dropped a shoulder. "If your husband, Inshushinak protect him, turns out to have left this world, you have the luxury of mourning him and taking a new husband who pleases you.

"I do not have that luxury. My son's a prince. My daughters are princesses. I must choose a husband wisely and wed quickly."

"Governor Ur-sag-enki would be a better father than either counselor. He's also handsome. I like him."

"I do too. But he may not be the best choice politically." She sighed. "You may tell both counselors they may return in two weeks to court me."

*

Later that morning, as Nindalla embroidered eight-pointed stars in red wool on a new skirt for Bar, a loud slap-slap-slap of bare feet made her stiffen. No servant woman walked so boldly or with such long strides. *Akkadian soldiers have come for us!*

She slid the hilt of her dagger into her palm and forced herself to straighten slowly. She would be dignified, as befitting a princess. She would show no fear no matter what they threatened.

She turned, and a sigh of relief escaped her lips. She let go of her dagger. Her visitor was Ur-sag-enki, his face creased with worry. He stopped beside her bed, standing so close that the flaps on his soldier's skirt brushed the sheets.

She dared not pull away. She must smile and call him "brother." She must speak only of pleasant things and of things of no matter. She must show her gratitude for his aid.

Daanan followed the governor in.

"Sister, you're soaking wet," Ur-sag-enki exclaimed. "Are you ill? Has the demoness Dimme cursed you with childbirth fever?"

She shook her head and smiled as much as her lassitude allowed.

Lady Midu called out an obsequious greeting to the governor.

Ignoring the concubine, Ur-sag-enki laid his hand on Nindalla's forehead. She sighed at its pleasing coolness, but his brow furrowed. "You're hot. I'll go fetch an incantation priest," he said as if he were not the governor, as if Daanan and other servants were not at hand to run errands at his command.

Her stomach fluttered at his concern. "Brother, do not worry. I dreamed; that is all."

His face lost its creases, and he nodded. "I understand," he whispered. "I still dream of Eridu burning." He pulled a stool over next to her bed and plunked himself down. He drew his face close to hers. "Sometimes the dream visits when I'm awake. I see the flames and smell the smoke and hear the screams."

"While you are awake?" She shuddered. Her hand reached out of its own accord toward him. She stopped it before it touched his skin, yet it was near enough to tingle from his warmth.

His gaze fell to her suspended hand. His lips softened and parted. He reached out and wrapped his huge hand around hers. He moved even closer to her, and his breath tickled her face. "I dreamed while awake just this morning."

She resisted the renewed urge to comfort him with her touch. After everything he had done for her, gratitude came easily and wariness did not. "To suffer nightmares while awake must be terrifying."

His face reddened. "Not anymore. Not after so long."

She did not believe him. She had never gotten used to her nightmares. Her heart raced now, pounding in her ears like the hooves of running onagers, just from talking about the dreams.

She changed the subject to something less disturbing and more appropriate. "Thank you for finding a wet nurse for Enki-kiag."

"Are her, uh, breasts, working well?" His face reddened, and he cleared his throat.

Her liver warmed. His shyness was endearing. She smiled and nodded "yes" to his question.

"I came to tell you news," he said, squeezing her hand.

A chill raced down her back. She shivered despite herself. "Bad news?"

He nodded curtly. "High Priestess Zana orders you to return to the birthing hut. You have to stay eight days to finish out your confinement." His voice got louder. "She knows it's dangerous. She doesn't care."

I made one mistake in ritual. . . . She immediately regretted the thought. She was a princess, born and bred. She was not allowed make a mistake. Ever. Not even in a ritual she'd never performed before, not even when the ritual was in a foreign language.

This time, though, the vindictive priestess had misjudged her desires.

"Will you make sure that my children stay safe while I'm in the birth hut?"

"Yes. I promise," he said immediately.

"Then your news is good. Truly, I need to rest and get to know my new son." A week in the birth hut would also give her a reprieve from his marriage proposals. She would have time to consider possible sanctuaries and who else she might marry if she stayed here.

Ur-sag-enki frowned, petulant. "But I need you *here*, in the palace, in the city. So you can advise me. So the people can see you and Enki-kiag with me and know that the city has continuity."

"You can stand outside the birth hut and shout your questions." She giggled, blaming her fatigue.

He grinned ruefully. "Chamberlain Dagu already thinks I'm not fit to be governor. Shouting questions at the birth hut would confirm his opinion."

"Dagu lives? How can this be?" Trepidation clutched her heart. She found herself gripping the governor's hand. She motioned for Daanan to bring her something to drink and gulped down the sweet juice.

"Why are you surprised?"

"Dagu marched out of the city in his place at the king's side. I assumed the councilors died with the king and his sons."

"They did."

"Then how . . . ?"

"The times I saw the king or princes during the battle, Dagu wasn't with them."

Nindalla digested the news, unease crawling along her spine like scorpions.

"Men in helmets look much alike," Midu volunteered.

"There could be an innocent explanation," Ur-sag-enki said as if he could not conceive of a single one.

Until she knew how Chamberlain Dagu survived, Nindalla could not trust him. "I've changed my mind. The birthing hut is too isolated. I will stay here, where it's safe. Or at least safer."

"The high priestess insists, and I need to win her good will. I am too new in my post to challenge her authority."

She twisted the sheet in her damp free hand. No ruler could afford to anger his city's patron deity. Especially not a new ruler like Ur-sag-enki. He had made the right decision. But it required him to betray his promise.

"You said you would protect me." It came out as a whine. She bowed her head quickly. "Forgive me, my lord. As I said, I am very tired. I know you have many responsibilities. You have been more than kind already to me and my children."

He crossed his arms. "I promised to protect you, and I will. I'll station guards in the courtyard."

She blurted out the fear that consumed her. "What if they are more loyal to Chamberlain Dagu than to you?"

He rocked back as if he had been hit with a war axe. His hand jerked free, and his face paled as if an axe were indeed draining his life's blood. She felt more alone than ever.

Daanan came to the bed. "I'll come with you, my lady. I started working in the kitchen when I was a tiny child. I can wield a cleaver as well as any man." She lifted her thick, muscular arm—it was indeed as thick as many a man's—and grinned. "In the kitchen we hear all the rumors. I know who is on the outs with the chamberlain and whom he tells his secrets to."

Nindalla laughed shakily and beamed at Daanan. "I have known you only a few hours, and already you are indispensible." She liked Daanan; she hoped the woman was not one of the chamberlain's spies.

She turned to Ur-sag-enki. He was still pale, but his color was recovering. "Brother, the hut is too small for the children to come with me. Daanan's sister Sukura is coming temporarily to be their nursemaid, but she does not know the palace or its staff."

He twisted around to look at the girls. They were still playing dolls with Midu.

Ur-sag-enki called across the room. "Lady Midu!"

She looked up, her face flooded with eagerness. A seductive half-smile played across her lips.

Nindalla rolled her eyes.

The governor said, "Princess Nindalla is returning to the birthing hut to recover. You will help Sukura the new nursemaid until the princess returns. I hold you personally responsible for their safety. If anything happens to them, you die."

Nindalla looked outraged, but Midu did not. Instead, she placed a finger on her lip as if she were calculating sums.

"I do not want *her* to care for them!" Nindalla protested.

Ur-sag-enki took her hand again and patted it. "I've heard some women do not like their husband to have a mistress," he said condescendingly. "But you must admit, we have no reason not to trust her."

She yanked her hand away. "Like Dagu, Midu came through the attack unharmed."

Midu turned wine-red, her angry face matching the expensive dye made from sea snails that she colored her lips with. She dropped the doll and stood up with her jaw clenched. "Unlike you, I grew up in Susa." She jabbed her finger toward Nindalla. "Unlike you, I would give my life for Susa. My friends are here. My family is here. I'm no traitor. I survived because I hid in the secret room in Prince Humba's quarters."

Nindalla bit back the childish retort that sprang to her tongue first, that she knew *all* of the secret passages throughout the palace. She did not want Midu to think her petty, let alone Ur-sag-enki.

She had to admit, Midu had been loyal to Humba, even when he was out of favor. The woman had no reason to harm her lover's children. They were all that was left of Humba. It might ease her grief to help care for the children and see bits of Humba in their faces.

Nindalla shook her head. She would save compassion for someone worth it. "She will not watch my children. I refuse to go back to the birthing hut unless you promise."

"As you wish," Ur-sag-enki said placatingly. "I'll check in on your children when I can. I'll also have a treat for you when you get back. After your purification at the temple, keep on your new clothes. Dress the children in their best. Have someone put up your hair and paint your face."

She had no idea how to respond. Humba had never brought her any treat, much less one that warranted such fuss to receive it. She looked down, suddenly shy. "A treat?"

"The finest beer. Juices. Sweet just-picked peas. Sweet barley cakes. Dates and fresh apricots and nuts. I'll have the kitchen prepare your favorite foods."

Nindalla tilted her head. "Whatever for? You have already done so much for me."

"It should be obvious," Midu cut in. She smirked, but her voice was ugly. "He intends to court you."

"That's right," Ur-sag-enki said. "You'll have no reason not to become my bride."

– Chapter 18 –

Early the next morning, Ur-sag-enki strode toward his audience hall, faking a confidence he didn't feel. Each morning he had to work harder to force his feet to the hall. But today he had a new plan. Today he would speak boldly, act with self-confidence, and learn everything he could without revealing he didn't know it already. He would pretend to be the governor he needed to be.

As he approached, servants bowed and opened the doors to the audience chamber. He stopped short in the doorway. An angry mob filled the room.

Men shouted, shoved, and waved clay tablets at each other. Some were in loincloths, some in wool skirts, and some in linen robes and jewelry. Above their deep voices rose an occasional bleat. The sound rang against the stone floor, walls, and ceiling.

Two prostitutes with hennaed hair, the only women in the room, argued shrilly. Scribes slid smoothly through the mob, saying calming words and trying fruitlessly to form the mob into a line. One scribe was shoved into a statue of some alien god or monster. The statue toppled, pulling down a rug hung on the wall behind and shattering into three pieces. Ur-sag-enki winced. No one seemed to notice.

A smell from his childhood tickled his nose. He stood on the balls of his feet, and his eyes confirmed what the bleats and smell had suggested: Some men had brought their goats to the palace.

Ur-sag-enki schooled his face to serenity, but his mind raced as he searched the room for hints about whether the rowdy crowd was usual or whether he should eject the mob.

"At last you arrive!" Chamberlain Dagu bustled toward him from a dark corner, tapping his nose in a perfunctory greeting and looking him up and down. He frowned like a sergeant reviewing a raw recruit. "Your body servant should not have let you leave your rooms dressed so unfittingly."

The question made Ur-sag-enki's back itch, but he resisted the urge to scratch. "I always wear a tunic," he said stiffly. He would not explain further, no matter how many questions the man asked. The chamberlain and everyone else would have to get used it.

"That short tunic is strange, yes. But the problem is greater than the tunic. None of your clothes are suitable."

Baffled, Ur-sag-enki looked down at his clothing. In addition to his brand-new linen tunic, he wore his soldier's cape and his best garment, a pleated leather skirt with brass studs. General Qisim had given it to him when he promoted him to captain. He touched it proudly. "Speak plainly."

Chamberlain Dagu huffed with irritation. "You look like a farmer, not a governor. You're about to hear petitions! Meet with important people! Yet you arrive in bare feet. You should be in your best linen robe and adorned with face paint and jewelry. Look at me, how I've dressed with care for meeting with the citizens, and I'm only the chamberlain." He pointed to Ur-sag-enki's chest with annoyance. "Why is your cylinder seal not around your neck? We cannot get business done if you cannot sign documents."

Ur-sag-enki drew himself up. "I dress as a captain in Sargon's army. I have no face paint but kohl. I have no jewelry. No robe. No sandals. No body servant. I don't even know what a 'cylinder seal' is. If these things are important, you as my chamberlain should have told me the first day or obtained them for me."

Dagu shook his head. "Pitiful. General Qisim assured me that it would not take much effort to turn you into a governor. He might as well have given me a goat."

Ur-sag-enki nodded. "A goat is a good comparison. Like a goat, I keep my footing in high places." Then he did what he thought General Qisim would do in his place: He chuckled at Dagu's exasperated expression. "I have every confidence in your ability to work with me." He threw his arm around the short man's shoulders, forcing the chamberlain to be in front of him, reminding him again of their encounter on top of the ziggurat. "Let's go to the king's chambers. On the way, you'll brief me, and then you'll choose appropriate clothes and jewelry from the king's treasure rooms. You'll have me looking and acting like a governor in no time."

Dagu sputtered, turned red, and finally said, "My lord, I have many duties."

"Yes, you're essential to the running of the palace. That's why I want *you* to brief me each morning."

Dagu puffed up like a courting bird.

"Later today, find me a body servant so that I no longer upset your digestion in the morning."

The chamberlain nodded.

"I warn you, I will wear my tunic and skirt. I am the military governor here and should look the part. I'm sure once you think about it, you'll agree."

Dagu looked taken aback.

Ur-sag-enki pressed his advantage. "Also, get me one of those seal things right away."

Dagu returned to his more arrogant persona of the previous day. "Once I find a jeweler who has reopened his shop, I will commission a seal. But it will take some time to carve it."

Ur-sag-enki still had no idea what a cylinder seal was. So he merely nodded. "Why is there a mob in the audience hall?"

"Those are citizens waiting for an audience."

Ur-sag-enki cursed, and Dagu snorted.

"You had not expected that, had you? You're the final source of judgment for the city."

"What do I do?" Ur-sag-enki asked with reluctance.

"Listen to each side. If a dispute involves a sales contract, marriage contract, or other contract, ask for the tablet and have a scribe read it out loud. It should be obvious who broke the terms. In other disputes, have neighbors brought in as character witnesses. You must appear firm but wise and merciful. Don't execute everyone who's in the wrong."

Ur-sag-enki frowned. "I should just cut off a hand?"

"Perhaps. Although you don't carry out the punishments yourself. Delegate." Dagu chuckled after throwing Ur-sag-enki's words back at him. "Say a man complains that his neighbor's pig ripped up his emmer field. You may execute the pig if you like. But the pig's owner should also fix his fence to prevent more pigs from escaping, till his neighbor's fields, and plant double what his pig destroyed."

Ur-sag-enki nodded slowly. "That makes sense." Could he have come up with that judgment on his own? Probably not. He would have to ask Nindalla to teach him how to make good decisions.

They reached the door to the king's chambers. This time, two armed guards stood there, two men he recognized as aides to General Qisim.

"Any trouble?" Dagu asked them.

"No, sir," the one on the left said. "Nothing that a spear jab in the rear didn't solve."

Dagu frowned. "You do remember to ask for a tablet impressed with my seal before spearing people?"

The man on the left shrugged. "I ask. But all the tablets look alike."

"Like chickens danced on them," added the other guard.

"So I send them away. If it's important, they can complain to you or the governor."

Ur-sag-enki laughed, but Dagu clearly didn't like their answer. He glared at them.

Ur-sag-enki already knew the expression; it was the one the chamberlain used before lecturing or hectoring. Mindful of the crowd waiting for him, he said, "Let's go inside, Chamberlain. We both will be busy today. What news do you have for me?"

Dagu rushed about the rooms of the late King Ebarti, collecting things for Ur-sag-enki while shouting the problems he had discovered since they had spoken the previous day. He had sent men to conscript citizens for repair, but many refused, fearing soldiers would ravage their wives and daughters in their absence. He had checked the palace food and beer supplies himself and discovered that soldiers had stolen much of the beer. His underlings brought reports of drunken soldiers still looting. Others reported that in the poorest section of the city, where they drank river water instead of beer, people were having sicknesses of the bowels. Several children had already died. A messenger had arrived from the ambassador of Nehesy, who was bringing ivory as gifts and trade goods. The ambassador would wait to arrive until order had been restored. The high priestess of the temple of Enki refused to accept the orphans without an official request from Princess Nindalla stamped with her cylinder seal.

Ur-sag-enki's head spun, but at least he now had a hint what a cylinder seal was. He interrupted the chamberlain. "Are you married?"

Dagu draped one collar of colored beads after another around Ur-sag-enki's neck, then chose one and fastened it around his neck before responding. "The gods blessed me with a wife. She was taken during childbirth."

"It's a dangerous time. Childbirth, that is."

"Yes."

"Princess Nindalla is again in the birthing hut at the order of the high priestess. But the turmoil in the city scares her. I would like to give one of your sisters or daughters the honor of getting Nindalla's stamp on the request for the temple of Enki and then joining the princess during her confinement."

Dagu stopped in the middle of comparing three rings with flat blue stones. The tendons stood out in his neck. "You do me too much honor. I cannot accept."

"I insist." He let Dagu mull that for several seconds, then added, "You may also choose guards for the birthing hut, since your sister or daughter will be there. Post guards around the bleeding hut too. We must keep the palace women safe."

Dagu swallowed visibly. "I will see to it. Close your eyes."

Ur-sag-enki removed Dagu's dagger from his sash first. The chamberlain grumbled as he rubbed something on Ur-sag-enki's eyelids and shoved rings onto two of his fingers.

"That should do for now," Dagu said.

Ur-sag-enki opened his eyes, glanced briefly at the gaudy rings, and guided Dagu to the door. On the way back to the audience chamber, he asked the chamberlain for his ideas on handling the problems he had reported. The chamberlain proved to have already thought out possible solutions.

If only I could trust him. He knows everything about running Susa, and I need to learn all of it. He approved most of Dagu's suggestions, hoping none of them was intended to unseat him or make him look foolish, and ordered Dagu to have them carried out.

When they reached the audience chamber, soldiers were clearing complaining citizens out.

Dagu grabbed a soldier by the shoulder. "I did not order this."

"The general did." The soldier jerked his thumb toward the front of the room.

They threaded their way through the crowd to the front, where General Qisim waited, dressed for travel and tapping his foot.

Ur-sag-enki touched his hand to his nose. "Are you leaving now for Anshan?"

"*We* are leaving. Anshan has rebelled against Sargon. Rebels are holding my wife hostage. I need you and the three companies intended for Susa to come with me. We must put down this rebellion and teach the Elamites a lesson they won't forget. Get your armor. We leave in an hour."

— Chapter 19 —

Confinement after a birth was a mixed blessing, Nindalla thought. Each time she found it wonderful to be free of duties and obligations, free of the scrutiny to which a princess was otherwise always subject, free to rest and enjoy her newest child.

Always before, with only a midwife and a wet nurse for company, she had been bored by the end of her eight days. She returned to the palace stiff and wobbly from not moving enough.

The flimsy reed walls of the birthing hut, unlike the thick clay walls of the palace, gave scarce protection against the weather. Of her three previous confinements, she had spent one shivering while cold winds blasted through the gaps between reeds. During another, she had sweltered in an unusually hot summer. Her one confinement during temperate weather had been miserable. A rainstorm flooded the birthing hut, turning the dirt floor into mud and adding fuzz to the bread.

This time, confinement was much different. Guards surrounded the hut, and their loud talking and laughing disrupted her sleep and made Enki-kiag cry. With no midwife to look after her, Nindalla worried that she would not heal properly.

State business did not stay away. On the contrary, she was startled and bemused when Chamberlain Dagu's pregnant daughter, Lady Intarza, brought a document to the birthing hut for her approval. Of all things, it was a request for the temple of Enki to house war orphans. It was an excellent idea, but Nindalla would have never thought of it. Perhaps only a peasant could truly understand the problems of peasants. Did Ur-sag-enki grasp that ruling a city required attending primarily to the problems of the powerful and the wealthy?

She was even more surprised when Intarza returned to the birthing hut at Ur-sag-enki's order, but did not protest. In fact, she deemed her presence an excellent idea. If Dagu had thought to harm her or her baby here, he would have to put his plans aside to keep his daughter and the child she carried safe.

Intarza appeared to have no idea she was a hostage for Nindalla's safety. She was eighteen but seemed much younger. Even though she had been married for three years, this child would be her first. In contrast to her formal and sometimes dour father, the joyful Intarza laughed often and shared her true thoughts—a dangerous habit for an upper-class woman, but refreshing and entertaining in a forced companion.

Enki-kiag fascinated Intarza. She played with him for hours, giving Daanan time to sleep between feedings as well as fetch necessities and serve the food left outside their door. Incessantly curious, Intarza pestered Daanan and Nindalla to tell her the function of every object in the birthing hut and every detail of giving birth.

The weather stayed hot but not unbearably so. To Nindalla's relief, Ur-sag-enki did not barge into the birthing hut to talk about marriage. He did not even shout at her from outside. After two days, Nindalla counted this confinement her most enjoyable ever.

That evening, Daanan went to the kitchen to gossip and returned to the birthing hut with a covered tray. She coughed to get the attention of the other women. Then silently and solemnly, she lifted the lid. Underneath lay several kitchen knives.

Intarza gasped and scooted away. "Are knives part of a confinement ritual?"

Daanan motioned to her to lower her voice.

Nindalla lay a calming hand on Intarza's arm and spoke softly so the guards could not hear her. "Have no fear of that. Confinement is just as you have seen, a time to rest and enjoy your baby." She turned to the wet nurse. "Daanan, why have you brought knives into our sanctuary of calm?"

"I should have been collecting gossip every day," she whispered. "Waiting this long was wrong. I failed you, my lady."

Nindalla's breath caught, and she brought a hand to her turtle amulet. Her thoughts rushed to her children in the palace. "What has happened? Speak quickly!"

"When the Akkadian general—" Daanan stopped to spit toward the corner "—left, he took Governor Ur-sag-enki with him. And all his soldiers too!"

"What does it mean?" Intarza asked. "Why do you look so worried?"

The girl was so naïve. Nindalla wondered at Chamberlain Dagu. How could he have neglected to teach his daughter the ways of court, how to behave, and how to advise her husband? Her own father had talked with her and her sisters daily about their responsibilities as princesses now and royal wives later.

Not that Prince Humba ever asked for her advice or thanked her when she gave it. He had not wanted to hear the gossip she collected either, deeming it "women's talk." Perhaps such was the way in Susa.

She shook her head. She would not leave her own daughters unprepared. She would give them the training she had received growing up in Eridu.

"What does it mean?" Intarza asked again.

Nindalla tore her thoughts away from the past. "It means that Susa has no protection against raiders or thieves. The Akkadians broke the walls, and now their army is gone. Anyone could attack us. You were right to bring us these, Daanan." She nodded at the knives.

"Are we free of the Akkadians now?" Intarza asked. Daanan nodded at the question and leaned closer.

Nindalla shook her head. Something was terribly wrong. Ur-sag-enki had talked as if he would be in Susa during her confinement, and he had promised her a feast afterward. Of course, he had lied to her before; his promises might have been a lie as well. "King Sargon never gives up a city he has captured. Something unexpected must have happened. Daanan, did you hear anything more?"

The wet nurse bit her lip, thinking. "One of the cooks said that the governor ran into the kitchen and ordered all the bread packed immediately into baskets for his men."

He didn't lie to me. Nindalla took a deep breath of relief. "Clearly he did not expect to go with the general until the last minute."

"How clever you are!" Intarza said.

"I remember something else," Daanan said. "A pot washer said he heard the general was going to Anshan to put down a rebellion." Her face brightened. "Maybe the Akkadians will be killed."

"While they're gone, we can take back Susa. There's no one to stop us," Intarza said.

Enki-kiag can be king! Nindalla's jubilation lasted only as long as a sigh. A city with damaged walls needed a warrior-king, not a queen-regent. Her father had taught her how to withstand a siege, but he had never told her how to defend a city without walls.

"Think, Intarza! We can't rebuild the walls in a day or a week. We would be independent only until another city heard about our lack of defenses," Nindalla said, fighting back tears of frustration. *It is all too much. Giving birth, being widowed, losing my children, being courted, having my protector go to war in Anshan, people plotting a pointless rebellion here. If I were a jar, I would be riddled with hairline cracks.*

"Besides, the new prince is too little to rule," Daanan said.

Intarza smiled artlessly. "My father could be Enki-kiag's regent. He worked side by side with King Ebarti for many years. He knows better than anyone how to rule Susa."

– Chapter 20 –

Now—with the gods-cursed Akkadians gone—is the best time to escape Susa and find asylum elsewhere, if that is what I want to do.

Nindalla's confinement now felt truly confining. The airy reed walls of the birthing hut seemed as solid as cedar planks, and the pleasant voices of her friends grated on her like her parrot's screeching.

With the army in Anshan, no one would stop her if she strolled out of the city. But she had to finish her eight days in the birthing hut. Each time she thought about it, her hands curled into fists. There was nothing she could do about High Priestess Zana's edict. And with Anshan only two days' march away, the Akkadians could return before her days were up.

With the city in danger, she longed to be with her children, and she fumed that she could not keep an eye on Chamberlain Dagu.

She needed to heal and recuperate so that when her confinement ended, her thoughts would be clear and her body strong. She needed to be ready to take the children away from the city or to protect them if there was a new battle.

Dutifully, she tried to rest, but her efforts were futile. She jerked awake from her naps, more tired than when she lay down. At night she stared into the darkness, wondering whether Ur-sag-enki was still alive. In the brief times she did sleep, she dreamed of her unwanted suitor.

Enki-kiag, who had been a quiet, observant baby, picked up her mood and fussed and whimpered. All three women became short-tempered.

Many times Nindalla had watched Humba and his father march off to war and felt only annoyance at the disruption in court life. Now she worried constantly. She worried that her children would lose their protector, that the next ruler of Susa would banish her or execute her baby, that Susa could not be rebuilt if the governor was gone indefinitely, that no one would ever again treat her as someone special as Ur-sag-enki had from the first time they met. She did not understand his concern and protectiveness, she did not completely trust him, and yet she missed him.

"He is like a tooth," she whispered into Enki-kiag's ear one day while the other women dozed in the heat and insects buzzed and droned outside the hut. "I took Ur-sag-enki for granted when he was around, but now he is gone, and I am constantly aware of his absence. Does that mean I care for him? Even though he fights for my enemy and hides things from me?"

Enki-kiag had no advice to offer.

She continued to stare into his face, which resembled his dead father's. Yet one face was beloved, and the other was not. Just as she had loved beautiful Eridu and its waters yet cared so little about Susa that it mattered little to her who ruled the city as long as her children were safe.

But in truth it should matter. Greatly.

"You're the rightful ruler, my princeling," she whispered. "What would you want me to do if you could reason? Keep you alive at the cost of your losing any chance to take your throne? Or fight against the Akkadians to take back Susa for you at the probable cost of your life? Have I been too shortsighted?"

The baby stilled and looked in her eyes with an intense, captivating gaze. Clearly he was a born leader.

"Ur-sag-enki may be a Sumerian, and he may have brought you into the world," she told the rightful king of Susa, "but he would be our worst enemy if you ever want to take your throne."

"I brought a guest who insisted on seeing you," Daanan said the next afternoon when she returned from collecting gossip.

Nindalla sat up, suddenly alert. She pinched her cheeks and smoothed her hair. "Ur-sag-enki is back already? Praise the gods!"

"No, my lady. It's Lady Midu. Should I let her in?"

Her hands balled into fists.

Intarza whispered, "My father told me that all men took concubines and that I should befriend my husband's women."

"Befriend them?" Nindalla asked, incredulous.

"He said it could prove useful."

"Begging your pardon, my lady," Daanan said, "but why hold a grudge? Your husband has returned to his earth. She's no longer your rival, and the poor thing doesn't even have any children."

"We could use some company," Intarza wheedled.

She was right. All three of them had been tense and irritable, so much so that Enki-kiag had been out of sorts. "Let her in," Nindalla commanded.

The Midu who came in was not a Midu she had seen before. Her eyes were red and puffy—from crying, not from the evil eye—and no color painted her cheeks or eyes. The dusty hem of her shift suggested she had been in the streets and not taken time to change.

"Welcome, Lady Midu," Nindalla said stiffly. "Would you like some beer or food?"

Shaking her head, the woman sat down without an invitation and, without bowing, wrapped her arms around her knees. "I'm not hungry. I may never be hungry again."

"What has happened?" Intarza asked.

"I have been going out each day to look for my mother and sisters. Today I found out their fates." Midu raised her hands to her face and dragged her long nails from her cheekbones to her jaw. Scarlet blood burst to the surface to fill the scratches.

"Someone has returned to the clay?" Intarza asked in a whisper.

Nindalla winced at her tactlessness. "You must be thirsty from being in the streets in the heat. Please, take some beer."

"The neighbors returned to the house next door," Midu continued in a monotone as if she had heard neither woman. "They told me that my sisters fought the Akkadians when they broke into our house.

They were killed right there. In their own home. Later, the soldiers dragged their bodies away to the pile in the square."

Is this what happened to Nu-nu when Eridu fell? Or did my little sister escape? Is she well and happy in hiding? Nindalla could not speak, could not breathe. She grabbed Enki-kiag from Daanan and squeezed him tightly.

The baby screamed and squirmed. She could not release her hold. She could not let the soldiers take her baby.

She rocked in place and shook her hair free. It would hide Enki-kiag from view.

She felt the gazes of the other women in the heavy silence. She forced words to tongue. "Hide. Hide before the soldiers arrive."

Someone sat next to her and put a heavy arm around her shoulders. Daanan. "The soldiers are gone. Enki-kiag is safe."

She shook her head.

Midu and Intarza resumed speaking. Their words sounded as if they came from far away or through a thick morning fog.

"What about your mother?" Intarza asked.

Midu grasped the bottom of her shift, sliced the edge with her knife, and tore. Twice more she tore her clothes before answering.

"The soldiers dragged my mother away. The neighbors told me she has not been back to her house." Cloth ripped again. "I pray to the great mother goddess Pinikir that my mother's spirit has been released, that she is not staked out in a soldier's tent."

Shuddering, Nindalla whimpered. *Or is this what happened to Nu-nu?*

"The soldiers went to Anshan," Intarza said. "Didn't you know? Go to the soldiers' camp and look for her."

"I'm afraid," Midu said.

"Ask my father, Lord Dagu, for help. Tell him I beg for his mercy."

All was silent then. Silent except for the occasional sound of Midu's knife ripping through linen.

Nindalla's spirit calmed and she remembered where she was. She made herself stop rocking, and she lifted her head. "May all the gods of Sumer and Elam strike the Akkadians dead."

The other women turned toward her and stared. Midu's face changed from grief-stricken to angry. "Yet you consider marrying a captain of their army."

And you tried to seduce him. "We have to live with the world as it is," Nindalla said.

Midu shook her head. "No. I do not believe that. You give in too easily, accept the degradation of Susa too easily. This is our city, and you have betrayed it."

Nindalla sat up straighter. "If that is what you think, why did you come here today? To scold me? If so, leave."

Midu twisted her hands together in her lap. The blood on her fingernails smeared on her shift. "No," she said softly. "I longed for Prince Humba in my dark hour. I could not find his children, so I came here. You are my next closest link to him."

Nindalla turned away. She hated Midu at this moment, hated her for using her as a substitute for Humba, hated her for reminding her of the horrors at Eridu, hated her for loving Susa as she herself had loved Eridu. She even hated Midu for her sisters' deaths. Nindalla wanted to be nothing like her enemy, but they had suffered similar losses.

She bit into her thumbnail. It felt good when her teeth met resistance; it felt good that she could control everything, whether she bit through it or not, whether she tore it quickly or slowly, and where she would drop the removed piece. She worried it with her teeth, then ripped it quickly off. The second nail she tore slowly. The third as well.

"When men make war," Nindalla finally said, "they turn all women into sisters."

— Chapter 21 —

The huge palace in Anshan loomed over the city like storm clouds made heavy and red with sand. It squatted on a mound almost as high as the temple mound, daring the gods with its arrogance.

Ur-sag-enki liked the inside even less. As he followed the messenger through the palace, its high ceilings dwarfed him. Its passages were even more confusing than those of the palace at Susa, especially since they kept having to backtrack when passages were blocked by rubble from a broken wall or, in one case, a small fire.

From under his copper helmet and his metal-studded leather cape, sweat dribbled down his neck and back, making his skin itch. He reached back, worked a finger under the edge of his helmet, and scratched the small area he could reach. It came back blackened with soot.

I hope the general is sending me back to Susa. Today. I am sick of fighting and past ready to settle down with Princess Nindalla.

They reached a door guarded by two soldiers in armor. The messenger made a sign, and the soldiers opened the door. The messenger led him into a large room smelling of resin and reeds.

"Wait for General Qisim here, Captain," the messenger said, then bowed and left.

The room appeared to be the general's office. Although it was empty now, several low reed tables for scribes stood parallel to the side walls, and baskets piled with clay tablets stood next to each. A grander table of cedar holding a small beer jar occupied the middle. The table's scent tickled Ur-sag-enki's nose.

He wiggled his nose to relieve the tickle. But his urge to sneeze only got worse. He looked around a second time to make sure he was alone, then sneezes exploded from him, one after another. He rubbed his nose hard with his fist until the tickle at last ended. He yanked his helmet off and scratched his itchy scalp with the nails of all ten fingers, closing his eyes with joy at the brief relief.

"Captain!" bellowed the general.

Ur-sag-enki blinked, jammed his helmet back on his head, and smartly touched his nose with his hand. *I didn't hear the door open. This palace must have secret passages too.*

"You wanted to see me, sir?"

The general sat down cross-legged behind his desk and motioned for Ur-sag-enki to sit in front.

"Anshan is well and truly subdued now. It will be a sunny day in the Underworld before these people revolt against me again."

The general took a drink of his beer. "I'm sending you back to Susa. I can spare two hundred of your troops to return with you."

Ur-sag-enki tried to hide his dismay. One company instead of three to hold a city of thirty thousand? Impossible. It would be hard to protect Susa against raiders with so few soldiers, let alone put down an uprising.

The general picked up a clay tablet from the table and gave it to him. "I want you to deliver this tablet to Chamberlain Dagu."

He took the tablet and stared at it. The general should not go around his back for city business. He looked up. "I don't think Chamberlain Dagu is trustworthy. It would be safer if you dealt directly with me."

The general's eyes narrowed, and his face flushed.

Ur-sag-enki waited to be struck or demoted for his insolence. But instead the general took several minutes to smother his anger and then forced a laugh. "The tablet is personal. It's none of your business, but I didn't have time to collect a gambling debt from your chamberlain before we left so quickly. Now, of course, I need the money to repair the palace and other important buildings."

"Of course."

"Have you finished your looting?"

Ur-sag-enki's face got hot. He rarely looted, and only from the dead. Even so, he always felt as if he were a thief.

An Akkadian.

"Yes. I got Princess Nindalla some jewelry."

"Which will belong to my wife when the princess is her slave." The general's smile was disagreeable: scornful, greedy, and hostile all at once.

Ur-sag-enki smiled amiably. "Only if Nindalla does not marry me. That was our bet."

The general's hyena grin widened. "You may leave me now. Your two hundred men are waiting for you in new temporary quarters."

"Where are those?"

"In Enki's shrine in the Sumerian Quarter."

What a desecration! As he stomped toward the Sumerian quarter, sending wary sons and daughters of Anshan scurrying for cover, Ur-sag-enki fumed at the insult to his patron god. Soldiers barracked in the temple of holy Enki, where only priests and priestesses belonged! It was an outrage.

But something prickled him beneath his anger, some internal warning of danger. Sometimes General Qisim acted as if he liked him and sometimes as if he despised him—like today.

I don't get it. He had always made himself useful to the general. He didn't like to brag, but he had been essential at several key battles. For example, his men had done more than their share of fighting in retaking Anshan from its rebels.

Yet the general had not rewarded him. He had not even acknowledged him. Instead, Qisim took most of his company for himself.

Probably the best men, he thought sourly.

No, I won't let the general sully the day. I've been victorious in battle. I'm going back to Nindalla. With the grace of the gods, I'll never fight again. I should be happy.

But the signs of the battle around him kept a cheerful mood away. Already, dogs skulked in the shadows of alleys and inside deserted or damaged houses, waiting their chance at the dead scattered in the streets. Akkadian soldiers patrolled in a group, taking a census. Children were everywhere, getting too close to bonfires, climbing on broken walls, harassing bricklayers and builders scurrying toward the palace under armed guard.

Pain erupted in his temple. He touched the area, and his already sooty fingers came away bright red. A bloody rock lay at his feet, and giggles came from the shop on his left.

He spun, whipping out his sword during his turn, and ran into the building. The children scrambled out of windows and over broken walls. He pivoted and chased the biggest boy until the child looked terrified.

Satisfied that he at least would not be their target again, he sheathed his sword and set his feet again toward the Sumerian quarter. Soon the Sumerian-style buildings came into view, and his spirits lifted.

Home. Or as close as I'll ever get to Eridu of the waters again.

The gate was guarded by two Sumerian men as large as he was, but a little younger.

Ur-sag-enki showed his empty palms and smiled. "I mean no harm here, brothers. My men are in the house of Enki. We'll be leaving tomorrow," he said in Sumerian.

The men stepped to the sides. But one glowered and said, "You're no brother of mine, traitor-son of Eridu." His own accent marked him as a son of Ur.

Ur-sag-enki swallowed. At least he himself had not been part of hurting this man's family; Ur fell before Eridu. "Yes, I'm a traitor . . . to a deserted city where seagulls occupy the harbor instead of boats and the House of the Aquifer fills with sand. I did what I had to do to survive," he said, and then he added, "Just as you did."

The man dropped his head.

His fellow guard moseyed over and clapped him on the shoulder. "The righteous are dead, Namazu. Those of us who lived pay the price of our sins in guilt. Right?"

"Yes," Namazu said. "But some of us took paths more righteous than others."

The other guard, by his speech a son of Uruk, rolled his eyes and turned to Ur-sag-enki. "Our shift ends soon. Why don't you join us in the tavern? We can sing songs and tell tales of the old days."

"Sounds great. But meanwhile, the Akkadians under my command could be doing who-knows-what to this little piece of Sumer," Ur-sag-enki said regretfully. "No, I need to keep my men in line until we leave. Another time, perhaps?"

The guard from Uruk turned to his friend. "See? We all pay in our own way. We suffer guilt, but this fellow has it worse. He must spend his time with Akkadians."

All three laughed. The guards waved Ur-sag-enki through the gate into the Sumerian district, where traveling Sumerian merchants and war-displaced families lived.

Beautiful Sumerian words surrounded him, gentler and happier than harsh Akkadian, whose guttural spitting sounds still grated on his ears. Praise Enki, the damage in the Sumerian district was minor. He saw no evidence of fire or massacre. A few shops were open, and several vendors had set up booths in the market square. No one ran from him, although no one was friendly either. Most stared with curiosity at his Akkadian uniform and Sumerian face and hair.

He turned down a narrow deserted alley, startling a brown lizard basking under the hot sun. Unbroken walls rose on either side, although delicious smells wafted over into the alley—garlic, onions, lamb. He hummed a song from his childhood, adding the few words he remembered. By the time he'd marched a few blocks, he was singing almost all the words.

"Dear son of Eridu," quavered an old man's voice from the other side of the wall. "We're eating. Come join us."

He hesitated, but the upper-class Eridu accent persuaded him to accept. "For a few minutes, fellow son of Eridu."

"Please turn at the next street, then. Find us at the second door."

He followed the directions, and the man and his wife met him at the door.

"Oh dear oh dear," said the man, eyeing Ur-sag-enki's Akkadian uniform with heavily kohled, watery red eyes. He put his hand over his gold bracelet as if to hide it. "I didn't realize—"

"Look how young he is, Brother," the woman murmured. "He was a boy when Sargon took Eridu."

"Still. . . ." He licked his lips.

Ur-sag-enki took a deep breath. "Your lady wife is right," he ground out. "I was a boy when the Akkadians took Eridu. They killed my family and destroyed my home."

The woman tilted her head and smiled at her husband. "Please let him in. I long to hear the sound of Sumerian on a new tongue."

"For you, then, Sister." The man gestured feebly for Ur-sag-enki to enter, saying to him, "We encounter so few new people."

"You are welcome in our house," the wife said.

Ur-sag-enki bowed. "You honor me. Thank you, Lady. Thank you, Lord. I am Ur-sag-enki."

"I am Earabi, and my wife is Gan-utu." They led him through the dark coolness of thick brick walls to a large open courtyard that smelled deliciously of the lamb roasting on a spit over a fire pit.

Gan-utu invited him to sit on a colorful woven rug at a low table under a rush sunshade. The table held what would have been a feast when he was a child: barley breads, melon slices, butter, cheeses, and roasted onions, all displayed in beautiful platters and bowls with black and red painted decorations. His mouth watering, he sat and grabbed a flatbread.

More slowly, wincing, Earabi lowered himself to the rug, his joints creaking and snapping. Gan-utu went to the lamb, carved off a large slice, and put it on a plate.

"Still beautiful, is she not?" Earabi asked. He gazed with pride on the wizened, hump-backed woman whose wispy white hair was neatly twisted and held with a jeweled pin.

Whatever beauty the man saw eluded Ur-sag-enki. But his mouth was too full of bread to respond. *Praise Enki, I have time to think of a polite reply!* By the time he could talk, he had remembered a proverb from his childhood.

"A woman is a man's future."

"Well said," Earabi answered. "I could not survive without her."

"Have you been married a long time?"

Gan-utu slipped a plate in front of him. The lamb slice now shimmered with an aromatic sauce his nose told him contained dill, vinegar, and oil. He cut it with his dagger, speared a piece, and brought it to his mouth. *The gods must eat food like this!*

"Fifty-two years," Earabi said. "We've been married fifty-two years."

"Through many tears and much laughter," she said. She poured wine into a beaker decorated with stripes and placed it in front of Ur-sag-enki. "And you, child? Do you have a wife?"

"Soon. A beautiful Sumerian woman from Eridu."

"Good. Sumerian women make the best wives." Earabi reached across the table to stroke his wife's cheek. She blushed and smiled.

"What is she like, your future wife?" Gan-utu asked.

"Black hair. Eyes like almonds. A long neck." Ur-sag-enki paused to think. "White teeth."

"Fie on you!" Gan-utu exclaimed. "Beauty does not last. What qualities does she have that will? Does she spin well? Weave well? Is her beer as good as mine?"

"I, uh, I don't know, Lady Gan-utu." He busied himself cutting his lamb.

Earabi chuckled. "Many things in the world change, but never young men."

Gan-utu huffed at her husband before continuing to harangue Ur-sag-enki. "If you do not know whether her skills are good, then why, in the names of Inanna, do you want to marry her? Besides her beauty, which the gods could take at any moment?"

This time he answered promptly. "I saw my lady once when I was little. I knew she was my destiny." He dared to look up to see whether destiny would redeem him in Gan-utu's opinion.

Earabi burst into laughter that shook his frail body.

Gan-utu shook her head, and her gold boat-shaped earrings swung. "Is there nothing about her, besides her beauty, that you admire or respect? How will you be content after one year of marriage, let alone fifty?" Her voice softened, broke. "How will you . . . how will you withstand the loss of a child or the need to go into exile?"

The world spun around him; the earth tilted under him. Ur-sag-enki dropped his knife onto his plate and braced himself. When he thought of his future with Nindalla, he pictured them sitting together in happy silence, several laughing children playing around their feet. Or he pictured them in bed, making more children.

He had never wondered about her skills, about whether a governor's wife would be expected to spin and weave and brew like other women. Never wondered what she liked to do when she had free time. Never wondered what their life would be like when the children were grown. Never considered that a disaster could befall them. Still. . . .

"I do know some things about her," he began slowly. "Both good things and bad things. She is arrogant and haughty and sometimes jealous. She doesn't forgive easily. She has been lonely a long time. But she is also brave and dignified. She's not often generous, but sometimes she is. She doesn't babble or shriek. She loves her children and would do anything for them." The whirling in his head stopped. He took a deep breath. "I don't know why, but I long to take care of her. I want her never to be lonely again or need to be brave. I need *these things,* deep in here." He thumped his chest.

"Well spoken, young son of Eridu," Earabi said.

He and Gan-utu exchanged smiles so tender that Ur-sag-enki wished to switch places with him. His love for his sisters and mother filled him and clogged his throat. He had loved his family without regard for their appearance, knowing each person's faults and loving despite them.

But he had loved Nindalla for her beauty.

And for the family she would bring with her to their marriage.

Did she know I was shallow and selfish in my love? Is that why she puts off agreeing to marry me?

Ur-sag-enki rested his elbows and forearms on the table and leaned toward the old couple. "Please. Tell me about your marriage. I need to learn how to be a good husband."

— Chapter 22 —

On the fourth or fifth night in the birth hut—Nindalla found it hard to keep track of time because she slept so irregularly and each day followed the same pattern—as Daanan snored, Midu blew bubbles in her sleep, and Intarza mumbled nonsense in her dreams, Nindalla had the most surprising visitor yet.

"Nindalla?" whispered a familiar deep voice on the other side of the flimsy wall at the back side of the hut.

The cold of a mountain-fed stream hit her deep inside and spread, numbing her limbs and lips. *No! This cannot be.* Sweat broke out on her forehead. She forced a name to her lips. "Humba?"

She hugged her arms to herself and rocked, regretting that she had never kissed Ur-sag-enki's handsome mouth while she was free. Now she was a wife again, with a wife's duties and restrictions.

"Nindalla, come to the wall."

Sighing, she crawled to the back of the hut. "Be careful, my lord. My lord king," she quickly corrected, speaking through a gap between the reeds. "The birth hut is guarded."

She ran her hand through her hair. The governor had told her Humba was dead. But she had not seen his body, and now he spoke to her. Had Ur-sag-enki deceived her in this matter as well?

Humba spoke again. "Let me in. The guards took a break, but they will return soon."

A new thought struck her, and the hair on her arms prickled and lifted. Could it be Humba's lonely ghost outside, come to take her or Enki-kiag to keep him company in the dark Underworld? Had his spirit come to berate her for his body's lying unburied and hungry in one of the Akkadians' grisly piles of corpses? Or for considering taking a new husband within days of his death?

"Meet me at the door." Her life's blood beat like a drum in her ears, and she had to force herself to breathe. To let a spirit into the birthing hut, if spirit he was, could spell disaster. But if he were her living husband, it was her duty to help him.

She went to the front of the hut, took a deep breath, and opened the door a thumb's width. No one was there. The hairs stood up even higher on her arms, and she covered her mouth with her hand to suppress a moan.

Then a man limped and lurched around the corner of the hut toward her. Even under the forgiving light of the quarter moon, he looked terrible, his expensive embroidered robe stained and his face pale and haggard.

Where was the relief, the joy, she should feel at her lord's return? The sorrow and indignation at his humbled state? Instead, confusion clouded her thoughts and feelings. As he neared, she pressed her weight against the door and peered at him through the narrow gap, her heart pounding so hard she feared it would break free.

When he was within a few steps, the musty, dusty smell of his robe reached her. Her hands shook so hard the door rattled. "My lord, you must tell me: Are you alive?"

The man took another step.

Nindalla fought the urge to shut and latch the door and pile the hut's furnishings against it. "Humba?" she asked again.

His breath rasped. "It's me, Kumdupum. Let me in."

She cried out, and her hand flew to her mouth to smother the sound. Kumdupum was her husband's youngest, and kindest, brother. He had taken to her when she first arrived in Susa. She had rarely seen him after he grew up, but he remained her favorite of her husband's family.

She threw open the door, ran out, and kissed him on the cheek. "Thank the gods you survived!" she whispered. She took his arm and propelled him inside, chastising herself for her bad memory. Abi had said her crippled Uncle Kumdupum hid her in the chest, but Nindalla had forgotten in the joy of the moment and through all the events since. She owed her brother-in-law a huge debt for saving her daughters. "Come in, Brother. Quickly. Please forgive me for touching you. If the guards should see you. . . ."

He snorted. "I am beyond caring about impurity." Once inside the hut, his body seemed to collapse into itself under its filthy robe as he crumpled to the floor. He could not keep his eyes open. He looked more beggar than prince.

She bent down and kissed his cheek again. "Thank you for saving my daughters. Whatever I can do for you, I will."

Nindalla stepped carefully over her sleeping companions and went to the beer jug. She dipped beer into a spouted beer bowl with shaking hands, sloshing beer on herself and all around. She darted a quick glance at the other women to make sure they still slept. Then she carried the beer bowl to Kumdupum and held it for him to drink.

"That's good," he mumbled halfway through the beer. He took the bowl from her and drank the rest on his own. "My vigor is coming back." His eyes opened to their normal width, and he sat up straighter.

"What are you doing here?" She shivered despite the stuffy warmth of the hut. "You can't trust the guards, even though they are palace staff. Your capture or death would be worth a lot to the Akkadians."

He struggled again to rise. "I'm hungry. I'm thirsty. And I had to warn you."

"Warn me?" Her stomach flipped over again. "First you must eat and drink. Allow me to help you up."

She knelt behind him and put her arms under his armpits. Clenching her jaw to keep from grunting, she heaved. His muscles tightened, he pushed down with his arms, and together they got him into a sitting position.

She kept him upright with arm around his shoulder and reached for the birthing bricks with her other arm. Hand clawed, she caught each brick with her nails and dragged it through the sand to them. She took several deep breaths. Then she put the bricks against his back, adjusting them to help prop him up. Panting, she pushed her hair away from her damp face.

Food. She looked for the most recent tray of food, found it, refilled the beer bowl, and placed them in front of him.

Her legs wobbled from the work. With relief, she lowered herself to the ground on the other side of the tray, facing him. She adjusted her shift around herself modestly, feeling awkward after touching him so intimately and serving him food as if he were her husband instead of her brother-in-law.

Kumdupum did not notice the impropriety or pretended to ignore it. He stuffed bread and dates into his mouth with both hands, swallowed, then lifted the bowl of beer and gulped straight from the rim, ignoring the spout.

"Ahhhhh," he sighed. "That was worth the risk of coming here." More delicately, he plucked meat chunks from the stew with his fingers and popped them in his mouth.

"What is your news? Will there be a rebellion against the Akkadians? Will you become king?" She wiped her damp palms on her shift.

"I can't be king." With his normal arm, he indicated the stunted leg and arm on his right side. "I can't fight, so I wasn't in the battle. That's how I survived. But who would support me as king when I can't defend my city?"

"What will you do? You cannot stay in Susa. The Akkadians are ruthless. They'll consider you a threat anyway."

"I planned to escape when I could find a way to get out of the city without being arrested. Now that the Akkadian soldiers are gone, it seems the perfect time."

She nodded. "Where will you go?"

"Perhaps Meluhha will welcome me. I handled much of Father's correspondence with his brother kings there. Do you want to come with me?"

"By the time I leave confinement, the Akkadians may have returned."

"As I said, I am not worried about impurity. Pick up the prince and walk out the door with me."

She blinked. She had not even considered breaking the taboo once she returned to the birth hut, even though she had done so without qualms the night Enki-kiag was born.

She could leave right now and go to Meluhha. Land of lapis lazuli, carnelian, and ivory. Of agate beads so finely cut and polished that each took a workman a week to make. Of fragrant exotic woods and strange animals such as the elephant and the peacock. Meluhha lay far across the sea. She and Enki-kiag would have a new life, far from Sargon and his armies. She would never suffer an Akkadian attack again.

"My girls. I can't go without them."

He ate silently until the platter was empty. Then he looked up. "Do you trust their nurse? Give me a message for her and a ring for proof. Meet me at the river gate at midnight. If I can sneak your daughters out of the palace before then, I will."

Chills swept through her, then fear. She could not decide without knowing whether her daughters would come along. She drew in the sand with her finger. "How did you avoid being discovered?"

"I hid in the secret passages during the day, foraged for food at night, and listened in on as many conversations as possible so I knew what was going on."

"Thus the warning you said you have for me."

He nodded. "I know the new governor intends to marry you."

"I must protect my children," she said. "I hope to find a better way, and perhaps leaving with you will be that way. But I will do what I must."

"You misunderstand. I don't blame you for considering him. I came to warn you that he may not last long as governor."

Fear prickled her arms, and she chafed them with her hands. "Why? What have you heard?"

"The general and Chamberlain Dagu met in secret at night several times. Sometimes they argued."

"How odd. Anything either wanted to say about running Susa should have been said to Ur-sag-enki."

"Exactly."

"What did they argue about?"

"Not sure. I don't know Akkadian. But whatever it was, it cannot bode well for the man you're thinking about marrying."

"Thank you for telling me." She twisted her hands together. Her decisions kept getting harder and more dangerous.

"I also overheard Dagu and Lady Midu talking in private."

Midu had been in the room when Ur-sag-enki told her that Dagu had not fought to protect Susa. Why would a patriot want anything to do with the chamberlain after that? "What does that have to do with me?"

"I didn't catch much. However, they mentioned four contracts of adoption."

"Ur-sag-enki has already said he would adopt my children when—if—we marry."

"If I heard correctly, Lady Midu plans to adopt four children while you're confined in the birth house."

"While I'm in the birth house? But why would she— " Nindalla gasped. You think she means the four living royal children? *My* children?" She stared at Midu. The woman looked harmless, even silly, as she slept, bubbles of saliva popping on her lips.

"Shhh," he cautioned, also looking toward the sleeping women. "You see why you need to leave here. You must decide quickly."

"Certainly. But not tonight. My father taught me hasty decisions often lead to unfavorable results."

"Tonight. Who knows when the Akkadians will return? What if they return tomorrow?"

She swallowed a lump in her throat. "Please, Kumdupum. One more day. Please. Come back tomorrow night if you can get my daughters out of the palace. I'll give you my answer then."

He frowned and made no answer.

— Chapter 23 —

The next morning, despite the already warm air blowing into the birthing hut, Nindalla made a pitcher of hot tea from mint leaves. As she devised a plan, she drank several beakers of it to slake her thirst and calm the occasional cramping in her womb.

When Daanan finally woke, Nindalla was feeling much better. She moved stealthily over to the wet nurse and spoke quietly in her ear. "I need a favor."

"I am yours, my lady." She stroked the baby's head as he nursed with loud sucking sounds and occasional murmurs.

Nindalla hugged her arms to herself. "You told me that the kitchen hears all the gossip. For my children's safety—for the safety of all of us here—I need you to go to the kitchen and listen. Perhaps ask some questions."

"What do you want to know?"

Nindalla glanced at Intarza's sleeping form and lowered her voice further. "Who are the children Lady Midu wants to adopt, and what claim does she have? What is the relationship between Dagu and Midu? Between Dagu and the general?"

"Sounds like plots. I hate plots. It's not just the kings and princes who die, but regular people." Daanan chewed her lip.

Daanan was old enough to remember Humba's uncle. The man had visited Eridu twice when Nindalla was small to arrange for her marriage. By the time she arrived in Susa, he had disappeared, and many people on the staff were new to their positions. No one had ever mentioned the uncle's name in her thirteen years here; she could not remember it herself.

But she had been on guard since and stayed attuned to the nuances of every conversation she heard in the palace.

"You'll need to be careful," she warned the wet nurse. "Careful and subtle. We do not want either the chamberlain or the general to know you asked about them."

"Or her either." She ducked her head toward Intarza. Daanan pulled Enki-kiag free from her breast with a loud plop. He squawked angrily, but she handed him to Nindalla. "I'll go now. I suspect it's best to stop lawsuits and plots early."

"I suspect so too. Thank you." Nindalla stroked the baby's soft hair and back. "I have to protect my son. I cannot do it on my own, not as long as I must stay in the birthing hut."

"When Ur-sag-enki returns, he will keep Enki-kiag safe." Daanan held up her palms as if to protect herself. "You don't want to hear it, but he would be the baby prince's best ally. He loves Enki-kiag. I can tell."

"He may not return soon enough. We may be his only protectors if he is in danger." Nindalla licked her dry lips. "Go now, and see what you may learn."

She talked nonsense to Enki-kiag, admiring his beauty. The pointed top of his head had rounded out, and his face was no longer red from the strain of entering the world. Daanan had oiled him until his pale skin glowed like the rising moon. He would be a strong, handsome man, everything a king should be.

Kumdupum had not returned last night. She expected him tonight and still pondered what to do. If she and the children left with him, Enki-kiag might end up a peasant or a shopkeeper.

If she stayed and married Ur-sag-enki, Enki-kiag would have a high status . . . if Ur-sag-enki held onto his governorship. Enki-kiag might end up governor himself. But he would not wear a crown, and he would have to bend his knee to Sargon.

She bounced Enki-kiag gently, cradling his soft head. She had only two ways to put him in his rightful role of king. She could support a successful rebellion against the Akkadians. Or she could leave Susa and marry a childless king elsewhere.

Ur-sag-enki had accused her of coldheartedness, but he misread her. She knew the cost of war. She knew it so well that she was like a soldier with an injury that didn't heal. Pain was a normal part of daily life, always there, always biting and clawing, but under the surface. Many people in Susa had already suffered. Many more people would suffer if there were a rebellion, even if the people of Susa somehow succeeded in holding their city against the Akkadians. And if they failed. . . .

She shuddered and held Enki-kiag tighter. If she supported a rebellion that failed, the Akkadians would kill Enki-kiag. They had given the few royal survivors one chance to be part of the future of Susa; they would not do so again.

She would leave with Kumdupum. Better a live son than a dead one.

After hours of fretting, Nindalla heard the soft footsteps of servants and rushed to the door. Intarza, who never did anything if Daanan or a servant could do it for her, gave her a curious look.

Nindalla opened the door, and Daanan stood outside. Several kitchen servants stood outside in the courtyard.

"My lady, I'm sorry for being away so long. But I thought we all needed more food than we've been getting." She gave Nindalla a wink before turning and gesturing to the servants.

As the guards watched with suspicion, the men set down two jugs of beer, another two jugs of foamy milk, and platters piled high with cucumbers, apricots, nuts, fresh spring peas, sheep-milk cheese, and sweet cakes with raisins. Nindalla's mouth watered. Daanan hauled everything in, one platter or jar at a time, since the men could not enter the birthing hut.

Nindalla, Intarza, and Daanan feasted, laughed, and talked about food and Enki-kiag. But the meal, like all meals, came to an end.

The rest of the day passed slowly, taking as long as three normal days. Daanan dozed on her mat in the afternoon heat with Enki-kiag on her chest. Nindalla had no chance to ask her in private what she had learned. Nindalla tried to nap as well so evening would arrive more quickly, but her thoughts whirled, her hands twisted together, and she rolled from one side to the other. For once, she welcomed Intarza's peppering her with questions about intimate matters, this time about ways she could please her husband better.

When dark fell at last, Nindalla sang lullabies to Enki-kiag and encouraged Intarza to drink more beer, pointing out that it would sour and go to waste if they didn't finish it.

Intarza drank three full beer pots and fell asleep before the baby did. Nindalla motioned to Daanan, and they retreated to the corner farthest from Dagu's daughter.

The bland mask Daanan had worn all day gave way to a face wrinkled by concern and worry. "Women who've just birthed shouldn't be disturbed by evil news," she said, biting her lip. "I don't want to harm you or the baby."

"These are not ordinary times." Nindalla clasped Daanan's hands. "Knowledge is safety."

It was as if she had opened the gate of an irrigation canal. Words gushed from Daanan. "I don't know how you guessed, but Chamberlain Dagu and Lady Midu *have* been spending time together. Not alone in his chambers or his office, mind, but off in corners and in empty courtyards, whispering.

"No messengers have come from the governor or from General Qisim. Dagu is taking on the governor's duties. He sits in the governor's chair, dispenses judgments, and gives orders. He says that court business needs to get done. He says that the governor might be away for days or for months. He says that rebuilding the city can't wait.

"People hear more in his words. They see hope that life will continue as it is now, with a son of Susa in charge."

Daanan stopped for breath.

Nindalla picked at the fringe on the hem of her shift. How carefully Dagu proceeded! Was he was being a good steward or was he slowly, quietly building support for himself while increasing hatred of the Akkadians?

"What about the concubine? Whom is Midu adopting?"

Daanan looked away. "The birthing hut should be a place of joy and recovery."

"My joy is already disturbed."

"My lady, the news is bad. Dagu has filed a petition with the court on behalf of Midu. She wants to adopt Abi, Bar, Habarane, and Enki-kiag."

Horror embraced her in a death grip, like a sand boa squeezing the life from a rat or chick. She struggled to force out even a few words. "How can she? Doesn't she need grounds?"

Daanan looked away. "She says you are an unworthy mother."

Nindalla's heartbeat pounded in her ears. "How dare she!"

"Hush," Daanan cautioned, jerking her head at the door and the guards beyond.

Nindalla lowered her voice. "Unfit to care for my own children? Ludicrous."

"She says you are not acting in their best interest. They will lose the rights and privileges of royal children if you marry the governor."

"I have always put my children's welfare first! Who in Susa does not know that? The concubine cannot win."

"My lady, please don't take this lawsuit lightly. Everyone says that if Ur-sag-enki doesn't return soon, Chamberlain Dagu will decide the case. You will lose your children."

✳

Nindalla lit a second lamp and, cupping it in her hand, blew gently on the wick until it caught. The squat clay lamp was nearly out of sesame oil, but it had enough for her purposes.

She wiped moisture from her forehead then padded over to each woman and lowered the lamp to view each face. All still slept peacefully despite the heat, even the conniving Midu.

If she had not been planning to leave with Kumdupum, she would have sent the insolent woman back to the palace after her insults this afternoon. But she wanted as few people with her daughters tonight as possible so that Kumdupum could more easily take them from the palace.

She padded over to the stacks of clean linen and set the lamp on a chest. She flipped through the folded packets of soft, worn cloth until she found a large piece. She knelt with difficulty, trying not to think about how much more painful traveling with Kumdupum would be. She spread the large piece of linen out on the dirt floor and smoothed it out. Then she piled folded linen in the middle until she could just bring the four edges of the bottom piece together to tie. Between her bleeding from the birth and Enki-kiag's peeing, she needed as much linen as possible.

Now she needed to put the bundle by the door. She stood and tried to heft it. It didn't budge.

She frowned. Kumdupum would have to come into the birthing hut to carry it out. His bad leg might bump into something or someone. She picked at a hangnail until she could rip it off with her teeth. It tasted metallic. There was no choice: She could not lift the linen, so Kumdupum would have to.

She took some more linen from a stack, picked up the lamp, and went over to the leftover food. What a night for everyone to be especially hungry! Still, a ball of sheep cheese and a flatbread were better than nothing. She wrapped each up separately and put them in the largest basket in the hut.

She turned to the tall jars of beer and milk. She filled mugs halfway full of beer and nestled them in the basket, stuffing wadded linen between the mugs so they would not clank together or break. She carried the basket to the door and set it down.

She blew out the lamp, leaving only one to keep a flame alive for the next day. She placed her hand over Enki-kiag's mouth and carried him to the door. She set it ajar by a finger's width and settled herself and the baby next to it to wait.

She fanned herself and Enki-kiag with her hand. Air blew through the reeds of the hut, but it was too warm to make her more comfortable. Outside, the guards grumbled about the heat. An owl whistled off and on. For several minutes, nightjars kept up a steady burst of trilling. A cricket chirped in the corner of the hut.

The air cooled. Stripes of moonlight moved across the floor and then disappeared altogether. The guards became quiet except for an occasional yawn.

Nindalla shifted from legs folded to her right to legs folded to the left. She pulled loose threads on the bottom of her shift and picked at a knot in the embroidery. A band of tightness around her forehead made her head ache, and she pushed her knuckles against it. She fed Enki-kiag each time he woke.

When the sky pinkened, she placed Enki-kiag back next to Daanan, emptied the mugs of beer back into the jar, and replaced the bread and cheese on the tray. The basket went back to its original place.

She sat on her blanket and buried her head in her hands. Kumdupum had left her behind.

– Chapter 24 –

The next morning, Nindalla told Midu to leave the birthing hut and not come back. Food came and was eaten; drink came and was drunk. She and her two companions slept at night and talked or brooded during the day. She gnawed her fingernails and worried the hem of her shift until it was as ragged as a beggar's.

After years and years in the birthing hut, the eighth and final day of Nindalla's confinement arrived. She would soon be free of what had become a prison.

Despite the need to be dignified in front of her lessers, Nindalla could not suppress her smiling lips or tame her joyful heart, which bounded in her chest like a young jerboa. Today she would become spiritually pure again, and demons would be less of a threat to her and baby Enki-kiag. She would rejoin her children and her household.

Daanan and Intarza were already awake, and a tray of food sat near the fire. Intarza held Nindalla's finest shift high, and Daanan hit the linen with her fists to knock any dust or dirt from it. Enki-kiag watched with wide eyes.

Nindalla rose, laughing. "Do not tear my shift, Daanan. It's the best one I have here in the birthing hut, as well as the only one that is clean."

Daanan turned. She was smiling and red-faced from exertion.

Intarza lowered her arms with a whoosh of breath. She, too, was smiling. As she lightly folded the fabric, her feet danced in place. "What happens next?"

Nindalla forgave her the sin of having Dagu as a father. "Come with me and see."

Intarza's face glowed. "May I?"

"I have no ladies to attend me. I would welcome your company."

Enki-kiag, his entertainment done, took one of the deep breaths that the three women had learned preceded a scream. Daanan snatched him up and put him to her breast. "No screaming on your mother's purification day," she mock-scolded him.

"Were you able to find a sacrifice?" Nindalla asked the wet nurse.

"Yes. It's a new lamb instead of a yearling. But the god should understand the state of his city. I tied it outside and ordered the guards to keep it safe."

"Thank you. Intarza, please help me dress and do my hair."

"But you have not eaten yet."

Nindalla cast another glance at the bread and dates. Her stomach seemed filled with butterflies. "I am too excited to eat now." Usually fasting before the ceremony did not matter because it was followed by a feast. But in this time of Akkadian occupation and food shortages, she did not expect any celebratory meal, even a small one.

Intarza crossed the hut and found a comb. Nindalla sat on the floor, and the young woman combed the knots from her hair and chattered about her husband.

After several minutes, Intarza stood and circled her, inspecting her hair. "There! No knots left. I'll finish after I help you dress."

"You were so gentle that I didn't feel a single tug. What was your job in the palace?" Nindalla asked.

Intarza beamed. "I was one of Queen Ri-ti's ladies. I was the only one she trusted to comb her hair. I did not hurt her as the other ladies did."

A woman should know her mother-in-law's ladies. Nindalla shifted her bent legs to her other side and pulled a thread in the hem of her shift. *My grief over Eridu blinded me to my obligations to her. Perhaps her rudeness to me is my own fault.*

"I hope the queen treated you well. You are a treasure," Nindalla said.

"She was kind to all her ladies." Intarza grinned. "Usually. She had a temper and held a grudge." She fingered Nindalla's hair and said wistfully, "I so wish the Akkadians had not killed her."

Is her death my fault as well? Nindalla imagined the queen as she had last seen her, arrogant in the birthing hut while battle raged outside the city. Then she pictured her own soft-spoken mother—so different from Queen Ri-ti in so many ways, but alike in their deaths: queens murdered by the Akkadians.

"It is the way of the Akkadians to murder innocents," she said.

"Why did the gods preserve us?" Intarza asked.

"I do not know. Perhaps someone needs to live to remember the dead."

"That's a good thought. In case you're right, I will remember the queen always." Intarza wiped at her nose. "Now if you would stand, please?" She helped Nindalla up and untied the knot that held Nindalla's shift together at her left shoulder. The garment dropped to the ground, and Nindalla kicked it away.

Intarza unfolded the clean shift, caressing the intricate embroidery along the edges, and then draped it over Nindalla.

"Please sit again. I'll put your hair up." Intarza worked quickly but gently. Nindalla felt the hairpins go in, but none gouged her scalp. After only a few minutes, the young woman announced, "Done!"

Nindalla reached back to feel her hairstyle. Elaborate, balanced, with not a hair out of place. "Excellent work. Thank you." She stood on her own and hugged the young woman.

Intarza not only smiled but bounced on her heels. "The sooner you are ready, the sooner we can go to the temple of Inshushinak. Do you want sandals?"

"No. I will go before the god in humility. Daanan, did you want to come to the temple as well?"

"I'd prefer to take the baby and get him settled in his room, if that is all right with you."

"Yes. Come, Intarza. Be ready to be overwhelmed." As they left the birthing hut, collected the lamb—which scampered eagerly after Intarza—and took little-used side passages through the palace to the temple hill, Nindalla told her how Zana the high priestess would be dressed in her best robe and all her jewelry, how the chapel would be scented with myrrh and other precious resins, how all the priests would attend Zana while she sacrificed the lamb, said prayers of thanks, and blessed Nindalla in the name of Inshushinak. The priests would sing hymns in-between each part of the ceremony that purified her spirit after giving birth.

"All for you," Intarza said, wonder in her voice. "Perhaps I should not come. I doubt I am worthy to be your attendant today."

Nindalla embraced her, careful not to disturb her hair or makeup. "You have already proven yourself in the birthing hut."

– Chapter 25 –

As Nindalla strode angrily away from the temple after her purification ceremony, not bothering or even wanting to be ladylike, her body vibrated with humiliation and her face burned. *How dare they? How dare they?* She felt as cheap and used as a beggar's discarded loincloth.

Having Dagu's daughter as her attendant—and a witness—doubled her shame; no doubt Intarza would hurry back to her father to tell him what happened.

Or had not happened.

Light footsteps sounded behind her. A woman, or perhaps a boy from the temple.

She stopped and turned.

Intarza hurried after her, her feet pattering in small, feminine steps.

She is not running to her father after all. Nindalla waited for her to catch up, suddenly glad for the company. They walked slowly together in silence through the ancient passageways that connected the temple and the palace.

At last Intarza said, in a small voice, "The priests sacrificed the lamb, but nothing else happened the way you said."

Nindalla's jaws clenched tightly, and her nails bit into her palms. She lifted her chin high, trying to reclaim her pride. A long minute passed before she could say, "I am not a princess anymore. At least not of Susa."

She was still a princess of Eridu, but E-kug's letters said that the desert and the marsh were swallowing the city. The only people left were a few priests who cared for Enki and his magnificent temple and ziggurat.

And Akkadian soldiers, of course.

"My father still refers to you as 'Princess Nindalla.'"

Her hands relaxed. "Your father plays the game of court politics like a master. He does not choose sides or burn bridges unless he has to."

"Why did High Priestess Zana snub you?"

"Because she has never liked Sumerians, and because for the moment I'm only another Sumerian in exile. Zana thinks only one step ahead, without considering the other players in the game."

"So she thinks she can be disrespectful without consequence?"

"Yes." A giggle burst from Nindalla's lips. She clapped her hand over her mouth. "She forgets that the Akkadians' chosen governor for Susa is a Sumerian."

It would almost be worth marrying Ur-sag-enki to spite High Priestess Zana and force her to treat me respectfully.

Almost.

Nindalla wanted to see her daughters as soon as possible, but she kept slowing down to look around. Much had changed since the night she and Ur-sag-enki had searched for the children. Bodies no longer littered the floors, which had been scrubbed clean. Vases stood upright with fresh palm branches in them. Scribes and household servants bustled through the halls. It was almost as if the battle had never happened. The life of the court went on as usual.

When she entered Humba's family quarters, the courtyard looked as it always had. The fountain was clean now; the water sparkled in the sunlight. Two servants she did not recognize stepped into a storeroom carrying baskets of wet linens.

Even the parrot knew he was no longer in danger. His bright-red beak no longer hid beneath his green wing, and he was squawking. When he saw her, he bounced up and down on his perch to attract her attention, squawking, "Bread! Bread!"

Nindalla laughed at his antics and laughed again to hear her own laughter sound the way it used to, genteel but free and unchoked by fear. She wanted to stop and talk to the parrot, but she wanted to see her children so much more. She smacked her lips at him and hurried to her bedchamber.

It was empty.

No gifts from well-wishers for the new baby. No children waiting. No evidence of the treat promised by Ur-sag-enki. *He must not be back yet.*

She returned to the courtyard. As she walked to her daughters' bedchamber, she listened for them over the parrot's screeching. As she neared the room, shrieks of laughter spilled out. Smiling, she rushed to the doorway and stood there for several minutes watching their happy play. Enki-kiag lay between his sisters, cooing and trying to kick his feet within his bindings.

Even orphaned Habarane looked happy. She made her pottery sheep cavort around the floor as if she had no worries. Soon, Nindalla would have to reinstall discipline and remind the girls again that princesses did not play on the floor. But not yet.

Abi was the first to spot her. She leapt up and threw her arms in the air. "Ama!"

The other children jumped up and ran to her. They hopped up and down as they hugged her, Habarane hanging back behind the others.

"I have missed you so much, Abi! You too, Bar, my reed, and you, Habarane."

"Where's Abba?" Bar asked.

"What about my Ama?" Habarane asked.

Nindalla swallowed hard. She gentled her voice. "They are not coming back. Remember?"

Abi stood back and put her hands on her hips. "The governor isn't coming back either; is he? He said he would protect us and then he left. Like Abba."

"Ur-sag-enki will be back. Soon, if the gods favor him. Our lives will settle down to normal soon." She smiled weakly, knowing her words to be a lie. Grieving for a father took years, maybe a lifetime.

"Did the new nursemaid take good care of you while I was in the birthing hut?"

Habarane stuck her thumb in her mouth and turned away, suddenly shy. "Yes. Ama Midu gave me many toys."

"Midu?" The word was a dagger to her heart. "You mean Sukura. I am your new mother. Sukura is only your nursemaid."

"I gave her—I gave all the children—permission to call me 'Ama Midu.'"

Nindalla spun at Midu's voice. The woman lounged on a bench in a dark corner as if she owned it and the room as well. Sukura was nowhere in sight.

"After all," Midu continued, "I will be their mother soon. After the adoption."

"Is it so hard being barren?"

Midu went white. Her hand flew to her throat.

"The city is full of orphans. Adopt some of them!"

"Susa is my city, and you don't care what happens to it. You never have," Midu said. "I want to protect the last of the royal family. You're a disgrace, catting around before Prince Humba is even in his grave. You have not even torn your shift."

"Perhaps I should have expected you to covet my children," Nindalla went on. "After all, you first stole my husband's affections."

Midu turned from white to red and back again. She stood and smoothed her shift.

Her arms and chest looked bony instead of soft, and only simple copper pins held her hair up and her shift together. *Who feeds her, I wonder? Where does she sleep? How does she pay?* Nindalla shook her head. How Midu got by was not her concern.

"You think I envy you." The knuckles of Midu's clenched fists gleamed white. You're wrong. I want the best for Humba's children."

"You want the political advantages of controlling the last remaining members of the Susan royal family," Nindalla snapped.

Midu turned her back on Nindalla, stood still long enough for even a halfwit to notice the insult, and then strode, head high, from the room.

Habarane burst into tears. "Ama Midu is sad!"

Bar scooted over, patted Habarane on the head with weighty thumps, and hugged her. Bar started crying in sympathy.

Enki-kiag's dark eyes opened wide at the sound. He pursed his lips and listened intently. Then he wailed.

Nindalla enclosed them all within her arms and knees. "Ahhhh, children. Don't cry. I am here now. Things will get better."

They only cried louder.

Nindalla sighed. *Another one of those days.* She thought of her own childhood and how she always joined in when her younger sisters cried. She was pleased her own children had the same bond, but today of all days, after her humiliation at the temple, she wanted a simple, uncomplicated, merry homecoming.

It was a foolish hope after the terrible disruptions the children had been through. She should expect a lot of pointless crying and excessively exuberant behavior in the weeks ahead.

Abi stood apart from the others, hugging her arms to herself. Her eyes held pain and confusion. "I do not like it when you fight with Lady Midu. It makes my stomach hurt."

Nindalla had no arms left to comfort her oldest daughter.

– Chapter 26 –

Nindalla was putting away the things she had taken to the birthing hut when the deep sound of a man's voice rumbled nearby.

Ur-sag-enki is here! He kept his promise! She spun.

Her smile died. Her visitor was Chamberlain Dagu, and he stood at the entrance to her bedchamber.

Sharp words rose to her lips. Then she remembered he had not been at his king's side during battle. She had to tread carefully.

"Good afternoon, Princess." He nodded. "I heard about this morning from Intarza. You were not treated in a way befitting your rank. I will speak to High Priestess Zana."

She blinked at him. "Thank you. And thank you also for allowing your daughter to attend me in the birthing hut. She was an excellent companion."

He gave a rare smile. "She is even more eager now for a child of her own after a week of playing with your son."

"May the gods grant her one soon." Nindalla set down the pile of linens. How strange for the chamberlain to see her private quarters and private things. She felt as if he had come upon her changing her clothes or taking a bath. She gestured toward the courtyard. "Please, let us go out there to talk. It is pleasant in the afternoon."

They sat on benches by the fountain, under palms that blocked the sun. The parrot looked at the stranger in his courtyard and began bouncing and screeching.

"Is your reunion with your children going well?" Chamberlain Dagu asked.

She wondered why he was delaying getting to his purpose here. "Yes, thank you. And your household is well, I trust?"

"It is just the servants and I now." He clasped his left hand in his right in front of his heart in an attitude of prayer. "In times of turmoil, not having young children is a blessing, not a curse. I was spared your worries."

"The city must overflow with widows. May you find a new wife soon and know the joys of children." He had not said what she most longed to hear. "Have you had a messenger from Governor Ur-sag-enki?"

"No. Have you heard from the governor?"

"No." She looked at him with narrowed eyes. "I thought you knew everything that went on in the palace."

Dagu smiled with obvious self-satisfaction. "Usually."

"Then may I have your advice?" She stretched out a pleading hand. "I have no one else to turn to."

His eyes sparked with interest, and his gaze rested on her uncovered right shoulder. "Certainly, my lady. How may I help you?"

"You filed a petition for Lady Midu to adopt my children. What can I do to persuade you to withdraw it?"

She had expected him to ask for a bribe or a favor. Instead, his face sombered. "It's a delicate matter. And withdrawing a petition is not always easy." He stood up abruptly and went to study the parrot. "What an interesting bird. Where did it come from?"

"Meluhha. It's called a 'parrot,'" she answered. When he said nothing about the petition, she went on. "You are a man of rank and power. Surely you can do something to stop the groundless lawsuit of a jumped-up concubine against a royal princess of Susa."

He clucked his tongue at the parrot.

Hoping to prick his pride and vanity, she added, "Or have you lost power under the Akkadians?"

He turned. A forked vein in his forehead pulsed as red as the parrot's bill. He took two noisy breaths before repeating, "It's a delicate matter."

"The very kind in which you are so expert," she flattered him, puzzled. *Why is he willing to help Midu but not me?*

"Please, my lord, have a seat." She called for a servant to fetch food and turned her question over in her mind as Dagu talked idly about the parrot. Gradually an answer came to her: a court power play that only his subtle, complex mind could conceive of and execute.

Ur-sag-enki hoped to gain legitimacy as governor in the eyes of the sons and daughters of Susa by marrying her and adopting her children. The people would find him a more palatable governor if he were father of the rightful but too-young heir than if he were merely the appointee of the hated Akkadians.

Dagu too sought legitimacy as a potential governor—but slyly, subtly, behind the backs of people who might oppose him.

The servant returned with a platter of food.

The luscious aromas made her stomach rumble, but she wanted Dagu occupied while she thought through Dagu's plan. She pasted on a smile. "Please, my lord, have it all. Eat and be well."

His eyebrows rose, but then he smiled back. "Thank you, my lady."

She nodded. She kept her smile on as she thought. According to Ur-sag-enki, Dagu kept information from him and sometimes made him look foolish. If Dagu wanted to be governor, it would help if Ur-sag-enki appeared to be incompetent.

Now Midu, a daughter of Susa, was trying to adopt her children. As their former nursemaid, she did care about them, Nindalla knew. But it was not her place to presume to even think about adopting them. The idea should never have occurred to her.

The lawsuit made more sense as Dagu's idea. In this time of chaos, few people cared about an adoption fight between a princess and the prince's concubine. But once Midu was the legal mother of the royal children, Dagu could marry her and be the father of the heir instead of Ur-sag-enki.

Her conjectures hung together. The people of Susa would prefer a son of Susa as governor, especially if he were the legal guardian of the rightful king. The Akkadians might then prefer Dagu as well, thinking Susa less likely to rebel. Even in Sumer, Sargon had occasionally appointed local elites as governors instead of his own men.

It was a plot as tangled as yarn after a cat had played with it. But its implications were clear. Dagu would, sooner or later, through violence or petition to King Sargon or an "accident," get rid of Governor Ur-sag-enki.

And possibly me as well.

She gripped the edge of the bench, fear settling in her stomach like a heavy rock. She had assumed her status as a royal widow would protect her. She had been wrong. Dagu had concocted a convoluted plan with Midu instead of simply courting Nindalla.

Her face got hot. *Once again, I take second place to Humba's concubine.*

She couldn't think about her damaged pride. Her life was at stake.

She could take the children and sneak out of the city tonight. But where could they go without help, on foot, with a new baby?

She could warn Ur-sag-enki when he returned, and together they could thwart Dagu. But men did not always come back from war, or they came back too late.

Her mouth went dry. Her best hope was to buy time for herself and Ur-sag-enki by encouraging Dagu to take an interest in her.

She swallowed and wiped her damp palms on her shift. Another balancing act, this time with Dagu instead of Ur-sag-enki. Could she pull it off? Could she bear to marry Dagu and let him command her body and every aspect of her life? Let his hands roam free on her body whenever he wanted? The thought sickened her stomach.

She admired Dagu's cleverness and knowledge, but he was not kind like Ur-sag-enki. The chamberlain of a king had to be a hard man who could make hard decisions and still be able to sleep. Dagu's grim, pinched face suggested he would not be a loving, affectionate father either. He would be a worse husband than Humba.

Yet to save her children, she had to try to sway Dagu's interest from Midu to her.

Her mouth tasted bitter. She swallowed and then swallowed again. It did not remove the taste of disgust.

The parrot shrieked. It rocked from foot to foot, squawking, "Bread, my lord! Bread, my lord!"

Dagu chuckled.

Nindalla joined in. "He's a funny bird, isn't he? He always makes the children laugh. Me as well."

Dagu walked to the cage and held out a piece of bread. The parrot's beak snapped it away from him. Still chuckling, Dagu returned.

Nindalla patted the bench immediately next to her. "You are going to spoil that parrot with so much attention, Lord Dagu."

His hunched shoulders relaxed, and he took her invitation to sit close to her. "As a Sumerian, my lady, you can understand that some people in Susa—not everyone, but some people—hate the Akkadians and don't want them ruling here."

She nodded and leaned toward him. "I hate the Akkadians more than anyone in Susa." Her fists clenched on their own. Her bitten-off nails were jagged against her soft palms. "My hate has had ten years to fester and grow."

"Then you can understand that some people—again, not everyone—are outraged by the rumors that Ur-sag-enki intends to marry you. They don't want the royal bloodline under the control of the Akkadians."

"But Ur-sag-enki is not an Akkadian. He is a Sumerian from Eridu. As am I."

"I must speak bluntly. Anyone who fights for the Akkadian army is as bad as an Akkadian."

She sighed. "Certainly. He betrayed Eridu by fighting for Sargon."

"But you entertain his courtship."

"What else can I do?" She sighed again. "I must protect my children."

"Of course. Of course you must." He scooted a little closer to her.

A jewel beetle scuttled toward the fountain, its back a rainbow in the sun. Dagu's gaze followed it. "My concern, as always, is Susa first and foremost. If she has to be under the thumb of the Akkadians—and that seems the fate of Elam now as it was for Sumer earlier—then she should have a good ruler. Preferably one from the city itself."

"You object to Ur-sag-enki as governor just because he is not a son of Susa? The Akkadians could have appointed someone worse, far worse. General Qisim, for example."

For an instant, Dagu's face twisted with anger, and his cold eyes grew colder. Then his face smoothed to its usual controlled visage, except the skin under his right eye jerked and twitched more than usual.

He hates General Qisim, yet he had secret meetings with him. Her intuition suggested that the general had made Dagu a promise and not followed through. She leaned closer, wanting for Ur-sag-enki's sake to learn more about the general.

But when Dagu spoke again, it was not about the general. "Ur-sag-enki grew up on a farm. It shows. He has no idea how to dress like a governor or hide his thoughts, let alone how to run a city." He swiveled toward her and spoke slowly, watching her face. "There are no Akkadian troops in Susa now. When—if—Ur-sag-enki comes back, he will have but one company of soldiers."

She feigned shock. "Chamberlain! Are you suggesting rebellion against the Akkadians?"

He feigned shock himself. "Not at all! I merely want to warn you that marrying Ur-sag-enki could be dangerous."

"I deeply appreciate your concern for me, but I do not see the danger."

"With so few soldiers, the city needs a strong, able ruler to keep order, quell rebellion, and protect her from raiders. Sooner or later, Ur-sag-enki will show he is not that man. General Qisim will have to replace him. If you were his wife, where would you be then?"

"In the desert without water." She hunched her shoulders in fright. She did not have to pretend; his alarming words chilled her to the bone. They suggested that the chamberlain had a backup plan to marrying Midu: Encourage a rebellion against the Akkadians.

If the rebels somehow succeeded, Dagu was the natural choice to be regent for Enki-kiag. If the rebellion failed, the Akkadians would replace Ur-sag-enki. Again, the natural choice was Dagu.

She shivered. "Help me, please. How can I protect the legitimate king and the rest of my children?"

"Legitimate king." He winked. "Now *you* seem to be suggesting rebellion."

"Never! But I have a duty to protect Susa's hereditary ruler. Just in case."

"You are well known for always doing your duty."

"Thank you, my lord."

"You asked for my advice. I urge you to plan for every contingency. I myself am."

Nindalla nearly snorted with laughter. *You surely are, you despicable man.* But she immediately sobered. He must have many more plots underway than she suspected. He was a spider in the middle of an unseen web.

Dagu scratched his neatly trimmed beard with unusual self-consciousness, in the process showing off several expensive rings on his hand. "The best way to protect your children and Susa is to marry someone other than our governor."

"Do you have a suggestion?"

"Someone native to this land. Someone well off. Someone powerful. Someone already well known by the people. Midu could not win in court if such a man were your children's father."

"Thank you, Chamberlain. You have been so kind to give me your wise advice." She touched his hand lightly and looked down with feigned modesty.

His foot tapped once, twice.

Quietly she said, giving her voice a little tremor, "Chamberlain, you may call here again. If you wish." She felt dirty for encouraging him.

"I do indeed so wish, Princess Nindalla." He rose. "I would stay in your beautiful and wise company longer, but I have duties to attend to."

She had hooked him. Soon she would need to decide whether to throw him back into the sea or keep him. She watched from under her eyelashes as the chamberlain left Humba's quarters with a self-satisfied strut.

Her stomach felt as if it were full of flopping fish. She returned to the children's room, picked up Enki-kiag, and slumped against the wall. Dangling one suitor had been hard enough. Now she had two.

As she chewed her fingernails, she thought back to the night she and Ur-sag-enki had searched for her children. Midu told him that widows could not remarry for ninety days after their husband's death. Nindalla believed her. The Sumerians had the same custom, and the two regions had interacted for many generations.

Dagu would know the purpose of the ninety-day wait—for the new husband to be certain that the widow did not carry her former husband's child.

But she clearly was not with child, having just birthed one. Like Ur-sag-enki, Dagu would not be willing to wait to marry. She had to decide her children's future soon.

Now.

— Chapter 27 —

The road from Anshan to Susa was not a true road, but a wide rut that ran through a rolling, often rocky desert for as far as Ur-sag-enki could see in front and behind. The landscape bore little resemblance to the flat, rich river lands of Sumer or to the marshes of Eridu, and it smelled bland and lifeless. Ur-sag-enki could shake neither his unease nor his longing for the comforting scenery of his childhood. He would give much to hear ducks quacking overhead or to see turtles basking on a log.

To the east, mountains topped with snow—frozen water that was fluffy like wool, one of his men had told him—stood like towers of the gods. Not even Sargon of Akkad could surmount such a barrier. The mountains also oppressed his mood as he led what remained of his company in a march under a hot, unyielding sun.

The closer they got to Susa, the more Ur-sag-enki thought about his inadequate force. Two hundred men! How under all the gods of the heavens did General Qisim expect him to hold Susa with only two hundred men?

Maybe he didn't. The cruel, capricious general had tested him before. Maybe he was again challenging Ur-sag-enki's leadership ability. It was not a big deal, at least to the general. He had many talented officers under him at Anshan. It would be a simple matter to send one to replace Ur-sag-enki if he failed.

It *was* a big deal for Ur-sag-enki. He had nowhere else to go.

He pulled out the turtle and lion amulets that the old couple in Anshan had given him at the end of their visit. He was glad to have a replacement for the turtle amulet he gave to baby Enki-kiag. He would need all the divine protection he could get when he returned to Susa.

His lieutenant, Idi-Ishtar, coughed and broke his thoughts. "Captain! The scouts return."

Ur-sag-enki shaded his eyes with his hand and squinted. The two men strode toward them at a jaunty pace; they had been droopy with fatigue when he sent them forward. His spirits lifted. "I think they found a stream or waterhole. Care to wager against me?"

"No, sir. I'd rather have water than win back any booty."

"Let's pick up the pace."

Lieutenant Idi-Ishtar turned and shouted to the rest of the men. Ur-sag-enki strode forward.

The scouts ran to meet him. They saluted him with a hand to the nose, and then one said, "We found a stream."

"A cold one from high in the mountains," the other said. He was baked as dark as a burnt brick.

The lieutenant shouted their words for the rest of the company to hear. The men cheered and marched faster. They reached the stream in less than an hour.

As soon as he gave the signal for his men to relax, they ran for the water, whooping and hollering. He motioned for the scouts to join him under a white willow. Its drooping, dancing branches gave almost as much privacy and protection from the sun's searing rays as a tent, but unlike a tent, they let the water-cooled air through.

He took a stick of leathery dried meat from his pack and offered some to them. "I don't remember this stream. I ordered that you take us back by the same road."

"We are on the same road," said the dark scout. "When we marched to Anshan, the stream was just a trickle. The snow in the mountains is melting and filling the channel."

The other scout added, "If we march until dusk and start again at dawn, we'll be in Susa by noon, if Inshushinak allows."

"You are a son of Susa?" Ur-sag-enki asked. The man had invoked Susa's patron god and had a heavy accent, but Lieutenant Idi-Ishtar had recruited only a handful of men from the just-conquered city.

"We both are from Susa. We have been friends since we were children. When you provided food and shelter for the orphans, my dark friend Kuk-kalla here said, 'Brother Il-alsu, the new governor is not like other Akkadians. Let us serve him and see whether the gods smile on us.'"

"I'm no Akkadian. I'm Sumerian."

"You were once in our sandals then," Il-alsu said.

Ur-sag-enki nodded. He could use the advice of a son of Susa. He chewed his stick of jerky, deciding how to ask his question. At last he just blurted it out, but softly, so that none of his other men would hear. "I don't know the customs of Susa, but I want to court a Susian widow. What should I do?"

The scouts looked at each other and shrugged their shoulders. "We both had arranged marriages with maidens. I never saw my wife until our wedding day," Kuk-kalla said.

"Your father wanted to make sure you didn't run away," Il-alsu said, earning himself a kick. He stood. Before Ur-sag-enki could guess what he would do and stop him, Il-alsu shouted toward the men at the stream, "The governor needs some tips on winning a woman!"

Raucous laughter greeted the announcement. Several men dunked themselves to soak their hair and kilts and then ran to crowd under the tree around Ur-sag-enki, shouting advice.

"Women like presents."

"Yes!" shouted another. "Show us the spoils you brought back from Anshan."

Il-alsu started a marching chant, substituting "Show us, show us" for "One, two, one, two."

After a moment of embarrassment, Ur-sag-enki clapped in time with the chant and laughed at their enthusiasm. Soldiers were predictable in so many ways, so unlike Nindalla.

"I did well in my plundering," he bragged to his men. He leapt up, took off his pleated leather skirt, and spread it on the ground. He held his pouch at a slight angle and let the contents gently roll out and onto the skirt.

He had chosen carefully from among the ornaments taken in the fighting, imagining each necklace around Nindalla's neck and each ring on her finger. The jewelry she wore showed fine workmanship, so he had looked for that in the spoils.

Lieutenant Idi-Ishtar had grabbed whatever was big and shiny. The pieces Ur-sag-enki had won from him in their wagers stood out for their crudeness. He brushed them to the side of the skirt, along with the tablet General Qisim had sent with him. "What should I give her first? I want to make a good impression."

His men argued the merits of various pieces and settled on a necklace with several strands of blue and orange stones. It was a masterpiece of craft: All the beads were exactly the same size and glistened in the sunlight as if they were wet. A god could have made it, so perfect it was. Like Nindalla herself.

"Good choice, men." He planned to give her a pair of earrings too. They were in his rooms at the palace, part of the bundle of jewelry from the king's rooms that Chamberlain Dagu had forced on him so that he could look like a governor.

He slipped everything back into his pouch and put his skirt on. "Time to march on," he said.

One of the men shouted, "Presents aren't enough. Women need compliments."

Ur-sag-enki recognized a delaying tactic when he heard one. Still, if women needed compliments, he needed to know what to say. "What traits are worthy of praise?"

The men crowded closer, each with something to say.

"Large dark eyes."

"A smooth, round belly."

"Courage."

"No beard."

"Goes without mentioning."

"Plump cheeks."

"Which ones?" The men laughed.

"Both!"

"Wisdom."

"A sweet smell."

"A bright face."

"Good ancestry."

"Brows like swords."

Kuk-kalla asked, "Does your woman have any of those traits, or will you have to lie?"

"She has all of them," Ur-sag-enki replied, wonderingly, amazed now that he had never had any doubt that he would one day possess this perfect woman.

The soldiers whistled and shouted his name as if they had just won a battle under his command.

"I'd like to see this goddess, captain," said Kuk-kalla. "Why don't you send me ahead with a message so that she knows you are safe and on your way?"

– Chapter 28 –

That evening, as Nindalla and Daanan were singing to the children, Sukura returned to the children's room leading a panting, sweating, sunburned soldier in Akkadian armor. "This messenger was in the kitchen asking for you. He speaks Elamite."

Nindalla leapt up from her bench, her hands clasped together to keep them from shaking. The messenger looked uninjured, although his news must be urgent for him to have run so hard. "Do you come from Ur-sag-enki? Is he safe?"

"Yes, my lady, to both questions." The soldier prostrated himself on the floor, to the delight of Bar, who joyfully grabbed his hair in both fists.

"Bar, my sweet reed, stop that! Princesses do not pull hair. Soldier, you may rise. What is your message?"

"Captain Ur-sag-enki said to tell you that he will be returning tomorrow midday and that he will call on you about dusk."

"Praise Enki for his great mercies!" she exclaimed. Daanan murmured her own thanks to Inshushinak.

Nindalla's knees quivered like calf's foot jelly. She sank back down onto the bench with a profound relief that surprised her. "We worried that he might have returned to the dust."

The soldier bounced from foot to foot, a grin growing on his face. "He is alive and coming to court you!"

"Oh!" Nindalla said. She looked at Daanan for a clue to how to respond to such an announcement.

The wet nurse laughed and winked at the soldier.

Heat rose in Nindalla's face. "The governor made you run a long way to deliver such a little message."

The soldier grinned wider.

Nindalla's gaze dropped to the floor. Although news that the governor would be in Susa soon was most welcome, his imminent courtship was no joking matter to her, who had never been courted before. She wondered whether Daanan had ever been courted and whether she could advise her how to act.

What was she thinking? It would be inappropriate to ask a servant for such advice. She would behave like a princess, as always.

Would she put him off if she did not laugh and giggle and wink?

She caught her thoughts short. *I have bigger worries than being courted.* The palace political game would change tomorrow . . . or tonight if she told the servants to spread the news of Ur-sag-enki's return.

No, it would be better to keep his return secret. And better, too, if Ur-sag-enki were warned of the plots and secrets before he arrived.

She looked back up at the soldier and stood. "Thank you for your service." She undid the abalone pin that secured her shift at the shoulder and handed it to him.

His eyes widened. "My lady! My thanks and eternal gratitude."

"You must be tired and looking forward to bed. But I have a message for Ur-sag-enki. I wish you return to him. Tonight. But first, go to the kitchen to eat and refresh yourself."

"Yes, my lady."

"Tell no one here of Ur-sag-enki's arrival. I want it to be a secret from his enemies. Say this to him: Be on your guard. Some believe Susa would be better off with a different governor."

The soldier's face hardened. "Name them. They will die."

She shook her head. "I will tell him all at dusk. Meanwhile, he should trust no one here."

The soldier slid her brooch into his waist pouch. "He is a good captain. I won't take time to eat or rest. I'll leave right away." He gave her a quick bow over his clasped hands and marched out.

Nindalla ran her hand over her hair. "Daanan, Sukura, tomorrow night I will eat early with the children and then bid them goodnight. I want no interruptions when I talk with Ur-sag-enki."

Daanan nodded, her broad face serious now. "May Inshushinak protect him from his enemies."

— Chapter 29 —

Ur-sag-enki turned to inspect his men one more time. Despite their long, dusty march, they stood at the broken gate of Susa looking alert and strong, soldiers to be proud to have serving under oneself.

Or to fear if you wished harm to their captain.

Lieutenant Idi-Ishtar said, "They are prepared, my lord."

Ur-sag-enki nodded. "Send the messengers ahead to proclaim a great feast tonight. Then raise the new banner."

As Il-alsu and Kuk-kalla ran through the gate toward the palace hill, the company's newly created hedgehog banner rose. His soldiers cheered.

Ur-sag-enki ordered them into formation again, and they marched slowly into Susa so that all could see their strong arms and the banner they marched under. News of the feast outpaced them. Halfway to the palace, they received their first cheer, from a blacksmith who also shouted out that he made fine swords.

As they marched, the crowds increased along the side of the road. When the reduced company at last reached the palace, many people were waiting. They cheered and sang hymns of praise to various gods to greet him.

Ur-sag-enki left his soldiers in the square to talk up the feast and went inside. He pulled off his helmet and went immediately to the audience hall.

Chamberlain Dagu sat in the governor's chair. Ur-sag-enki slunk along the side of the hall until he reached the front. No one noticed him. One of the tricks he had learned as a slave was how to be inconspicuous.

He stepped onto the dais and dropped a casual, fatherly hand on Dagu's shoulder. The chamberlain lurched under his hand. Ur-sag-enki interrupted Dagu's remarks, speaking in a booming voice so all those waiting for an audience could hear as well as see him. "Go home. Put on your best clothes. I sponsor a feast tonight in front of the palace to celebrate my homecoming to Susa."

Under the loud murmurs of the people leaving, Dagu protested. "How will we feed the whole city? Our stores won't last the winter if we do."

"Send to Anshan for beer and grain to replenish our supplies for the winter. Anshan has more than enough. As for the details of the feast, you taught me to delegate." He patted Dagu's shoulder. "I leave it to you to prepare a splendid feast for this evening. I expect to be amazed."

Dagu delegated, as Dagu liked to do. He said it was more important to brief Ur-sag-enki on the city since he had left than to see to the feast himself.

Two hours later, Ur-sag-enki left the palace, his head spinning from Dagu's confusing, complicated, contradictory report. Already he remembered only a blur of sounds.

He might not be educated, but he wasn't stupid. Dagu and his scribes had purposely sped through their explanations of the accounting records so fast and in so much detail to confuse him. And when he asked a second time for an explanation of the progress of the rebuilding, the scribe consulted a tablet with a different shape from the first time and told him something different.

He could not count on Dagu or anyone who had worked for him to tell him the truth. He had to be able to look at the tablets and know what was what.

He needed to learn his numbers and how to add and subtract.

A passing merchant, his paunch and gold earrings marking him as successful, greeted him with a smile and a touch to the nose.

Ur-sag-enki touched his nose in return and stopped him. "A beautiful day, isn't it?"

"Very fine, my lord. And the feast—what a fine idea. Makes people think you will be a fine governor. Fine traffic at my shop since you got back this afternoon, very fine."

"I'm glad of it. Our citizens need the businesses running again. You have helped by opening your shop already. May the gods bring Susa peace and prosperity."

"Lord Governor, peace and prosperity depend on you as well as the gods."

"I have many ideas for making Susa more secure and more prosperous than before. I didn't accept the governorship to become rich at the citizens' expense. Susa will be my home, and I will do what is best for her."

The merchant played with an earring. "As should we all."

"I have a favor to ask. A favor important for the future of Susa."

The merchant studied Ur-sag-enki's face, his own impassive, as if he wanted to be polite but expected to be asked for silver and barley. "You may ask, my lord."

"If I wanted to hire a master scribe for the palace, where would I find one?"

The merchant broke into a wide smile, clearly relieved. "The tablet house my sons went to had a fine master. He's a Sumerian, but all the finest are. May I escort you to him?"

Ur-sag-enki held out his hand.

The merchant grasped it and led him on a long, rambling stroll on the largest avenues—they walked some of them twice—as if he wanted off his closeness to the governor. He gossiped about the palace staff all the way, so Ur-sag-enki did not hurry him or chastise him for leading him in circles. The more he knew about palace feuds and alliances, the better.

"How do you know so much about the palace?" Ur-sag-enki asked.

"My neighbors and fellow merchants are terrible, terrible. I have sought audiences with the king and the chamberlain many times to seek justice." He squeezed the governor's hand tighter. "I look forward to bringing my future suits before you, my friend."

At last they arrived at the tablet house, a well-kept house of two stories. A servant showed them in, and the merchant introduced him to Master Gunidu, master of the tablet house, before leaving.

Master Gunidu led him into a large courtyard, invited him to sit, and bid a servant fetch jugs of cucumber water and pomegranate juice with honey.

Several finely dressed women sat in the north corner. Some had spindles and spun yarn. Nearby, the oldest woman sat at a loom and wove. Servants or slaves stood behind each woman, awaiting orders.

In the north corner, which held a built-in brick stove, a woman busied herself with brewing equipment and supplies just like the ones his mother had had. He closed his eyes and remembered. One huge jar held water and another the fermenting wort. The smaller jars held dates, honey, or fruits or herbs to flavor the beer. Three large baskets held barley, emmer wheat, and a hard, overbaked bread, made from roasted hulled grains, his mother had called *bappir*. As a child, he had often been given the jobs of stripping the husks from barley and of breaking the cooked *bappir* into small pieces that his mother would soak in water in a large bowl.

He inhaled deeply. The mouthwatering perfume of a finished batch of *kash-sa*, red beer, scented the air even here on the other side of the open courtyard.

Tablet House Master Gunida laughed.

Ur-sag-enki's eyes flew open. "Please excuse my inattention, Master. Seeing the breweress at work brought back good memories of my childhood."

Gunida nodded. "It's perfectly understandable. All Sumerians smile when they smell good beer. It is in our nature."

Two servants arrived. One set down a rack holding two beakers onto a low table, and the other placed two pitchers on the table. A third servant put out a plate of dried apples and fresh apricots.

"What drink is to your taste?" Gunida asked.

"Pomegranate, please."

A servant poured drinks into the beaker and handed them to each.

As they drank, Gunidu said, "I hear rumors that you may marry our wise Princess Nindalla. Do you wish to hire new tutors for her children?"

"I do hope to marry the princess, but I'm not here today about tutors for her children."

"Then for whom?"

Ur-sag-enki gazed into the brilliant pomegranate juice. *My face is probably the same color.* "For me. I need to know what the chicken-foot marks mean, and I need to learn to speak Elamite."

Gunidu rubbed his chin. "Someone who grew up here might be a better teacher of the language. As for learning to read, it's a hard task. Most rulers don't bother to learn. They rely on their scribes."

"I don't know whom in the palace I can trust. Except for Princess Nindalla."

"Ahh! I understand." The master nodded. "Many people hope to improve their position during the turmoil."

"Some at my expense. To govern wisely, I need to talk face to face with the citizens. I must be able to look at the tablets myself and know their secrets."

"Not everyone has a scholar's mind, and I assume you have little time for studying. To be blunt, Governor, I fear I would waste my time teaching you."

"Does it matter, if I pay you well?"

"Hmm." Gunida gestured to a servant to refill his beaker of cucumber water.

The servant attending the breweress padded over and whispered in Gunidu's ear.

"My wife urges me to accept you as a student, and she is ever a good counselor. She points out that, unlike my usual students, you won't throw clay when my back is turned or make eyes at our beautiful daughters and daughters-in-law."

Light laughter sparkled in the busy corners of the courtyard.

"Then you'll teach me?" *Won't Nindalla be proud when I tell her I am learning to read!*

"Yes. Can you come at dawn every morning for an hour?"

"I'll be here, Master. Thank you for taking me as your student. I'll work hard."

They finished their juice and fruit. Before Ur-sag-enki could say goodbye, Gunidu ordered cheese and grape wine brought and asked, "Did the Princess Nindalla recommend me?"

The mention of the princess's name made Ur-sag-enki's heart pound. He drew a deep breath so his voice would be steady. "No. The merchant did. Do you know Princess Nindalla?"

The master smiled fondly. "I was her tutor in Eridu. When she married, I came here with her to finish her education. Of course, after Eridu burned—" his voice hitched "—I had nowhere else to go. I made Susa my home."

Ur-sag-enki clutched his smooth buff beaker and studied the red ducks painted on it. "Then you must know her well. And you must be a wise man who knows about many things. Tell me, how do I win her love? Or at least her hand in marriage?"

"Consider her upbringing: Her parents taught her to put duty first and her own feelings and desires last."

"I want to be a good governor and a good father. But I don't want her to choose me because she thinks it's her duty."

The master dipped his head in acknowledgment.

"No matter what I do, she remains distant," Ur-sag-enki continued. "Should I threaten to beat her if she refuses me? Should I recite my great deeds? Should I invite her to watch me fight against my best swordsman?"

Shaking his head, Gunidu put his mug down and leaned closer. "Nindalla is not a silly young girl who thinks battles and soldiers are glorious and exciting. She's a grown woman, mature and sensible, who hates your masters, the Akkadians."

"I can't change my past. I can't change that the Akkadians made me governor. What can I do?"

"Show her you have the traits she admires. Loyalty. Honesty. Be a man of your word. Keep your duty to the city uppermost in your thoughts and deeds."

He slumped, his now-heavy heart weighing him down. *She thinks I am neither loyal nor honest. I shouldn't have hidden the truth from her.* "How should I act when we're together?"

"Do what the wisest men have written down: Respect her, ask her opinion, trust her judgment, and rely on her courage. A wise wife is better than any jewel."

"She is the best jewel of all," Ur-sag-enki said softly. "She is the Jewel of Eridu."

— Chapter 30 —

Ur-sag-enki was late. Nindalla paced her front chamber, waiting for him, closing and unclosing her damp hands. She promised herself she would not chastise him for his tardiness. He was probably seeing to the great feast.

What a brilliant idea to throw a feast in this city of hungry, devastated people. He is a good shepherd to his people, despite what Dagu says. He may win the love of the city.

But I must harden my liver against him. I must choose the future that is best for my children.

She had dressed carefully, choosing a clean, blue linen shift embroidered around the hem with gold thread. A large gold pin held the shift together at her shoulder. She had kohled her eyes and painted the lids with malachite crushed with gold.

She still had no maid, so she had asked Daanan and her sister to roll out a clean reed mat on the floor and to bring a jar of beer and platters of fruits and cheeses. Two torches lit the room, and myrrh and cedar burned in a copper tray to perfume the air with sweetness.

Everything is ready. Where is he? Has he forgotten?

"The palace is empty and dark. The only brightness is in this room," Ur-sag-enki said from the doorway.

She started. "Come in, my lord." She fussed with the drape of her shift and then clasped her hands behind her back to keep them still.

The governor of Susa entered her chambers like a god, tall and strong, smelling of mint and rose petals. His freshly washed hair shone, the black as glossy as bitumen bubbling from the ground on a sunny day.

As always, he wore a half-shift instead of going bare-chested. He carried something wrapped in orange. He smiled at her tentatively and then looked around the room. "Where are the children?"

"In bed, my lord. So we can talk of adult matters." She gestured for him to sit by the beer jar.

"Thank you. I had a long and tiring day." He shoved his package behind him and took several sips of beer through the silver straw. "How is Enki-kiag?"

Nindalla sat on the opposite side of the beer jar and arranged the folds of her shift to look more graceful. "He has grown much since you saw him last. He has a calm temperament and smiles often. He is beautiful."

"Like, uh, like his mother."

Nindalla stared down at the mat. *What does he mean? What should I say?*

"Your eyes are dark and plump," he continued.

Plump? Does he mean swollen? Have I gotten the evil eye?

He cleared his throat. "Uh, I mean your eyes are dark and large. Your thighs are plump, and you come from good breeding stock."

He is trying to compliment me! She stifled a giggle and erupted into a coughing fit instead. She pulled the straw toward herself and sucked down some beer to halt her hacking.

Prince Humba had never complimented her. Not once. When she first arrived in Susa, he had looked her up and down and grunted, "She'll do."

Ur-sag-enki grabbed a hunk of cheese and stuffed it in his mouth, looking at her as if waiting for a response.

Nindalla's mind went blank. Her mother had taught her nothing about responding to compliments. She fumbled for a response. Finally she said, "Your eyes are dark and large too."

Ur-sag-enki choked.

She dropped her gaze and folded her hands. Minutes passed, the only sound that of Ur-sag-enki sucking beer noisily and rudely through the straw.

"Have you wooed many women before?" she asked.

"Some. Well, not very many. Uh, actually none. Can you tell?"

"Not at all," she said with more politeness than truth.

He let out a large breath. "How about you? With men, I mean."

She shook her head. "I was betrothed to Prince Humba when I was only six years old. I came here at fourteen."

"Did he make you happy?"

Nindalla shrugged. "He gave me children and did not beat me."

"But were you happy with him?"

"He preferred Midu. He visited me only to get me with child."

"He must have been a fool. How could he not love you?"

"My mother told me that lust is for the lower classes and animals. Not for princesses, who have higher duties."

"I'm talking about love, not lust. You love your children. My parents grew to love each other after they married. Their love made our home happy."

"I know nothing of the love between men and women. Or of how it differs from animal lust."

"Maybe I shouldn't talk of love, but affection. When I came in, you looked glad to see me. I think you are fond of me, at least a little?"

"Of course not! That would be selfish." She had behaved properly and with self-control, putting her children's needs first. "You delivered my son and rescued my daughters. I owe you their lives."

"Thankfulness is all you feel toward me? You named me your brother."

She chewed her lip. "You should be happy. The gratitude of a princess is no little thing. It is my duty to show my appreciation of your many kindnesses."

"Duty," he repeated, disappointment in his voice. He looked away. He finished the jar of beer and looked around for more without success. He ate the almonds, crunching them with his mouth open. He ate apricots and spat out the pits onto the floor.

Nindalla watched his crude manners with appalled fascination until he had finished every bite of food.

"I can teach you the eating habits of the upper-class Susians," she offered.

"There are many things I need to learn to be governor," he said, wiping his mouth off with his arms. "Did I tell you? I brought you gifts."

"Gifts? For me? Why?" Prince Humba had never given her presents.

"I want you to be happy. You've had too much sadness in your life."

What a sweet gesture! Tears sprang to her eyes.

Ur-sag-enki did not notice. He looked behind him and picked up two small bundles wrapped in orange linen. He offered them to her.

She took them and stared at them, savoring the warm, comforting feeling of having someone think about her.

"Open them," he urged.

Her hands trembled as she peeled the linen away from the first gift. Inside nestled a necklace with several strands of beads, beautiful beads of the highest quality lapis and carnelian, polished to a high shine. Her hands shook outright as she placed it over her head and adjusted it on her chest.

"Do you like it? It's pretty, huh? You're not saying anything. I'll give you something else if you don't like it." He took a pouch from his belt and started to empty it on the mat.

She put her hand up to stop him. "No, I love the beads. I cannot believe you commissioned a necklace for me. For me!" She giggled, startling herself. She had not giggled since she was a girl in Eridu. "It's wonderful that you are patronizing the artists of Susa."

His brow creased, and his ears turned red. He turned away and picked through the items from his pouch that had spilled onto the mat. She looked at them too. They were an odd assortment.

"Why do you have a tablet?" she asked.

He shook his head as if to wake himself and touched the small rectangle of dried clay. "The general sent it for Chamberlain Dagu. I was so eager to see you I forgot to give it to him." He looked at her from beneath his dark eyelashes, like a shy gazelle. "Why don't you open your other present?"

It was hard to maintain her dignity while unwrapping the linen. She wanted to yank it off to see what else he had commissioned for her at the jeweler. But she took her time and was glad because the earrings inside were delicate and could have been damaged. They, too, were beautiful, made of gold beaten thin into the shape of laurel leaves. She picked them up to examine them more closely.

They look familiar . . . .

She covered her mouth with her hand. "These earrings belonged to Prince Humba's mother."

She dropped them as if they were made of fire. Then she tore off her new necklace and threw it at him.

"You deceived me again," she said, choking on the words. She reached for the beer straw, but the beer jug was empty. He had finished it without asking whether she wanted any more. "You did not have a jeweler make these presents for me. They're plunder. You stole them from Queen Ri-ti and other people the Akkadians killed."

"Your mother by marriage? Please forgive—"

She shook her head.

"Look around," he said gently. "All the beautiful things in your room, in your children's rooms, that aren't from Susa. Where do you think they came from?"

It took her a minute to grasp what he implied. Then heat flushed her face. "Get out!"

His shoulders hunched, and he clutched the rejected beads to his chest. He looked at her like a puppy that had chewed up a sandal.

"It was bad enough that you killed my husband. But now you imply he was a thief! Please leave. I am tired of talking to you."

— Chapter 31 —

Nindalla stormed around the room, tearing out her hairpins and throwing them against the walls. If she were a peasant, she would have shouted at Ur-sag-enki, thrown food scraps at him, perhaps whacked him with the wicker tray. But she was born a princess and she must behave like one, even when she was not wearing the title. Ur-sag-enki had no idea how angry she was. To ask for forgiveness after giving her Queen Ri-ti's looted earrings . . . she shook her head. Chamberlain Dagu would never have been so crude.

When she calmed, she hiked up her shift and began tidying up after her rare rampage. There, on the mat, still lay Ur-sag-enki's bag and the things he had emptied out. Now she would have to see him again to return them.

No, she could not bear to look at him again. Daanan could return his bag.

She squatted on the mat, picked up the bag, and began filling it. Her nose wrinkled on its own as if the objects were animal droppings instead of rings, bracelets, necklaces, amulets, and oddities such as a river-polished stone and part of a turtle shell. Halfway through, she got up and rinsed her hands in a basin. She still felt unclean, thinking of how he acquired these things. She scrubbed her hands roughly dry with some linen.

A thought popped into her head, unbidden: *Where did King Ebarti get the gold laurel-leaf earrings for his wife?* They were not in the style of any jeweler in Susa.

Perhaps Ur-sag-enki was right, that many of the beautiful things she took for granted, perhaps some of her own jewelry, were spoils of war? Some had to be, considering how often the king and his sons had gone off to conquer and pillage.

Men and their wars.

Chastened, she squatted again on the mat and continued filling Ur-sag-enki's bag. The last item was the cuneiform tablet he had said was for Chamberlain Dagu from the general.

She weighed it in her hand. It would have been simpler for the general to tell Ur-sag-enki the message rather than find a scribe to write it down. General Qisim must have wanted to keep the message secret.

But what could be secret from the city governor and not from the chamberlain?

She found the beginning and began parsing the characters. They were crudely written, and the letter did not start with the customary lines of formal greeting. She pronounced the various sounds for each character out loud, trying different combinations until the message made sense.

"No further use for Ur-sag-enki. Kill him. I said you would be governor. Now is your time."

A chill ran down her spine. She closed her fist around the general's message. "May demons confound his senses! May his bowels twist and his eyes shrivel! Great Inanna, keep General Qisim from success in love and war!"

Now she knew why the general and Dagu had whispered secrets in corners. Why Dagu had not been at King Ebarti's side when Susa fought Sargon's armies. Why Dagu sought to undermine Ur-sag-enki.

Dagu had betrayed his king so that he could rule Susa as governor under the Akkadians.

The gods must be watching over Ur-sag-enki: Because she had the tablet, she, not Dagu, controlled his fate.

She licked her lips. It was time to decide which man would be her husband and the father of her children: the shrewd politician with the ruthlessness to seize the staff of office, or the naïve farmboy-turned-soldier determined to do his best for Susa.

❋

Dawn arrived with cool, sweet air. Nindalla had not slept. Now that the sun had emerged from the Underworld to grace the living for another day, she did not think she could. She dressed her hair simply, put on a fresh shift, and went out into the courtyard to enjoy the colors of the sunrise reflected in the fountain and wait for the children to wake. The parrot unfolded, ruffled its wings, looked at her, and then went back to sleep.

Nindalla still had not decided whom she should marry, but she owed it to Ur-sag-enki to tell him what the tablet said. She was working up the courage to knock on his chamber door.

Daanan rushed out of the girls' chamber, shrieking and rubbing her eyes.

Sukura stumbled after her and both ran into Enki-kiag's chamber. After a moment, both screamed.

Nindalla leapt up. Every bit of her, inside and out, clarioned an alarm. "What's wrong? Is it the children?" she called.

Daanan came out of Enki-kiag's room, crying, and sagged against the doorframe. "They're gone. Just gone. They all fell asleep so fast last night, but I didn't guess anything was wrong."

"What are you saying?"

"We slept solid through the night, both of us. I can hardly keep my eyes open, and my mouth feels as if it is full of linen. We were poisoned."

Not poison. Poppy juice. Prince Humba and some of his friends used to sit in the courtyard for hours or even days, their eyes glazed over from the juice of the poppy. They would doze off and wake, demanding beer, wine, even water, anything to quench their thirst.

She shook her head. No. Daanan had to be mistaken. The children were playing a joke on her, just as she and her sisters had played jokes on their nursemaids.

Nindalla strolled into the girls' chamber. She looked under every bench and bed and behind every chest. Daanan and Sukura followed her, grimly shadowing her footsteps as she then went to Enki-kiag's room and searched it just as thoroughly. Then the servants' rooms. The bathing room. The storage room.

The children *were* gone. Just as they had been after Enki-kiag's birth.

She stumbled drunkenly back out into the courtyard. Shaking, she wrapped her cold arms around herself. They knew not to leave the family quarters, yet she had searched everywhere.

She dropped to her knees onto the morning-cold bricks and looked up at the brightening sky. "Lord Enki!" she called out in Sumerian. "Why have you forsaken me? Have pity on your daughter. Bring back my children, and I will sacrifice to you many sheep."

Daanan wrung her hands. "I am so sorry, my lady. I am so sorry," Daanan repeated between sobs. "Who could have taken the children? Who could have done such a sinful thing?"

Cold rippled down Nindalla's spine. "It had to be Midu. But how?"

"She visited the children last night," Sukura mumbled. Her eyes closed, and she stumbled.

Daanan caught her sister and shook her. "She brought our beer! Remember?" She turned to Nindalla. "Oh, my lady, what'll we do?"

"Tell the governor." He had helped her find the children before. He would do so again.

Guilt washed over her. She had not said yes to his proposal, but she continued to seek his help during every trouble.

Even so, he would help her. She was sure of it. Her legs regained their strength. She rose from her knees, hurried to his door, and pounded. As she waited for him to answer, she pressed her forehead against the cool wood of the door, taking deep breaths of its scent of cedar.

He did not answer.

He had marched a long way and was probably exhausted. She pounded again, harder, and shouted.

Still no answer.

She tried the door. It opened. She pushed it open and checked every room. He was not home.

She went through his rooms again, this time searching for the children. She had not thought to search there before because Humba forbade the girls to ever go in his rooms.

But still she did not find them.

"Daanan, the messenger from the other night. The one the color of burnt bricks. Go to the soldiers' camp and find him. Ask whether he knows where Ur-sag-enki is. I will go to the audience chamber to see whether he is at work early."

"Yes, my lady." Daanan ran out.

Nindalla composed her face into calm and followed.

Servants and slaves were up and about, busy about their chores, but all denied seeing her children or the governor. She had almost reached the audience chamber when Chamberlain Dagu hurried out from a side hall and nearly bumped into her.

"My apologies, Princess Nindalla." He bowed over his hands.

"You are forgiven, Chamberlain. Have you seen the governor? I am on my way to the audience chamber to see whether he is there."

"I'll walk with you, my lady. I need to give him his morning briefing. But I doubt he's there yet. He arrived early at the feast and stayed until it was over. I have never seen a man so drunk. I had some slaves carry him to his room. He will probably sleep until noon."

Dagu lied so smoothly that she might have believed him if the governor had not spent the evening with her and if she had not just searched his rooms.

She shook her head. "Peasants!" she exclaimed. She had no need to feign disgust; right now, she would sooner marry a scorpion than the chamberlain.

Dagu made noises of agreement. "He never had any chance of being a good governor. I have been covering up his mistakes since he got here."

"Is that so?"

"Yes." Dagu smoothed his beard with self-satisfaction. "He's not going to last as governor. He wasn't even a good soldier."

"His men seem to admire him."

Dagu spat on the floor. "He's a weakling. During the battle, he refused to kill any women or children. The general gave him an order and he refused. Imagine that! Why the general gave him Susa I have no idea."

Nindalla schooled her face to blandness. Dagu *had* been at the battle, just not with King Ebarti. He had betrayed his city.

The chamberlain turned toward her, dismay at his revelation clear on his face.

Her blood pounded. What would this proud man not do to protect his reputation and his life? Nindalla played the fool. "I am truly surprised General Qisim let Ur-sag-enki live after he refused an order."

Dagu peered at her then shook his head. "You are no innocent. Do not pretend with me!"

She took tiny steps backward, away from him, counting victory in each thumb's width she distanced herself from him. "I do not understand you."

"Yes, you do." He leaned toward her, scowling.

She shrugged in what she hoped was a carefree manner. "What is done is done. Good day, Chamberlain." She nodded and turned. If she could just get to the audience chamber and find Ur-sag-enki before Dagu thought through the implications of her knowledge. . . .

He seized her arm in a grip strong enough to kill a feathered viper and forced her to stop.

"I am Susa's most loyal man," he said in her ear.

She flinched from his hot breath. "I have been in Susa eleven years. I know your loyalty."

"Everything I have ever done has been in the interests of Susa." He gripped tighter. "After I tell you what happened, you'll understand."

She went rigid with rage. "You're hurting me." Her voice rang in the hall. "Let go. Then I will listen."

He loosened his grip and looked around, as if to see whether anyone had heard her.

She pulled free and turned to face him. She dropped all womanly modesty and looked him straight in the eyes.

He did not quail at her anger or the challenge in her eyes. "General Qisim approached me several weeks ago with an offer," he said softly. "If I helped him conquer Susa, he would install me as its governor."

Nindalla's mouth burned with a sour taste. "What did he ask you to do?"

"You must remember, Susa would have fallen whether I helped or not. No city withstands Sargon's army."

She wanted to slap him, knock all the self-justification from his mouth. "So what did you do?" she demanded.

"Only enough to make the conquest quick and save many lives. Before the battle started, I ordered the soldiers at the west gate to man the other gates. Then I unbarred the gate and slipped across the river to General Qisim. I told him the king's battle plans and where the king and his sons would be."

Her mouth fell open. Horrified, she could think of nothing to say.

The twitch under the chamberlain's right eye worsened as he waited for her to speak. His foot tapped faster and faster.

She found her voice. "Then the general betrayed you and made Ur-sag-enki governor. Everything you did was for nothing."

"No! Through my efforts, a corrupt king is dead, and the slums have been cleared of riffraff. Soon, Susa will have a competent governor, rich trade with the Akkadians, and new buildings. We'll be richer and greater than ever before. You are a most dutiful woman. You more than anyone can understand that I was doing my duty to Susa."

She could only look at him.

He smiled and touched her cheek. "You can be part of the new Susa. You can be the most powerful woman in the city if you marry me."

She jerked away, gaping. "Marry you? You just admitted you are responsible for my husband's death!"

He smiled slyly. "Ur-sag-enki bears that responsibility."

She shook her head. "No."

"Yes. He was the one who stuck the knife between Humba's ribs."

Nindalla's hands flew to her mouth, then to her head. The corridor spun around her, and she staggered to the wall and leaned against it to keep from falling. "No! He could not have. He would have told me."

"I heard the general order him to kill the king and his sons." His words beat against her relentlessly. "I watched him do it."

She drew in a sobbing breath. "No. No." The tightening knot in her stomach told her she did not believe her own words. She sagged against the wall and buried her spinning head in her hands.

Ur-sag-enki had hidden many things from her, starting from the first moment when she met him when he allowed her to think he was a soldier of Susa.

But Chamberlain Dagu had deceived her too. He had deceived the entire city. What could she believe? Whom could she trust?

She was adrift in the desert. There was no landmark to guide her, no familiar scent or sound to follow. The sun hid behind heavy clouds so that she knew not what direction she faced. She was adrift, lost, abandoned.

She slid down the wall and squeezed her eyes together tightly. She put her hands over her ears.

It was no use. The world still intruded. The bricks of the wall and floor were rough against her skin. The cool morning air carried the scent of baking bread, flowers in vases, and sweaty servants.

She could not escape the world. It demanded answers.

She searched her spirit for one true thing to hang on to.

She found a solid truth and grasped it. No matter what else Ur-sag-enki had done, he had delivered her baby and done her and her children many other kindnesses.

Behind her shut eyelids, those kindnesses glowed brighter and brighter. She followed them out of the desert and back to herself.

She gulped air and opened her eyes. The corridor had stopped spinning.

Dagu's face crinkled with worry. "Are you ill?" He reached down a hand to help her up.

She shook her head and slowly stood on her own. She took a step away from the wall. "I am going to marry Ur-sag-enki." Her liver warmed as she said the words.

His brows lowered and drew together. "I have been patient with you, and I'll give you time to get used to the idea." He smirked as if he was certain she would choose him. "Remember Lady Midu's lawsuit. Your children will belong to whomever I choose. If you won't have me, Midu will."

She leaned back, away from his foulness. Her vision darkened at the edges, and her stomach twisted. She clutched her belly.

"Ur-sag-enki will stop the adoption, will stop you."

"He can't. He knows nothing of our laws and customs. He depends on me for everything. He is governor in name only."

The smugness on his face squeezed her chest and twisted her entrails. "Are you a demon? I asked you for help."

He lifted his shoulders high and let them drop.

"Please help me get my children back," she whispered, her chin trembling. "I will not tell anyone. As I said, what's done is done."

He backed her against the wall and put his hands on it, above her shoulders, trapping her. "It's not that easy. You have to do something for me. Trade favor for favor. What will you do to get your children back?"

She bowed her head. She had failed. She was trapped like a lioness in a pit. "Anything. I'll do anything."

"Prove it. Kill Ur-sag-enki and marry me."

— Chapter 32 —

Heavy-hearted, Ur-sag-enki trudged back toward the palace under the pink dawn sky, hailing the citizens he passed but avoiding conversations.

He had thought he would learn to read at his first lesson with Master Gunidu and would go home ready to throw Dagu's lies in his face. Instead, he had spent the entire hour kneading clay and smoothing it into four-sided shapes. Not three sided. Not five sided. Each tablet had to have four straight sides and be smooth on the writing surfaces.

He now was covered in clay to his elbows.

Tomorrow, Master Gunidu had promised, Ur-sag-enki would learn how to cut a reed.

He took a roundabout route to clear his mind. More shops were open today, and more people were in the streets. Several men hailed him and asked after his health. A poor man knelt and kissed his feet, thanking him for the feast and for filling his children's empty bellies.

He looked about and realized that, unlike Eridu after the Akkadian attack, no children with empty eyes wandered the streets. His mood improved, and he headed for the palace.

As he climbed the broad steps, a servant ran over and whispered, "Princess Nindalla awaits you in your private quarters."

He thrust his dagger in the air with a fervent, "Yes!" Then he remembered her anger from the night before. It was too soon for her to have forgiven him for giving her war booty. Unease sped his steps.

A slave opened a door for him. As soon as he entered the palace, another servant stopped him and whispered in his ear, "Princess Nindalla awaits you in your private quarters."

He was late, and dozens of men were already lined up outside the audience chamber. He still needed to wash the clay from his arms. Nindalla would have to wait.

A woman from the kitchen stopped him just before he entered. She looked in both directions, then whispered, "Lord Governor, Princess Nindalla awaits you in your private quarters."

Ants crawled over his skin. Something must be really wrong for her to have rallied so many staff to give him her message. He made a sharp turn and hurried toward his quarters. He pulled open the door to the family courtyard.

A spear poked his belly. "Halt!" a deep voice in the shadows growled.

He halted. With each exhale, the spear tip brushed his expanding belly. Slowly he straightened his shoulders. "Stand aside. These are my rooms," he said crisply.

"Thank the gods it's you, captain." His assailant stepped back into the sunlight and slapped his fingers to his nose in a hasty salute. His scout Kuk-kalla stood dressed in full armor, including his helmet. He dropped to his knees. "Forgive me, my lord. Your lady needed protection."

Ur-sag-enki set his hand on the scout's soldier. "Stay at your post. Let no one enter." He ran into the courtyard.

Nindalla sat in the shade, shoulder to shoulder and head to head with the wet nurse. The princess's face was as pale as the moon, and the nurse's eyes were red and swollen.

"Sister?"

Nindalla's gaze lifted and locked with his. Her eyes were swollen almost shut. "Ur-sag-enki? Is it you? At last?" She stood and rushed to him.

He clasped Nindalla's shaking hands. "My lady, what happened?"

She gripped his hands, despite the slippery, cold clay caking them. Her mouth opened and closed, wordless.

He tugged one hand free of her terrified grip and grasped her shoulder to steady her. "Peace, my sister, peace. Tell me what's wrong."

"Midu has stolen the children and she is going to adopt them and Dagu is going to help her and the general and Dagu are conspiring to make him governor and I will marry you or do whatever you want if you will get my children back."

Battle rage exploded in him. The muscles in his arms and legs strengthened and urged him to action. But first he had to find out more.

He stroked her hair. "Peace, Sister. Tell me what happened, beginning to end."

"We have no time! We must find them."

"I need to know everything. Otherwise, how can I fix what is wrong?"

She took another breath and pressed her hand to her stomach. "You are right." Now her words poured out. Midu's petition to adopt the four children. Dagu's secret conversations with General Qisim. Dagu and Midu's secret relationship.

He interrupted. "How did you find these things out while you were in the birthing hut?"

She didn't answer, but continued talking, shocking him to the bone with the contents of the general's letter to Dagu and the disappearance of the children.

Bitterness rose in his throat. He clenched his jaw. General Qisim had used him like a game piece and sacrificed him as easily. The general was one of Sargon's favorites. Did he dare send an assassin to kill the man who had betrayed his loyalty?

Later. The children had to be his first concern. "Don't fret. We'll find where the children wandered off to."

"They're not lost. Dagu and Midu kidnapped them."

"Those hyenas! May their patrons gods desert them!" Banging his fist against his palm, he strode across the courtyard and back again.

"There's more you should know." She told him of Dagu's admission that he had betrayed Susa to the Akkadians because he wanted to be governor. Dagu's blackmail. Her agreement to kill Ur-sag-enki so Dagu would give her children back.

He slumped onto a bench and put his head in his hands. Nearly the whole world was aligned against him. He had so few people on his side. Was Nindalla even one of them? Could she be planning to kill him when he turned his back?

He shook his head. He would not, could not, believe she would murder him. She had thrown "loyalty" and "duty" in his face too often. She would not kill him after all he had done for her children.

Slowly he sat up, braced his hands against his knees, and leaned forward. "You should have told me your suspicions about Dagu and Midu last night. So many times you've accused me of lying. Yet last night you deceived me."

She knelt in front of him. She had the grace to blush in penitence and drop her head. "Smaller deceptions than yours, my lord."

"My deceptions protected you. Yours put me—put both of us—in danger."

"You are twisting words to make me sound as false as you. But do not chide me for little sins. You are the king of liars." Her head flew up; her eyes flashed in anger. "You still have not admitted to your biggest deception. You never told me you killed my husband!"

He forgot how to breathe. *Was it true he hadn't told her?* He had protected her from so many harsh truths he could not remember which ones he still hid from her. His gaze slid away, unable to meet hers.

The wet nurse plodded over and knelt beside the princess. "Many pardons, my lady, my lord. May I speak?"

"What?" Nindalla snapped.

"The children have been stolen," she said bluntly. "Don't you think it might be better to argue later? And look for the children now?"

He and Nindalla looked at the wet nurse, then at each other.

"You are right, of course, Daanan." Nindalla held out her hand, and Ur-sag-enki helped her stand. Her eyes pleaded for his help. "Governor—Brother—you are the only person I can count on. Have you thought of a plan?"

He rubbed the back of his neck. What was he going to do? He wanted to storm out of his quarters, find Dagu, and wring his neck. But what if the chancellor had hidden the children? Then he might never find them.

He might never find them anyway. He hadn't yet learned the layout of the palace, and his partial knowledge of which palace staff might help Dagu instead of him came from gossip, that of the kitchen workers and of the merchant who took him to Master Gunidu.

"Brother?" Nindalla's voice trembled.

He straightened up. He was a captain in the Akkadian army. Rescuing kidnapped children was no different from rescuing hostages or prisoners taken by an enemy army. The situation became clear in his head. He could imagine the layout of the battlefield and probable locations of the enemy and of the hostages.

He spoke with the tone he used with his troops. "You told me there were secret passages in the palace. We'll use those to find the children and keep out of sight of the enemy until we surprise them."

Nodding, the princess stood, head high. She wiped her eyes and smiled tremulously. "I knew you would know what to do."

Crying, Daanan fell onto his feet and hugged his calves. "Thank you, my lord governor, thank you. I will tell everyone in the city about what a hero you are."

"Not yet, Daanan. Everything must be secret for now." He helped her to her feet and stood her next to Nindalla. "Princess, fetch your dagger. Danaan, light a lamp with unscented oil. Meanwhile, I'll put on the rest of my armor and get my weapons. Dagu and Midu have greatly underestimated me."

"Underestimated both of us," Nindalla said, a dangerous glint in her eye.

– Chapter 33 –

Nindalla wanted to race through every passage hidden in the walls, but Ur-sag-enki was adamant: caution, quiet, and painstaking diligence. He handed her the lamp to carry and padded ahead of her like a leopard, silent but lethal. He found the peepholes without her help; in the dark, they shone as brightly as the small lamp.

Every few steps he stopped, put his ear to the wall, and sniffed for food, burning lamp oil, and other signs someone had been nearby recently. At every peephole, he listened first and then eased into a position from which he could look through the hole and sniff the air.

She copied his movements and tapped his arm to alert him each time he came near a secret door. Most of the doors were holes under large pieces of furniture or were hidden behind decorative panels or weavings. But a few were full-size openings in obscure places. If someone happened to be in one of those places, they would clearly see anyone in the tunnel who passed the door.

After an hour of careful, tedious searching, they reached a section of tunnel with more peepholes than elsewhere. A faint whiff of a baby left in its bindings too long wafted from one hole.

Her heart nearly doubled its speed. *Praise Enki!* She reached forward and tugged on Ur-sag-enki's tunic, whispering, "Enki-kiag's been in this room."

Ur-sag-enki looked through the hole. "No one's in here now, but there are several small pallets on the floor." He craned his neck at an angle. "I see Bar's toy sheep. Do you recognize the room?"

She exchanged places with him quietly and looked through the peephole. Lamplight illuminated jars stacked high against the left wall, and old chests and benches were piled against the wall across from her. A thick layer of dust coated everything and tickled her nose, making her want to sneeze. "It looks like a storeroom."

"Storerooms don't need a bed or window."

She gave him the lamp and clamped her nose shut with her thumb and pointer finger. She put her eye as close to the peephole as it would go. He was right—behind the stacked furniture, which she now realized was made of expensive imported cedar, sunlight shone through a high, barred window. A large bed stood in the middle of the room. The room did not open onto a courtyard, as a usual bedchamber did, but onto another room. Ornate bronze torch holders were plentiful, but only a single gleaming bronze lamp lit the room now. "You're right. It's a bedchamber. For someone important. But I do not recognize it."

"Retrace our steps. When you find a room you do recognize, figure out where we are. I'll keep going and see what I find."

She turned away from him and the lamp. Ahead, the peepholes would be her only light. She kept her hand on the wall to avoid getting turned around or running into anything.

Her hand hit a stretch of fired bricks mortared in place at different angles. She stopped and brushed both hands over them. They were regularly spaced; a decoration? In a tunnel? No, this part of the palace was ancient. The wall was probably outside once.

She moved on, looking in each peephole. The rooms were unfamiliar but more richly decorated than the one with Bar's toy. None were occupied. Some had been looted.

But the Akkadians had left some valuables behind. A familiar sword half-hidden behind a bench in one room and some small pieces of familiar jewelry on the floor in another identified the rooms as the most private of the private quarters of the king and queen.

The late king and queen.

She hurried forward to catch up to Ur-sag-enki, stopping quickly to peek in succeeding peepholes. They revealed more luxurious rooms, also deserted. "We are near King Ebarti's chambers. These other rooms must be where the foreign ambassadors are housed."

"Shhhh," he warned. "The children are in the next room. With Midu."

"Praise Enki!" She darted forward to the peephole, but he darted after her and stopped her with an arm around her waist.

"Stand aside," she ordered.

He placed his fingers over her lips and pulled her several feet down the hall. "Peace, Sister. Soon we'll have them in our arms. Don't let haste undermine our plan. How do we get to this room's courtyard?"

"It has none."

"No courtyard?"

"Ambassadors are sometimes also spies. Their quarters are set up so the ambassadors cannot escape. That is why there are no doors from the tunnel into the rooms."

"Where are the ways in?"

"The only entrance to the ambassadorial quarters I know of is in the outermost of the king's chambers."

He groaned and ran his hand down his face. "Dagu has guards stationed at the door to the king's chambers. We can't trust any of those men, but they should let us in if I order it."

"Not a good idea. The door to the ambassadors' quarters has a heavy bar on each side. The guards could trap us inside."

Ur-sag-enki slid down a wall to sit on the floor and motioned for her to sit too. "It works both ways. Once inside, I could hold these quarters against an army."

"Yes?"

"If I were king, I would want some way to get in and out. To get to ambassadors who were spies or working with my enemies."

She thought about his words. "The door would have to be cleverly hidden. A king could not take the chance that an ambassador or servant would discover it." She lifted her hair off of her back so that the dampness underneath would dry. All the passages in the walls were stuffy and hot, but here the air was especially bad, probably because there were no courtyards to provide fresh air and no trees or fountains for cooling.

"You've lived in two palaces. Where would you expect to find a door?"

"In a storeroom that was out of the way and little used," she answered, then frowned. "But . . ."

"But what?"

"Supplies enter and leave storerooms all the time. One might need a door and find bags of barley stacked against it."

"Even in a bedchamber, people might move the furniture. So the secret door can't be on a wall." Ur-sag-enki looked up at the ceiling. "Lift the lamp high."

Nindalla stood and held the lamp above her head.

Ur-sag-enki said, "The ceilings here are higher than in the other passages."

"We must be near the audience chamber."

"If I were king, I would take advantage of the height."

"That explains something," she said. "Come."

She led him to the section of wall with fired bricks. She held the lamp up, and her eyes told her what her fingers had not.

"It is a ladder," she announced. She set down the lamp, grasped a brick above her head, and climbed halfway up the wall. "See? The bricks that stick out are at just the right spacing and depth for climbing."

"Come down. Let me climb."

She ignored him and kept going. The ladder-like bricks stopped at a dim tunnel that ran above the ambassadors' rooms. "We can crawl above every room from here!" she whispered down to Ur-sag-enki from the top brick. "Perhaps there are ways to get into the rooms as well."

He clambered up to stand next to her. "I see patches of light. But they could be arrow slits. If you can kill the people inside, you don't need to be able to get in."

"They would start to stink after a while," she pointed out. "We have to look for a door." Her heart pounded. The children were so close, so close.

Ur-sag-enki bent his knees, then lunged up, swinging one leg up and into the tunnel. He pulled the rest of himself up and then lifted her from the top step and into the space as easily as if she were a child.

He pointed down the tunnel. "Let's see what's over the room where the children are."

They crawled until they reached a spot where the high voices of children were clear. Diffuse light glimmered here and there through cracks in the plastered ceilings, but there were no obvious doors or even peepholes.

There has to be a way to get into the room. There has to be. She ran her hands over the floor on all sides of her, moved forward, and did it again. In one spot, the bricks had a different texture.

She explored the area carefully and slowly. She found indentations and gasped.

"Shhhh," Ur-sag-enki cautioned. "What did you find?"

She put her fingers in the indentations and tugged.

A piece of the tunnel floor lifted away. The hatch was made, not of bricks, but of reeds tied together into a panel and plastered with mud on both sides. In the dark, it could have eluded anyone but a mother desperate to get to her children.

She felt inside the hatch. About a foot down, she found another panel that could be lifted. "I found the door," she said softly.

He motioned for them to crawl back toward the light of their oil lamp. When they were above an empty room, he signaled a stop. "If we can reach the children, I'll pull them up into this ceiling. You will hide them in the tunnels until I come for you."

She nodded. "What will you be doing while we hide?"

"I'll gather some men loyal to me. Then I'll arrest Dagu and his supporters. Kill them if I need to."

"And Midu?"

His breath roughened and sped up. "I don't kill women."

"If you do not, she will find someone else to manipulate to give her power."

"I'll banish her."

"She might come back to steal my children again."

He touched warm fingers to her lips. "Don't worry. I'll find a way to deal with Midu. Right now I'm going to get a rope. Go back to the hatch. Listen carefully so you know who comes and goes. I want to rescue the children when they're alone."

She nodded again. What a relief it was to have him by her side. If she had to have a husband, he would not be so bad to have around. She was glad she had chosen him instead of Dagu.

Ur-sag-enki climbed down the wall, taking the oil lamp with him. The flickering light got softer and softer until she could no longer see it at all.

She crawled back to the hatch above the room where the children were. She did not like being alone in the dusty half-light above the ceiling and below the roof. She felt as if she were in the Underworld. There were noises she did not make, noises that sounded like the slithering of snakes and the scritch-scritching of rats. Insects and scorpions probably lived in this dark space as well. Her skin crawled and itched.

She flicked at each spot where she felt something brush against her. She never found anything there, but then the sensation would jump to another part of her body and she would flick again.

A deep voice sounded directly beneath her.

She started. Dagu! He stood right below her.

He might know of the secret passage in the ceiling. He might know of the hatch. He might check it. She could not move; he might hear her.

She felt dozens of creatures run over her arms and legs and under her nose. Skin all over her body twitched from the tickle of tiny vermin legs. Her stomach wanted to retch; her skin wanted her to scratch it. She fought the urges and closed her eyes so she would not see any rats or snakes.

Breathe! Count to sixty and Ur-sag-enki will be here. She counted to sixty. Counted again. And again. And again.

– Chapter 34 –

At last, faint light illuminated the tomblike space above the ambassadorial quarters where Nindalla lay, and the scent of sesame oil reached her. As Ur-sag-enki crawled over to her, her eyes filled with tears of relief.

He adjusted his position to be next to her, arm against arm, leg against leg, flesh to flesh, his warmth suffusing her skin and relieving the tickle of vermin that the dim light from the small lamp showed did not exist.

This closeness is unseemly. I should move away from him. We are not yet betrothed, let alone married. But Nindalla didn't dare take a chance of making a noise that would be heard below. Besides, his nearness and his warmth calmed and comforted her. Together, they would rescue the children.

Habarane's high voice penetrated the ceiling and her words were clear. "Where are you going, Ama Midu?"

Nindalla flinched at the endearment. She longed to strangle the woman. Knowing about Midu's dead family did not soften her hate. She nudged Ur-sag-enki with her elbow, and they drew their heads together, over the hatch, to listen.

"Girls, Chamberlain Dagu and I are going to get more food," Midu said. "Be good girls and play nicely until we come back." Footsteps left the room.

After sixty times three seconds, she reached down into the hole to the second hatch and grasped the two sturdy, criss-crossed reeds that served as its handles. She held her breath and lifted the hatch slowly, a thumb's thickness at a time, until she could set it on the tunnel floor and look down on her daughters.

Her gaze ran fearfully, hungrily, greedily, over every part of them. They played calmly, without fear. Thank the gods they had not been hurt! Enki-kiag lay on Abi's lap, fast asleep, still in his bindings from yesterday.

Nindalla wrinkled her nose at the stench. "It is a long drop," she whispered to Ur-sag-enki.

He unbuckled his sword and pulled out his mace, laying both on the floor of the tunnel. "I'll jump down holding one end of the rope. You hold the other end. I'll tie the rope to each girl, and you'll pull them up one at a time. I'll find a basket or jar to put Enki-kiag in so you can pull him up too."

It would take a lot of strength. She had just spent a week wasting away in the birthing hut. She still needed rest breaks during the day.

She closed her eyes briefly. She had to pull them up. She had no choice. She imagined each step. The hardest would be pulling them over the edge into the passage.

"Do it."

Ur-sag-enki jumped into the room, landing almost silently on his bare feet. The girls jumped up with excitement, but he motioned them to silence and pointed up at the ceiling.

Nindalla leaned into the hole, stretched her arm down, and waved.

Ur-sag-enki moved to tie the rope around Abi.

Shaking her head, she squirmed away.

Ur-sag-enki put down the rope and went to her. He leaned over and whispered into her ear. Seconds went by while he talked and she shook her head.

At last Abi nodded. Ur-sag-enki quickly secured the rope under her armpits and signaled for Nindalla to pull her up. The other girls watched with wide eyes.

Abi was heavy, heavier than Nindalla expected, but she managed to haul the girl over onto the floor. Her arms burned with the effort, and she could not stop puffing loudly. *How can I do this three more times?*

"Isn't this a fun game?" she gasped.

Abi's lip quivered.

"When the little girls come up, you must keep them close to you and quiet. Do you understand, my sweet?"

"Yes, Ama." Her voice trembled. "Ama Midu and Chamberlain Dagu told us you didn't want us anymore. I thought it was true."

"Never," she reassured Abi. Again she let down the rope.

Ur-sag-enki tied it around Habarane and signaled.

"Here comes Habarane. Help me pull her over the edge." She and Abi lifted the girl up and into the tunnel, with Abi doing most of the work.

Ur-sag-enki's plan is working. The rope went down again, and Abi pulled Bar up.

At last it was Enki-kiag's turn.

"I need a basket," Ur-sag-enki said.

As he searched the chambers, Nindalla bit her lip until it was raw. At last, Ur-sag-enki reappeared with a sturdy reed basket. He tied the rope to the handles, placed Enki-kiag inside, and tied him to the basket.

Nindalla and Abi pulled him up into the ceiling and quickly unwrapped the rope. Nindalla hugged him tightly. "We're all safe, thanks to Ur-sag-enki," she whispered to him.

"Ama?"

"Yes, my honeycomb?"

"You forgot to pull the governor up."

We made no plan to get him out. Her mouth tasted of metal and dust. She leaned dangerously low in the hole. "You're too heavy for me to pull out."

"I know. Take the girls away from here and hide in the passage. I'll find you later."

"But—"

"Give me my sword and mace. I must deal with Dagu."

Pain blossomed in her chest. She could not argue; Dagu was a threat to both of them for as long as he lived. *I may never see him again.* The governor's lies now seemed laughably minor compared with his sacrifices for her.

She used the rope to lower his weapons into the room. "Take care, Brother. I meant what I said. I'll marry you for saving my children."

He had never looked as handsome as he did now, his face lit with determination and courage.

"Go on. Hide," he said.

She didn't want to leave him, to have him out of her sight. She looked at him, memorizing every feature of his face in case it was the last time she saw him.

"Don't give into fear now," he urged. "Close the hatch and get the children to safety. Dagu could return at any moment."

After a final look of longing and regret, she replaced the hatch covers and led the children to the ladder of bricks.

– Chapter 35 –

Ur-sag-enki reconnoitered the ambassadorial quarters, picking up Bar's toy sheep and sticking it in his waist bag in his pass through the room with sleeping pallets. Nindalla was right: There was only one way in and out. No courtyard opened to the sky, and no window opening was bigger than his two hands put together. He wondered whether the ambassadors noticed these security measures amid the luxury of cedar chairs, inlaid wood chests, and plastered walls painted with gold and lapis lazuli pigments.

He waited in a small, dark room just off the entry. He would be able to see Dagu and Midu, but they would not notice him.

His sweaty tunic stuck to the rough skin on his back. He resisted the urge to scratch his scars. He had thrown away too many tunics after blood spots ruined them.

He stepped in place and lifted and lowered his arms to keep his body loose while he waited and to distract himself from the itch on his back.

Wood groaned as it scraped against wood. The guards must be lifting the bar on the door. As Ur-sag-enki melted against the wall of the dark room, the door opened.

Dagu strutted in, Midu behind him. They were talking about her petition to adopt Nindalla's children. Servants carried in jugs and a tray of breads and sliced meat, set them on a table, and left.

Dagu barred the door from the inside. "By the way, I will not be ruling on your case as soon as I expected."

Midu rolled a strand of hair around her finger. "We need to hurry. I worry that Ur-sag-enki—" She stopped midsentence and wrinkled her brow. "Do you hear the children? I don't."

Dagu shrugged. "Perhaps they are napping."

"Without being nagged? They are full of vigor like their father." She set down her tray and sashayed the periphery of the entry hall, glancing in every room.

Dagu said, "I do not expect the governor to interfere with your case."

"How can you be sure?" She finished her survey of the quarters. "The children! They're not here!"

"They have to be here. My most-trusted guards kept the door bolted the whole time we were gone."

Ur-sag-enki raised his stone-headed mace overhead with both hands and strode into the entry hall. "The children aren't here. I've returned them to their mother, and you'll never see them again. I'll make sure of it."

Midu gasped. Her gaze high, on his mace, she backed toward the door.

Dagu turned toward him with raised eyebrows. "I expected you to be dead by now."

He still underestimates me.

Midu struggled to lift the bar on the door, but it was too heavy. She pounded on the door and screamed for help.

"Chamberlain, you shouldn't leave my death up to other people," Ur-sag-enki said. "If you want me dead, kill me yourself."

Dagu sneered and pulled his dagger. Longer than a man's foot, it had a straight edge—a crude stabbing instrument. On the battlefield, such a weapon was no match for Ur-sag-enki's Akkadian-issue long sickle-sword.

But in a room with furniture, with men fighting at close quarters, the dagger's lightness and maneuverability made it more dangerous than his sword and a match for his mace.

The fight would be quick. Whoever landed a good blow first walked away governor of Susa.

Outside, the guards shouted. The door shook in its socket.

"Once I kill you, I will leave you here," Dagu said with a sneer. "I'll tell Nindalla you ran away in fear, like the ignorant farm boy you are. You'll be forgotten by all, and vermin will eat your carcass."

At the door, the guards worked a bronze sword between the door and its frame and struggled to lift the bar.

Ur-sag-enki took a step to the left to balance his weight and swung the mace in the air.

Dagu looked up at Ur-sag-enki's greater height and brawn, and his smile faded. He took a tentative step forward. Then he lunged straight at his belly.

Ur-sag-enki knew what Dagu would do before Dagu did. He shifted his weight to his right foot and swung the mace down in a rapid curve.

Dagu's knife flew across the room and clattered off the painted wall, flaking off some of the gold leaf. The chamberlain's legs gave way, and he hit the baked brick floor hard. Wailing like a tortured animal, he bent over, protecting his crushed hands between his chest and knees.

Ur-sag-enki glanced at the door. Dagu's guards had not succeeded in lifting the bar with the sword. They would need to find a different way to open the door.

Sweat poured down him from the exertion, and his throat burned with thirst. He lowered the mace, grabbed a jar of beer, and guzzled the liquid portion on top.

Dagu's wailing echoed from the stone floor and brick walls. Midu crouched behind him and glared at Ur-sag-enki.

He focused his attention on the chamberlain. "A man with crippled hands can't lead an army, so you can't be governor. Give up, Dagu."

The chamberlain rocked back and forth. Midu put her arms around him, as if her body could shield him from the mace.

Ur-sag-enki squatted next to him. He grabbed Dagu's chin and lifted it until they looked eye to eye. "You told Nindalla that you are loyal to Susa. Prove it! Give up. Be my chamberlain again."

Dagu drew his head back as if preparing to strike Ur-sag-enki with his skull. The unskilled move gave Ur-sag-enki time to stand and step back.

Dagu's forehead connected with nothing. He tumbled forward under his own weight. "You son of a goat and a demon," Dagu cursed. "May Inshushinak give you a lingering, painful death."

"The gods decreed my fate when my navel cord was cut," Ur-sag-enki said, pulling out his new turtle amulet and holding it. "Lord Enki has watched over me since."

Dagu struggled to rise, his face contorted with anger and streaked with tears. Midu helped him up, supporting him under his armpits. He groaned each time his hands brushed against anything.

Bile rose in Ur-sag-enki's throat, and he swallowed. Dagu had great strength of will to overcome such horrible pain.

"Don't be a power-mad fool. Give up," Ur-sag-enki pleaded. "I'll fetch a physician and an incantation priest."

Swaying, Dagu stood nearly upright, holding his swelling, red hands out away from his body. "You are a peasant unworthy to lick my sandals."

Screaming in agony, he threw himself toward Ur-sag-enki and kicked him in the knee.

Ur-sag-enki staggered backward and tripped over a covered drain. He tried to regain his balance, but his injured knee would not do his bidding. His head hit the hard baked-brick floor. White lights danced in front of his eyes. Then blackness ate his vision.

He fought the blackness and the overwhelming urge to close his eyes and sleep. When he came fully to, he couldn't breathe. Something heavy pressed on his throat, and panic made him flail.

The weight lifted long enough for him to take a big gulp of air. Then heaviness pressed down on his throat again. This time, he was alert enough to reach for his throat. He touched flesh and forced his eyes open. The weight on his throat was Dagu's foot.

He grabbed the ankle with both hands and lifted with all his strength. Standing, he could have picked up the chamberlain easily. Lying on the floor, he could not even remove his foot. Dagu just pressed harder. He tried pushing the foot off

Dagu lifted his foot again, just long enough for Ur-sag-enki to snatch a breath; then he let the weight of the foot fall.

Dagu was playing with him. He could have crushed his throat with a stomp. Instead, he was making Ur-sag-enki die slowly.

One of us must die. I can't show any more mercy. Ur-sag-enki bent his knees so that his feet rested flat on the floor, and then he lunged upward and twisted. He had practiced the maneuver many times with his troops; his muscles knew exactly what to do.

His lunge threw Dagu off balance. The chamberlain fell to the side, screaming when his hands hit the floor.

Ur-sag-enki gulped air and staggered around the room drunkenly, blinking his eyes to clear the black spots from his vision. He found his mace only when he tripped over it.

He grabbed a bench with one hand to steady himself. With the other hand, he hoisted his mace and bashed Dagu's skull. It cracked like a hot rock thrown in a stream.

Dagu collapsed like a cloth doll. His spirit departed, leaving behind a jumble of cloth and skin.

"You fool," Ur-sag-enki rasped. The chamberlain could have been useful to his home city for decades more, but he squandered his life rather than serve under Ur-sag-enki.

He touched his throat and winced. It was tender everywhere. He would have heavy bruises around it tomorrow, and many other places too, because of his hard fall. His injured head throbbed. He slumped onto the bench and put his head in his hands.

Sharp, sudden pain lanced from his upper arm to his elbow. He turned.

Midu now had Dagu's long dagger, and from it his own blood dripped.

"Dagu's dead," he said, the words scraping his swelling throat like a knife. "You can't save him."

"I can get rid of you," she said, eyes narrowed and cold. "You will never approve my adoption petition now. A new governor might."

"The Akkadians orphaned many children," he whispered. "I'll find some for you to adopt. You can leave the city and start over."

"I loved Prince Humba. He was my life. Do you understand, prince-slayer? He was my *life*. I want to raise *his* children. In *our* city." Her eyes shone with tears. "Why should that Sumerian cow Nindalla have the heirs of Susa? She never loved this city or her husband."

She never loved her husband. Ur-sag-enki's chest tightened. Nindalla had agreed to marry him if he rescued her children. She had not agreed to love him. He had won the woman, but not her love . . . and maybe he never would.

"She does not love you either," Midu taunted.

He gazed at her, unblinking.

She changed her tactic, softening her eyes and licking her lips. "I loved passionately before. I could learn to love you." The hand without the dagger moved to slip her shift a little off her shoulder, revealing smooth, unmarked brown skin that shone where her collarbone lifted it to catch the light.

He struggled to lift his gaze from that perfect skin to her face, a face that had charmed the crown prince of Susa.

The prince had been foolish to love a woman without honor, a woman who cared only about her own desires. A pathetic woman who would offer herself to her lover's killer to gain some power.

I might be only a jumped-up farm boy, but even I know better.

He answered Midu with a firm voice. "It's not you I want."

Anger and humiliation suffused her face, turning it a dark, sullen red.

Ur-sag-enki had seen this look before, the look of an enemy who had lost everything and no longer feared death. She was particularly dangerous because she had no training in fighting and might do anything.

She shoved her hand through her hair. Pins fell out, and hair clumps fell, giving her the look of a demon. She licked her lips, and her eyes darted to the door. Then she swung the knife with wild abandon, like a hill tribesman. It came within a finger's width of his throat.

Her uneducated attack left her front unguarded.

He stepped back, not able to bring himself to hurt a woman.

She swung the long knife again and again, advancing, backing him into a corner far from the door, getting more accurate with each strike.

Now he wished for the guards. He spared a quick glance at the door. From the loud thuds, he guessed that the guards were throwing themselves against the door. The bar could withstand hours of such attempts.

He was on his own unless he could get to the door and lift the bar.

Her blade sliced again, this time at his face.

He dodged, but not quickly enough. The blade carved through his nose. Blood slithered into his mouth.

"Midu, stop," he croaked. His hand still held the mace; he lifted it sideways in front of himself to parry her strokes.

She smiled, guessing his reluctance to hurt her. Taking advantage of the awkward weight he held, she swooped in low and stabbed him deep in the thigh.

Groaning, he shifted his weight to his other leg and let the mace drop behind him before it pulled him to the floor. His battle lust was giving way quickly to exhaustion.

Thank the gods his sickle-sword was light, sharp, and evenly balanced. He pulled it from its scabbard and fended off her strikes. But injured, in a corner, he was at a disadvantage.

"You are throwing your life away," he said. "Accept banishment. Live to see your grandchildren."

"What a donkey you are! I'm a woman without a protector. Banishment is the same as killing me." Midu kicked his wounded leg.

Pain blazed through his body and darkened his vision. He threw himself against the wall and hopped on the other leg, trying to keep his balance.

She slashed at his face.

He fell to avoid the blade.

The dagger missed, but he now lay on the floor. He struggled to rise. His slashed leg refused to obey him.

Midu dropped onto his sliced thigh, and he howled.

She put the dagger to his throat and pricked him. Her smile blazed with triumph.

Eyes tearing, he tightened his grasp on his sickle-sword.

Midu's face blurred and vanished. He saw instead his sister Shatirra, not the happy Shatirra of his childhood but the bruised, skinny Shatirra who had lost everything to the Akkadians.

Just as Midu had.

He released his sword.

— Chapter 36 —

The passage was dark and dusty, and the cool bricks did not make up for the stale warm air. It was not a good place for four little children to wait.

"Ama, I'm bored," Bar complained.

"Me too," Habarane said, stretching and yawning. "There's nothing in this dark, dirty place to do."

"Being a princess is often boring. You must learn to hide your boredom and look interested," Nindalla said, jiggling Enki-kiag to keep him from crying. She had chosen to wait for Ur-sag-enki in a spot in the walls near their own quarters, away from peepholes. Still, the cries of a bawling baby could carry far, especially in a passage of bricks.

"Lady Midu said that we were not princesses anymore," Abi said. "If we are not princesses, we can be bored and not have to pretend."

"You were all born princesses. No one can take that from you, not Midu, not even the Akkadians." Nindalla pressed her back against the hard, lumpy wall, hoping her shift would absorb the nervous perspiration running down her back. She had expected Ur-sag-enki to have returned by now. Her hands were shaking, and every breath was an effort. "You like Governor Ur-sag-enki. Soon, I will marry him. Then you will be governor's daughters as well. Won't you like that?"

"Perhaps." Abi narrowed her eyes. "Chamberlain Dagu said the governor killed Abba. Why did he do that? Why do you want to marry him if he killed Abba?"

It was as if Abi had stuck a spear through her chest.

"Bad things happen in war, and war can change many things, important things. Ur-sag-enki used to be Susa's enemy." Nindalla took a deep breath. Abi was old enough to understand but perhaps not to forgive. "Now Ur-sag-enki is Susa's governor. Now you need a new father. I decided Ur-sag-enki was the best choice."

Abi frowned. "I wish things could be the way they were."

"Me too." Habarane gave an exaggerated sigh, her little shoulders drawing up to touch her ears before falling. "When will my ama and abba come back for me?"

Nindalla freed one hand and pulled her niece close. She stroked her hair. She had explained death to her twice, but the girl was too young to understand.

Lips pursed, Bar stared at Habarane. Then she stomped over and sat on Nindalla's other side. She crossed her arms and pressed against her mother hard, as if nothing could make her move.

"Abi, come join us. You children can nap to make the time pass faster."

Abi curled up next to her. The children dozed, but Nindalla worried her lip until a blood drop dribbled down her chin. She switched to chewing on the inside of her cheek. *He should be here by now. What is taking him so long?*

She fidgeted. *Perhaps I should have stayed with him. But I'm still sore and tired from the baby. I would have been in the way.*

Minutes passed. She had to do something. The children would be safe in the tunnel for a short time. But what could she do?

Kuk-kalla! Ur-sag-enki trusts him. I will ask him for help.

Midu grabbed Ur-sag-enki's chin and forced him to look straight at her. Her weight on his wounded leg kept him in agony. "The Akkadians killed my lover, my mother, and my sisters. Think about that as you die."

"I'm not an uncivilized Akkadian. I've never killed women or children," he protested.

"If a dog chooses to live with jackals, it is no better than a jackal."

He jerked back as if struck. He had stayed with the army after his family was dead. He still proudly wore the skirt General Qisim had given him. *I'm no better than an Akkadian.*

Outside the door, Kuk-kalla's voice broke through the shouts of the guards trying to open the door. The banging stopped.

Midu glanced toward the door. The pressure of the knife let up. "They have given up. You have no hope of rescue."

Vigor filled him to the brim as if he were a large jug. He tried to keep his elation off his face. Help was coming. All he had to do was buy a little time. He grabbed Midu by the waist and tossed her across the room.

Her knife fell, clattering against the brick floor. She landed on her bottom with a jolt. Her eyes glazed.

Grunting, he heaved himself up into a sitting position.

Midu shook her head. Her eyes focused. She threw herself toward her knife.

Ur-sag-enki lifted his sickle-sword in front of him.

Something heavy thudded against the heavy wood door, then again. The bar across it split.

Midu stood and danced toward him around his sword.

The door exploded. A stone statue of Inshushinak flew into the room and crushed a table into splinters when it landed. Roaring men tumbled in after it.

They had used the statue as an improvised Akkadian weapon, the battering ram.

Midu kicked his thigh again.

His eyes briefly squeezed shut.

She threw herself around the sword and scrambled to put the knife to his throat.

"No! Don't!" Nindalla cried. She squeezed between two guards and ran toward him.

Midu stood and turned. She braced her feet and held her knife out with two hands, aiming it right at Nindalla's belly.

"Brother! You're bleeding! You're hurt!" Nindalla looked only at him. She would impale herself on the knife.

I promised to protect her.

"No!" he roared. The agony in his thigh became a thorn prick. He threw himself up to his feet.

He swung his sickle-sword.

Midu's head fell to the floor. It rolled until it bumped into a jar. Her body collapsed.

Time resumed its normal speed. In an eyeblink, Kuk-kalla was supporting him, and Nindalla had her arm around his waist.

"Why don't you lean on me," she said, as if she weren't one-third his size.

He chuckled. Then, as relief and joy flooded him, he roared with laughter.

Kuk-kalla shook Ur-sag-enki. "The guards," the scout said, warning in his voice.

Ur-sag-enki sobered from his laughing fit. "Help me walk to them." Nindalla stayed close to his side.

The men crowded together in two clusters in a room too small for so many. Ten of Dagu's guards, bulky men in wool kilts, hovered to his left behind the fallen statue. Six of his own soldiers, armed, stood to his right.

A guard inched forward and examined Dagu's and Midu's bodies. He looked at their wounds, turned them over, and listened to their chests. "They're dead," he announced.

Ur-sag-enki's soldiers came to attention and drew their weapons.

The guards whispered among themselves, glancing occasionally at Ur-sag-enki's short tunic and leather skirt.

He glanced down. Blood soaked his clothes and stained the bronze studs on his skirt. With Kuk-kalla's help, Ur-sag-enki stood straight and tall before them.

The guard who had examined the bodies asked, "My lord, what happened?"

His throat was raw, and every word hurt. But he forced himself to speak loudly and boldly. "I killed Chamberlain Dagu in self-defense. Before he betrayed me, he betrayed King Ebarti."

"How?" asked his scout Il-alsu.

"Dagu opened the west gate for our army and told General Qisim the king's battle plans."

Il-alsu crossed his arms. "Why would he do that?"

"The general promised him that there would be only limited looting and killing of civilians. He also promised him he would be governor of Susa."

"Snake!" exclaimed one guard.

"Scorpion!" said another.

Several other men hissed their outrage.

"Hey!" One of the guards held up his hands for quiet. "No city can withstand Sargon. By opening the gate, Dagu saved lives. Would you rather be dead? He's a hero, not a traitor. The governor shouldn't have killed him."

Ur-sag-enki's men moved to stand in front of him. Nindalla kept her arm around him but slipped backward.

Another guard spat on the floor. "Dagu was King Ebarti's most trusted advisor. Had been for years. How could he betray his friend?"

"His ambition was greater than his loyalty," Ur-sag-enki said flatly.

"Then he met a fitting end," Il-alsu said. "I'm glad he's wearing feathers and eating dirt in the Underworld."

Some of the palace guards muttered under their breath.

"I know some of you didn't want me as your governor. I know some of you supported Dagu against me," Ur-sag-enki said. "Rebellion ends right here, right now. Swear loyalty.

"Or fight me."

Nindalla gasped.

His soldiers prostrated themselves on the brick floor.

He held his breath. He couldn't even stand, let alone fight.

The palace guards looked at each other and at the bodies on the floor. One guard dropped. The others muttered together. Then, by twos and threes, they also knelt.

When no one was left standing, he nodded. "Good. You may rise. Il-alsu, fetch the company's physician and then some clean clothes for me. I want to look strong and fit when I announce to the city that I will marry Princess Nindalla."

Nindalla let out a whoosh of breath. She had expected some of the palace guards to take Ur-sag-enki up on his challenge. Despite their obeisance, she shook.

Warmth under her arm reminded her she still had her arm around the governor . . . in front of many men. And he had announced their betrothal to them! Blushing, she pulled away and turned toward the nearest stool. She needed to sit. She looked at the food Dagu and Midu had brought in but had not eaten. Her stomach was empty. She should eat something—she needed to regain her strength—but merely looking at the food made her feel sick.

Ur-sag-enki caught her arm. "Guards, two of you remove the bodies. Make sure they get a proper burial with many mourners. The rest of you, you're dismissed." Under his breath he added, "Kuk-kalla, stay. I'll need your help to get back to my chambers after the physician sees to my wounds."

Ur-sag-enki tugged on Nindalla's arm until she faced him. She saw now that in addition to his other wounds, his neck was mottled with purple. Had Dagu or Midu tried to strangle him?

She looked at her feet. "You almost died for me. Why had you not killed Midu?"

"I swore long ago that I would never kill women or children," he croaked.

"You are a man of honor after all." She tilted her head and looked into his eyes. "You broke your oath to save me. I am . . . humbled."

He laid his hands on her shoulders; she shivered when bare skin met bare skin. "I promised to keep you and the children safe. I have done so. We will marry, and no one will threaten you again."

"Hush. Don't speak. You will injure your throat even more."

He bent down and pressed his burning lips against hers.

Before her gasp ended, he stood up, pulled her against his chest, and rested his chin on her head. His arms folded around her.

"The physician is coming." Her voice sounded as if it came from far away. "We need to get the children from their hiding place."

"Hmmmm." He did not let her go.

He was a boulder. Her trembling stopped. She leaned against him, savoring his warmth, his strength, his presence. They stood there for several minutes, ignoring Kuk-kalla, who looked at the wall.

Her chest loosened, and her breathing eased.

To her surprise, she was reluctant to step away when the army physician arrived.

— Chapter 37 —

Nindalla sat on a bench in the courtyard while Ur-sag-enki handed the children over to Daanan and Sukura with a terse explanation. She did not bother listening. Sometime, she would want to know what had happened in the ambassadorial chambers, but right now it was enough to sit under the palms, watch the fountain ripple, and know that Dagu and Midu would never cause her trouble again.

"Come, Sister."

She started and gasped. *Why am I so jumpy lately?*

"Come. We have some time to ourselves at last." Ur-sag-enki took her hand and pulled her to her feet.

She took a step and swayed, dizzy. She closed her eyes and put her hand to her forehead.

His arm immediately steadied her. "Are you hurt? Are you sick?"

"No, no. I am fine. I am better than fine. I have my children again." She did feel better. She must have stood up too fast.

He took her hand again and led her into his chambers, barring the heavy door behind them.

She stopped in the entry room, suddenly shy.

"Come." He tugged on her hand. "I won't hurt you."

"I know," she said, letting him lead her into his sleeping chamber. He sat on the bed and patted the thick stuffed mattress.

She sat at the opposite end, nervously smoothing the linens in-between them with her hand.

"Ahhh," he sighed, tipping his head back. "It's good to be home."

"How badly injured is your leg?" she asked.

"It'll heal completely, gods willing. A physician put a balm on my leg, my arm, and my neck. He said my voice will heal too."

"Did you see an incantation priest?"

"No. In the army, we had only physicians. I did not think to call a priest. Do you think I should?"

"Perhaps."

"Maybe I will, if it's someone besides High Priestess Zana."

They sat in silence again. Then he scooted over next to her.

She crossed her arms over her chest.

Slowly, he pulled the pins from her hair, laying them one by one in a line on the bed. Then he worked on her hair, freeing the interlaced strands and combing them with his fingers. When all her hair hung loose and heavy on her back, he ran his fingers through it, over and over, his occasional touch on her bare back jolting her.

She uncrossed her arms. Timidly, she walked her fingers across the linens to his leg. She hesitated and then let her fingers climb up his sheep-fur kilt and continue onto his bare leg.

"You are not wearing your soldier's skirt," she whispered.

"I will never wear it again. I will have a robe made," he said into the hair at her neck. He grasped it in his fist and buried his face in it. "I saw you once. In Eridu. I have dreamed of your hair ever since."

"It is yours now, my lord."

"Your voice quavers. Are you afraid of marrying me? I will treat you better than your husband did. I promise."

"It's not that I am afraid." Another wave of dizziness passed over her. She braced herself with her hand. "Everything has happened so fast. I know little about you, not even whether you like to hunt or to wrestle or to listen to music. I am also still exhausted from the birth."

"Time will soon fix those problems." He lay on his side and pulled her face to his.

At first she merely lay there, letting him kiss her, enjoying the texture of his lips and comparing his kisses to Prince Humba's. Ur-sag-enki kissed her and caressed her face as if he enjoyed it and wanted her to enjoy it, not as if he were in a hurry to warm her up.

She smiled when his breath got faster and louder and his lips heated.

Her own breath sped up to match his. Desire blossomed within her. She yearned for him; she longed to please him. She rolled toward him. Without shame or fear, she returned his kisses and caresses in kind—gentle for gentle, eager for eager, hungry for hungry.

"Fetch us some beer, my dove," he rasped. "My throat is raw."

"Yes, my lord." Nindalla kissed the tip of his nose and stood up. Her knees buckled, and the world went dark.

Ur-sag-enki stroked Nindalla's face with shaking hands. His chest tingled as if the time for battle approached. "Wake up. Please wake up."

She opened her eyes a sliver.

He looked up, toward the heavens beyond the ceiling. "Praise Enki! I will take a sheep to your temple in thanks."

She touched his cheek. "There are few sheep to be found in Susa. I think the army may have eaten them all."

"Then the god will have something else for restoring you. When you fainted, I, well, it was like nothing I had ever felt."

"I am fine." She tried to sit up.

He pressed her back down to the bed. "No, you're not. When did you last eat?"

"Sometime yesterday."

"Your face is pale. You've chewed off your nails. You jumped when I spoke to you earlier. Tell me what's wrong."

"I do not know what is wrong." She picked at her shift. "But I do not feel . . . right."

"What feels wrong?"

"I need to escape, but no cage encloses me. I need to run, but I have no place in mind to go. I jump at the slightest noise. I cannot sleep at night without a lamp burning. Sometimes I have trouble breathing. My own simple life, the little things I do every day, has become overwhelming."

"Have you seen an incantation priest?" he joked.

She smiled weakly at hearing her own words turned against her. "No. But perhaps I will, if it's someone besides High Priestess Zana."

He turned serious again. "I've known men with similar feelings." He lifted her wrist and felt the place where her blood pulsed. "The harmony of your body is off. Your blood pounds too fast."

She clutched at her hair. "Who were these men?"

"Soldiers who have been in many terrible battles." He swallowed. "Also, some people who survived the sack of Eridu."

"Did they die?"

"No." He stroked her hand. "But some wanted to."

"I have been so tired since Enki-kiag's birth. I have not had enough rest. So many bad things keep happening, but they do not feel real. I see everything through a fog. I have trouble telling my nightmares from my life."

"Is agreeing to marry me one of the nightmares?"

"I did not say that."

"You think I betrayed Eridu by becoming a soldier. You think I deceived you when I didn't tell you everything at once. You say you know little about me. Hiding things has been my habit for a long time." It was a habit he would have to break to make Nindalla happy. "But now I will tell you only truth, the full truth of my past."

He sat on the edge of the bed and pulled off his tunic, revealing his back. His biggest secret.

She gasped. "Who did that?" She reached out and ran a tentative finger down one of the ropey white scars that crisscrossed his skin like mountain ridges.

"General Qisim. After the sack of Eridu."

"Why?"

He looked over his shoulder at her. "Because I refused to let his men have my mother or sisters. Because I picked up a sword and hacked at his men even though I was a farmer's boy and had no right to a warrior's weapon. Because I would not surrender even when six sword tips pressed against my belly."

She covered her mouth with her hand. "Why are you still alive?"

"The general offered to spare my mother and sisters if I would be his slave. I was desperate to protect them. I said 'yes.' Then he beat me for my insolence, for defying him, for behaving above my station, for bargaining with a superior. I lay in a fever for days. I almost died."

"The Akkadians are demons," she snarled. She looked everywhere but his back.

"Are you disgusted by my scars?" He pulled his tunic back on. "You must be. Any woman would be. I am sorry I will bring such an ugly sight, such a demonstration of my shame, to our marriage bed. If you like, I will always wear my tunic to bed."

She reached for his hand and held it between her two small ones. "I am not disgusted. I am proud of my betrothed for doing his duty to his family."

"They would have been better off if I hadn't."

She kissed his hand. "How could that be possible?"

His voice could not last much longer. He hoped it would keep its strength until he could finish his story. "The armies of Sargon swept through Sumer like locusts through fields of grain. City after city fell. I marched barefoot with the other slaves, following the armies. My job was to set up the general's tent and make sure he had clean water, good beer, and fresh bread. After battles, I cleaned his weapons as he bragged about the terrible things he had done that day."

Nindalla drew a shuddering breath. "I would not have helped my enemies," she said. "I would have run away."

"Not if your mother and sisters were among the slaves that followed at the rear." Ur-sag-enki laughed bitterly and then broke into a coughing fit. His throat felt as if it were on fire.

Nindalla rose shakily and poured him a beaker of watered yogurt from the jug on a nearby table. Her hands shook so much that yogurt sloshed over the edge of the beaker. She handed it to him and slumped onto the bed.

He gulped the watered yogurt; it calmed his cough and cooled his throat. He leaned over to set the beaker in its rack. He pulled Nindalla closer and continued his story. "I bargained for the lives of my mother and sister, not knowing that living would be worse than going to the Underworld."

"They did not fare well?"

"My mother was old, maybe thirty-five summers. Most of her teeth were gone. The men weren't interested in her, so she had to work with the asses, hauling burdens. The overseers made sure she hauled just as much as the animals. It was too much. One day she fell over and never got up."

"And your sisters?" She grew rigid, as if she knew their fate.

He changed the subject. "The general saw potential in my spirit and my height and size. Because I was a boy, he thought he could mold me into the perfect Akkadian soldier. And when he thought he had done so, he freed me on the condition I join the army and fight beside him."

"Why do you say 'he thought he had done so'? You fought and killed with the Akkadian army."

"I vowed I would not be like them, that I would never kill women or children. I vowed that one day I would make my own choices, have a family, make things grow instead of destroying them." He dropped his head. "Somehow, I became like the Akkadians after all."

She stroked his cheek. "Your sisters survived?"

He leaned his face into the caress. "Because they were young and pretty, they were spared the heavy work Ama did," he choked out. "I negotiated badly. I asked the general only to let my family live. My sisters were assigned to, to, to service the soldiers. Shatirra couldn't bear it. She hung herself. Bau-iggal killed a man and ran away."

"That is terrible. How old were they?"

"Shatirra was twenty. Bau-iggal was ten."

She buried her face in his neck. "I lost three brothers and one sister, maybe two, to the Akkadians. Also my mother and father." Her body shook.

He stroked her hair. "Don't talk about it. Let's talk about our future."

"My sister Nu-nu disappeared. She may yet live." Nindalla shook as if with a fever. "I heard that General Qisim cut the cylinder seal from my mother's neck. The soldiers stripped my mother and my sister of their jewelry and ornaments. The general executed them in public as if they were criminals. My sister who was executed had seen only ten New Year celebrations."

"Peace, peace," he soothed. "Our families are beyond suffering now, my princess."

She turned too-brilliant eyes to him. How had he not noticed the tired shadows under them? "Our families hunger and thirst in the Underworld because we cannot take food and beer to their graves."

He pulled her closer. "I know," he whispered.

"We who remain behind should suffer with them. And yet we are getting married."

"We shouldn't make ourselves suffer for their sake. We'll join them in the Underworld soon enough. We should be joyful now. Together."

"Would that it could be so." She sighed, closing her eyes and leaning against his massive arm. "We have a duty to those who died. A duty to mourn and remember."

"The sack of Eridu and the conquest of Susa will be nothing but old stories to our grandchildren, just like the stories of Gilgamesh and Enkidu. We can't help the unburied dead, much as we'd like to. Why suffer for no reason? Why deny your children a joyful mother?"

"I have a duty to mourn and remember," she repeated. "And hate . . . hate consumes me."

He looked at her tired face and thought about her words and her new baby, not even two weeks old, though it seemed months since he had helped him into the world.

She had battle fatigue.

He had never suffered it, but he had seen it in some of his soldiers after they had fought in several bloody battles in a row with little sleep or food and lost many friends. They turned melancholy and lethargic, and they believed that life was too difficult or even unbearable.

Nindalla needed rest—a true rest, uninterrupted by gossip about plots and worries about her children. Good sleep. Good food. Good news. No new burdens or trials. Time to remember reasons to live and be happy.

He chastised himself for distressing her. "I shouldn't have told you my story yet. The attack on Susa is too fresh. You haven't had a chance to mourn your husband or his family or your servants."

She looked away and twisted her hands together. "Prince Humba did not love me. He preferred Midu."

"He was a fool. Forget him. Your future husband does love you. I am going to make sure you have a good rest, with lots of pampering and no worries. You can mourn and head forward with your life."

"I do not think I can." Her hand clutched the sheet and twisted it.

He kissed her forehead and stood. He went to a chest and dug through clothes and packages to find what he wanted. Then he came back to the bed.

Her hand still worried the sheet. Gently, he separated them and placed an amulet in her hand.

She looked in her hand and her face lit briefly with joy. She ran her fingers over the carving and then brought the amulet to her lips. "A lion! I did not realize you worshipped Inanna."

He closed her fingers around the amulet and stroked her hair. "I think after a rest you will again be the woman I met in the birthing hut, a lioness to rival Inanna in beauty and strength."

"May the gods bless you for your belief in me!" Her worried, overwrought look returned. "But what if I never get better?" she sobbed.

She is so fragile and overwhelmed. Just as my soldiers were. He took her hand and brought it to his lips. "My dove, I will take care of you. We can wait to marry until you are ready. As long as it takes." He paused and then said quietly, "If it will take one burden from you and let you heal faster, I release you from your promise to marry me."

— Chapter 38 —

Roses. I smell roses.

Nindalla woke alone in Ur-sag-enki's bed. A sheet covered her. *It is sweet the way he always protects me, even from the night chill.*

She smiled. As she sat up, yellow rose petals puffed into the air from the sheet and piled in soft drifts. She scooped up a handful, held them to her nose, and inhaled the heavy scent. *Sweet, like him.*

Her liver warmed, and she rubbed a rose petal between her fingers, relishing the smooth, almost plush, feel. Did he know that the rose was the symbol of Inanna, goddess of love? Or was he merely being practical, using the smell of roses to calm her spirit? Whichever, she already felt more cheerful.

She looked around. A bench now sat next to the bed, and it held trays and dishes of food—lentils, quail eggs, poached fish, lamb stewed in milk, fresh soft cheeses studded with raisins, and other delights that would be easy on her stomach. She looked in the pitchers. One held watered yogurt, and the other, beer.

If she were still a little girl, she would jump up and down and clap her hands. Ur-sag-enki had sent her a feast as good as a goddess received in her temple. Even though she had little appetite, everything looked and smelled delicious.

I will at least eat a quail egg.

Daanan came in as she swallowed. "My lady, I am relieved to see you awake and eating."

Nindalla sat fully up and swung her feet to the floor. "My children—Where are they? Who is taking care of them? Where is Ur-sag-enki? How is—"

Daanan frowned and put her hands on her hips. "The governor says you are not to worry about anything. Everything is being taken care of. He says you must rest and eat to regain your strength. I'm not supposed to tell you about anything outside his rooms."

Nindalla raised her eyebrows. "Daanan! What a severe nurse you are!"

The wet nurse winked and leaned close. "Don't tell the lord I told you, but he is sleeping in your room. Intarza is helping to take care of Enki-kiag so I can care for you." She lowered her voice. "The governor has asked Intarza if she would like to be one of your ladies."

"That's wonderful! I hope she said 'yes.'"

Daanan nodded. "But remember, be surprised when the governor tells you."

Nindalla winked herself. "All will be our secret. I feel better that you have told me. Otherwise I would have worried, despite your 'orders.'"

"I thought so. I didn't spend a week in the birthing hut with you without learning a little about you." Daanan's voice held satisfaction. "I'll leave you to your rest now. Is there any food or drink you crave? Any distraction?"

"No," Nindalla said. "I want for nothing." *And I long for nothingness.* "This time alone is just what I need."

"My lady, if you pardon my impertinence, I think the governor sometimes knows you better than you know yourself."

Nindalla tilted her head. "I think you are right." Her liver warmed even more toward him, and she wished he had visited her instead of Daanan. "You know, suddenly I have a bit of an appetite."

As Daanan beamed over her, Nindalla reached for another quail egg.

Days passed. Nindalla slept when she was tired and ate when she was hungry. She chatted about nothings with Daanan when she felt like talking and was silent when she felt like silence. She prayed often, to both Sumerian and Elamite gods, asking them to watch over her children and Ur-sag-enki.

To regain her strength, she drank lots of beer. Her appetite slowly came back, and she ate more and more of the food Daanan brought her. Her breathing eased, and her hands stopped shaking.

She padded around Ur-sag-enki's chambers, touching his weapons and drinking deeply of his scent, which had already replaced Humba's, even in his reception room and bedchamber.

She felt herself healing from the birth. Her *murub* was less sore with each day, now that she was not sitting on hard floors and climbing ladders.

As her body felt better, her mood improved. She had good dreams instead of nightmares. She could not forgive Humba, but she followed Ur-sag-enki's advice not to think about him. She took time each day to mourn her family and those of Susa who had died.

Then, one night, she thought she heard steps in a storeroom, one that connected to the network of passages within the walls. She grabbed her knife and a lamp, slipped close to the door, and peeked inside.

"Kumdupum! I thought you left the city days ago," she exclaimed, lowering her knife and going into the room. He looked worse than before. Thin, bony arms dangled limply from bowed shoulders. He stood on one leg, his good one, as if he no longer trusted the deformed leg to support any weight.

She set the lamp down on the floor. "Please, sit, and I will bring you some beer and food." The small storeroom had only a couple of worn benches with broken reeds for furnishings, but she dared not take him into the reception room. She did not want anyone to discover that a son of King Ebarti still lived.

Nindalla went back to the bedroom, filled a mug with beer, and carried it to the storeroom along with a platter of food.

As he ate and drank, she sat on the other bench and smoothed her shift over and over until the linen lost its crinkles. She had started to find some peace for her spirit. His visit disrupted that peace.

Kumdupum wiped his mouth with his arm and looked at her with worried eyes. "You've gotten thinner, and you look pale."

She twisted her fingers together. "I am feeling much better than I was a few days ago. Ur-sag-enki is very kind to me."

He nodded, but the worried look remained. "I am sorry I did not come back to you that night I told you I was leaving."

Shrugging, she said, "Prince Humba's family always found me easy to overlook."

"I didn't forget you! My plans fell through. It has taken me this long to find a new way out of Susa. A spice trader has agreed to take me in his caravan in exchange for my labor. I will see the four corners of the world."

"I am glad to hear it. May the gods protect you on your journeys."

"They have blessed me so far." He cleared his throat. "I know you have agreed to marry Ur-sag-enki. But a betrothed woman should be joyous and glowing, not hiding in a room looking ill. I ask again: Would you prefer to leave with me and find a new home?"

"I cannot. I gave the governor my word." She scratched her arms, realized what she was doing, and folded her arms to stop herself. "Besides, Ur-sag-enki is not the reason I became ill. There have been so many changes. So many worries. The conquest stirred up memories of friends and relatives the Akkadians killed when they took Eridu."

His eyes crinkled in pain. "Such is what the future holds for me, you think?"

She immediately regretted her words. His losses were so much newer and raw.

Metal hinges squealed. *The door of Ur-sag-enki's reception room—Someone enters!*

"Nindalla?"

It was Ur-sag-enki himself. She clutched the lion amulet he had given her, which she had tied to her wrist, and thought a quick prayer to the goddess.

She pointed to the lamp and mouthed "Hide!" to Kumdupum. She moved some bottles and baskets around to cover the sound of Kumdupum's dragging foot as he shuffled back into the passage.

She went back into the bedroom, sat on the bed, and called out, "Good evening, Governor."

"So formal, Sister." His voice was much improved, but when he limped into the room, she winced at the green bruises that mottled his neck. Then she looked lower, and warmness grew in her chest and abdomen. He wore a white linen robe edged with simple embroidery of turtles, one of the symbols of Enki. The right shoulder was pinned together with a turtle of gold.

He looks so handsome! The straight drape of the robe emphasized his unusual height and broad shoulders. *He must dominate his receiving hall now. I cannot wait to see him there.*

He looked her over as well and then smiled broadly. "You look so much better."

"I feel better. You were right. I needed rest and time to mourn."

"I'm glad. Your children are well and happy. Are you ready to leave this room and rejoin them?"

She looked at her feet. "Not quite yet."

"Oh." One short word filled with a world of disappointment.

They were an awkward arm's length apart. She did not invite him to sit by her. She remained silent and tried not to fidget or look toward the storeroom.

"I have a present for you."

She clasped her hands together. A smile pulled at her lips. "A present! That was not necessary, Brother. You have given me so much already."

He chuckled. "To be honest, this is a present for me as well."

His hands were empty. *What can he mean?*

"I found out that in Susa, the ruler appoints the high priestess of Inshushinak."

Her hand flew to her chest, and she raised her head. She leaned a little toward him. "Do you mean—"

"Yes! Zana is no longer high priestess. To compensate her for the loss of her position, I have married her to Lord Zag-Sudta of Uruk, who sits on my council."

"You are my hero!"

He grinned. "I thought you'd be pleased. When you return to the world, would you help me choose a new high priestess?"

"With happiness."

Silence fell. Minutes passed.

"You're out of beer and food both. I'll send Daanan right away."

"Thank you, my lord."

He bent down and kissed her. When he pulled back, she surprised herself by reaching up to pull him closer and extend the kiss. It felt good. More importantly, it felt right.

"I'll see you soon, my dove." His voice was husky and sweet. He left.

She waited for Daanan. And waited. The wet nurse finally arrived with a tray, eager to chat.

Smiling, Nindalla cut her off with an upraised hand. "Thank you. Please just leave everything on the bench."

When the reception room door clapped shut, she ran to the storeroom.

Kumdupum was already sitting on the bench. "The Akkadian surprises me. I assumed he would be brutal and that you would be better off far away from here."

"Perhaps an Akkadian would be." She folded her hands in her lap and stared at them. "Ur-sag-enki is Sumerian. From my home city." She took a deep breath. "And I am content to marry him."

"Why speak so somberly? He loves you. I heard it in his voice and in his words."

Heaviness fell from her shoulders, as if she shed burdens she had forgotten she was carrying. "You think so? He certainly loves the children. Marrying him is what is best for them."

"Better than a life in a spice caravan," he said. "Do you love him?"

"He is kind and brave and will take care of us."

"But do you love him?" he repeated.

"I do not know." She covered her mouth to suppress a giggle. "I respect him. I like him. He makes me feel safe. Safe and cared about."

He smiled affectionately. "Then I can leave you without worries. Unless you want me to delay until you are well?"

"Go! Find your new life. Write and let me know what it is and how you are." She closed her eyes and wet her lips. "I am a Sumerian princess. I can endure the life the gods bestowed on me at the cutting of my navel cord."

"I hope they decreed a happy life. Goodbye, Nindalla." He kissed her forehead. The sound of his lame foot dragging across the floor and into the secret passage got softer and softer until she could hear it no more.

She let her head fall back and released a huge breath. She felt light enough to float.

She had no option left but one: Marry Ur-sag-enki. But instead of feeling locked in, she felt free. After all her years in Susa, she would finally make the city her home. *Their* home, together.

She would dare to stop worrying about what blow would strike her next and hope for happiness.

No, not *hope*. She would strive for happiness. The governor had tried hard to please her and make her happy. Now she would do the same for him.

She clasped her hands to her chest and smiled.

– Chapter 39 –

This is the best part of the day, Ur-sag-enki thought two days later as he went through the door into his complex. Evening sun lit the courtyard. The little girls ran to greet him with happy shrieks and hugs, and Daanan brought out Enki-kiag for a kiss. No matter how tedious or difficult court business was, his evening welcome home made up for it.

"Can we play now?" Bar asked.

"Did the three of you eat?" They nodded their heads, and Sukura gave a confirmatory nod. "Then come in."

He led them into Nindalla's chambers, where he was still staying, and unrolled a mat for them to sit on. "What do you want to play tonight?"

"Tell us how you and Ama rescued us," Abi said, as she did every night. It was her favorite story.

"No!" Bar said. "Too scary. I want to play farm."

"It just so happens that I know a lot about farms." Ur-sag-enki opened a chest and took out the bag of small pottery animals—goats, sheep, chickens, asses, pigs, cattle, and hedgehogs. The collection also included a wooden soldier Kuk-kalla had carved for the children. "It's evening. Should we milk the cows?"

"No!" Bar scrunched her face in thought. "I want the father bull and the mother goat to get married."

"I don't think that marriage will work out well, Bar." He looked up at Abi and winked.

She rolled her eyes, a habit he was sure her mother would not approve of.

"I want the hedgehogs to prepare the wedding feast." Bar marched the hedgehogs across the mat, two at a time. "They'll cook right here. It will be just like our wedding feast. Except the mother goat will be there."

As he chuckled, his stomach clenched. "I promise you, your mother will be at our wedding." *She has to get well. She is my destiny.*

Ur-sag-enki picked up an ass and held it in both hands. "She will be there even if I have to carry her there myself, like this."

He tromped across the mat on his knees, carrying the ass and pretending that it was getting heavier and heavier. At last he collapsed onto his elbows with an "ooof!" *Maybe it was a mistake to release her from her promise to marry.* Unlike the ass, she had a choice, and he had to honor it.

The girls giggled. "Show us again!"

So again he crawled across the mat with the ever-heavier ass that stood in for Nindalla.

The girls giggled even harder.

He roared with laughter. He swept his arms around them and pulled them into a tight hug.

"An ass?" Nindalla stood in the doorway wearing a shift embroidered with triangles. She wore a small smile that made Ur-sag-enki's insides turn over. "Of all the animals you could choose to stand in for me, you chose an *ass*?"

"That's what you get for not being here to help out. Girls, clear some space for your ama so she can play too."

Her dark eyebrows flew up. "The children should not even be playing on the floor. I am not going to set a bad example of how princesses behave."

"I'm governor of a major city, and *I* am playing on the floor." Wiggling his eyebrows, he motioned again for her to join them.

She sat primly on a bench and tucked her shift beneath her. "We are about to create a new home, a new family, together. *Someone* has to demonstrate from the first how to behave with dignity."

Her voice held a lightness, a hint of humor, that he had never heard before. A smile seemed to tug at her lips, and when she looked at him, her eyes twinkled.

"You're just going to sit there while we play?"

"One of the parents has to behave responsibly." She truly smiled now.

"Is that so?" *She's one parent. And the other is . . . me?* He sat very still. If he moved or said anything, he could ruin this magical moment of hope.

"Yes. One parent has to be responsible." Her voice turned stern. "Preferably *both* parents." Her gaze belied her tone. She looked at him as tenderly as she always looked at Enki-kiag.

She is going to marry me after all! His breathing stopped, and the ass tumbled from his shaking hand. He stared at her glowing face. The air felt thick, as if all the gods had joined them to share his happiness. He wanted to stay in this moment forever, bathed in the glow of her gaze.

Abi poked him. The mood shattered. "Are you asleep?" she asked.

"Uh, no. Just, uh, enjoying the evening."

"I hope you are not going to be a responsible parent too." She imitated her mother's fake-stern voice.

"I'll be the best father I can be."

Nindalla continued to smile silently at him.

Why doesn't she tell me outright she'll marry me? But what else could her gaze and smile and teasing mean? He shrugged and played along with her game. "My lady, if you won't join us on the floor, then this ass will continue to represent you."

He picked up the clay animal and talked to it. "You must not eat anything until the wedding. My leg is not completely healed yet. I need you to weigh as little as possible. Otherwise I might not be able to carry you and would have to drag you."

The girls shrieked with laughter. Bar rolled on the mat in a frenzy of giggles that turned to hiccoughs.

At last Nindalla rose. She stalked toward him and snatched the toy ass from his hands. "You will not have to carry me to our wedding feast."

His blood pounded in his ears. "Why not? You have been a reluctant bride so far."

"No more. I will walk to the feast willingly."

She's mine at last! Yes! Praise the gods! He mimed astonishment, raising his eyebrows and gasping. Then he grabbed her hands and tugged.

She tried to pull away. "Stop it. No. I am not going to sit on the floor. No. No, I am not."

He tugged harder.

"No. Stop it," she said, kneeling next to him.

Abi, Bar, and Habarane flew off his lap and onto their mother's. Bar stood on her thighs and kissed her with loud smacks.

As Nindalla embraced each, tears shone in her eyes. "I have missed you so much, my little ones."

Ur-sag-enki swallowed and dared to ask, "What about me?"

The Jewel of Eridu dropped her gaze and blushed the color of fresh, sweet cherries.

His entrails fluttering, he leaned toward her. "I love you," he said, then lifted her chin with one finger and kissed her full, smooth lips.

Her body startled, then became soft and yielding. She leaned into the kiss.

He threaded his fingers through the silky mass of her hair. The day he had dreamed of had finally come: He had a family again.

"You say you will walk willingly to our wedding feast. Solely out of duty, right?"

Nindalla laughed, a throaty, womanly laugh, and she cupped his cheek in her soft, warm palm. Love shone in her eyes. "Of course. Don't I always do my duty?"

— end —

— By Shauna Roberts —

Ice Magic, Fire Magic
fantasy
Hadley Rille Books, forthcoming

The Measure of a Man
historical fantasy (novelette; Kindle book only)
Nicobar Press, 2014

Claimed by the Enemy
historical fiction set in ancient Mesopotamia
Nicobar Press, 2014

The Hunt
science fiction (novelette; Kindle book only)
Nicobar Press, 2012

Like Mayflies in a Stream
historical fiction set in ancient Mesopotamia
Hadley Rille Books, 2009

— About the Author —

Shauna Roberts is an author of fantasy, science fiction, historical fiction, and romance. She grew up in Beavercreek, Ohio. She was a copy editor and an award-winning freelance medical writer for 21 years before retiring to write fiction.

Mesopotamia has fascinated her since high school. She earned a BA in anthropology (with an emphasis in Near Eastern archaeology) from the University of Pennsylvania (Philadelphia) and an MA and a PhD in anthropology from Northwestern University (Evanston, Illinois). She has taught classes on ancient Mesopotamia in the University of California at Riverside's Osher Lifelong Learning Institute.

She attended the Clarion Science Fiction and Fantasy Writers' Workshop in 2009, and she now serves on the Clarion Foundation Board of Directors. In 2011 she won the Speculative Literature Foundation's Older Writers' Grant.

If you'd like a signed bookplate, please email her with your address.

Her social media links are:
Website: http://www.ShaunaRoberts.com
Email: ShaunaRoberts@ShaunaRoberts.com.
Twitter: @ShaunaRoberts5
Facebook: https://www.facebook.com/pages/Shauna-Roberts-author/194876117254102
Pinterest: http://www.pinterest.com/shaunasroberts/

— Acknowledgments —

Many people provided inspiration and comments on various drafts: my critique group in New Orleans: Farrah Rochon, Laurie Bolaños, Rosalind M. Green-Holmes, Margaret Hauck; my husband, David A. Malueg; my niece Alexandra Smith; the Writers Orbit of Orange County, especially Dave Moore; and my friend Claire Merriam Hoffman and other members of the Orange County Chapter of the Romance Writers of America.

My thanks also to Heather Comen of Heather G. Comen Editing Services for reviewing the manuscript and to Nicholas Stenner for copy editing it.

— Colophon —

Title page type: Snell Roundhand and Cochin

Body type: Cochin

Cuneiform type: Cuneiform Composite, created by Steve Tinney, with help on glyphs from Michael Everson. The font is based on Ur III forms and is released under the terms of the SIL Open Font License.

Printed and bound by CreateSpace